INSPECTOR WITHERSPOON ALWAYS TRIUMPHS ... HOW DOES HE DO IT?

Even the Inspector himself doesn't know—because his secret weapon is as ladylike as she is clever. She's Mrs Jeffries—the determined, delightful detective who stars in this unique Victorian mystery series! Be sure to read them all ...

The Inspector and Mrs. Jeffries
A doctor is found dead in his own office—and Mrs Jeffries must scour the premises to find the prescription for murder!

Mrs. Jeffries Dusts for Clues
One case is solved and another is opened when the Inspector finds a missing brooch—pinned to a dead woman's gown. But Mrs. Jeffries never cleans a room without dusting under the bed—and never gives up on a case before every lose end is tightly tied ...

The Ghost and Mrs. Jeffries
Death is unpredictable . . . but the murder of Mrs. Hodges was foreseen at a spooky seance. The practical-minded housekeeper may not be able to see the future—but she can look into the past and put things in order to solve this haunting crime!

Mrs. Jeffries Take Stock
A businessman has been murdered—and it could be because he cheated his stockholders. The housekeeper's interest is piqued . . . and when it comes to catching killers, the smart money's on Mrs. Jeffries!

Mrs. Jeffries On the Ball
A festive Jubilee celebration turns into a fatal affair—and Mrs. Jeffries must find the guilty party . . .

Mrs. Jeffries on the Trail
Why was Annie Shields out selling flowers so late on a foggy night? And more importantly, who killed her while she was doing it? It's up to Mrs. Jeffries to sniff out the clues . . .

MRS. JEFFRIES
QUESTIONS THE ANSWER

EMILY BRIGHTWELL

BERKLEY PRIME CRIME, NEW YORK

MRS. JEFFRIES QUESTIONS THE ANSWER

A Berkley Prime Crime Book / published by arrangement with the author

PRINTING HISTORY
Berkley Prime Crime edition / November 1997

The Putnam Berkley World Wide Web site address is
http://www.berkley.com

ISBN: 0-425-16093-9

Berkley Prime Crime Books are published
by The Berkley Publishing Group, a member of Penguin Putnam Inc.,
200 Madison Avenue, New York, NY 10016.

PRINTED IN THE UNITED STATES OF AMERICA

10 9 8 7 6 5 4 3 2 1

This Book is dedicated to Amanda Belle Arguile
The sunshine of my life.

MRS. JEFFRIES
QUESTIONS THE ANSWER

CHAPTER 1

Hannah Cameron smiled slyly as she stepped into the darkened room. Good, she thought, it's black as sin in here. No one would be able to see a thing. That should make the surprise even better. Hannah patted the pocket of her emerald-green velvet gown, making sure the box of matches was still secure on her person. It wouldn't do to let a small detail like forgetting the matches cause her to ruin the plan. No, she'd waited too long for this night, planned too hard to let it go awry now.

Moving cautiously, she edged further into the darkness, toward the French doors on the opposite side. Her heart pounded and her dress rustled loudly when it brushed against the settee as she eased past. She stopped, turned and looked toward the closed door through which she'd just come. It wouldn't do for one of the servants to come snooping about now. Not when she was so close to

achieving her goal. But she heard nothing. Most of
the servants should be fast asleep. That was one of
the reasons the little tart felt so safe. The silly minx
didn't realize anyone was on to her tricks. But by
heaven, she'd find out differently tonight.

Her eyes adjusted to the darkness and through
the faint light filtering in from the balcony, she
could see the outline of the lamp she'd carefully
placed on the table. Next to the table was the balloon-backed chair she'd put there earlier that evening. She wanted to be comfortable while she
waited. Who knew what time the little tramp would
actually come home? Reaching into her pocket
again, she pulled the matches out and set them
down next to the lamp. Then, wanting to be certain
that everything was going according to schedule,
she went to the French doors and peered out into
the night. Across the garden, she could see the faint
glow of a gas lamp rising above the high walls.
She squinted, trying to see if the lock was still disengaged as it had been earlier. But there wasn't
enough light to see. She had to be sure. Holding
her breath, she eased the door open and shut it
again. The door made the faintest of noises in the
quiet house. But she was satisfied. It was still un-
locked.

She giggled softly and then her laughter died
abruptly as she heard a faint creak. She whirled
around and peered through the blackness to the
door leading to the hall. No sign of light there, so
it must still be closed, she thought. But Hannah
wasn't taking any chances. She glanced to her left,
squinting hard to make sure the only other door in
the small sitting room, a door that led to a rarely

used guest room, was still closed. Nothing there either. Hannah shrugged, decided the creak she heard must have been the house settling and turned back toward the window to continue her vigil. She concentrated on staring out into the garden, watching the shadows and wondering when her quarry would arrive.

The thick carpet masked the sound of the footsteps creeping up behind her. Suddenly, she gasped and made a strangling noise deep in her throat. But the knife that had been plunged into her back had struck true and deep. Her heart stopped pumping. In an agony of pain, she couldn't find the breath to scream for help. She wheezed and choked, her hands flailing wildly in the air until finally, her knees buckled and she collapsed upon the floor.

Hannah Cameron wouldn't be surprising anyone tonight.

"I tell you, it's just not convenient now," Mrs. Goodge grumbled. The cook nodded her gray head emphatically, pushed her spectacles back up her nose and gazed around the table at the rest of the household of Upper Edmonton Gardens, home of Inspector Gerald Witherspoon of Scotland Yard.

"But Mrs. Goodge," Mrs. Jeffries, the housekeeper, said softly, "I don't think you've any choice in the matter. Your Aunt Elberta will be here tomorrow." She was a plump, kindly looking woman with dark auburn hair liberally sprinkled with gray at the temples, intelligent brown eyes and a fair complexion that contrasted nicely with the bronze-colored bombazine dress she wore.

"I could send her a telegram tonight," Mrs.

Goodge said quickly. She glanced at the clock. "Wiggins here could nip out and get one off . . ."

"That might 'urt the lady's feelin's," Wiggins, the footman, pointed out. "She's already done 'er packin' and all. Not that I mind goin' out fer ya. I don't. But ya told us a fortnight ago she'd be comin'." The footman was a sturdy young man of nineteen, with dark hair, blue eyes and round apple cheeks that blushed easily.

"Why don't you want her to come and visit?" Betsy, the pretty blond-haired maid, asked. "The inspector's already said he doesn't mind. There's plenty of room in the house for her."

Smythe, the black-haired coachman, crossed his arms over his massive chest. His brown eyes twinkled with amusement. His features were heavy, almost brutal looking, belying an easygoing nature and a kind heart. "What's all the fuss, Mrs. Goodge? I thought you liked your old auntie."

"I do like her," the cook shot back, "but it's just not convenient for her to come visiting now. We've got that dinner party for the inspector coming up and we've got. . . . we've got. . . ." She broke off, for in truth, except for one dinner party a few weeks hence, there was nothing else of any importance coming up for the household. Inspector Witherspoon, one of Scotland Yard's foremost detectives, was an exceptionally easy employer. Having not been born with a silver spoon in his mouth, he didn't expect his cook to cater to his every culinary whim. "We've got plenty on our plates right now," she finished lamely. "Besides, we might get us another murder and then where would I be? Hamstrung"—she nodded vigourously—"that's what I'd be. I can't have my sources in and out of this kitchen with a gossiping old woman under my feet, now, can I?''

Mrs. Jeffries sighed inwardly. The cook had a point, but as they didn't have a murder to investigate, it was rather a weak argument. "But Mrs. Goodge," she pointed out, "we don't have anything to investigate right at the moment."

"More's the pity," Mrs. Goodge snapped impatiently. "But that doesn't mean we won't get one, does it? If you don't mind my saying so, I don't want to have to miss another one because of my auntie! A woman her age shouldn't be out gallivanting all over the place anyway. She should be safely home."

"So that's it then." Smythe laughed. "You're afraid that dear old Auntie Elberta'll diddle ya out of a murder."

"It wouldn't be the first time," the cook replied darkly.

"But Mrs. Goodge," Mrs. Jeffries said kindly, "it wasn't your aunt's fault she became ill. . . .''

"Never said it was." Mrs. Goodge set her chin stubbornly. "But the fact is, I'm one murder short on the lot of you and it isn't fair. If I hadn't had to go off to see her last year, I'd not have missed that Barrett murder. She only had a touch of bronchitis, and here she had me dashing about thinkin' she was at death's door and causin' me to miss my fair share of the investigatin'. Well, I'll not be taking a risk like that again. I've got a feeling in my bones that sure as rice needs water, the minute Elberta shows up on our doorstep, we'll have us a fine murder."

"But sayin' we do get us one." Wiggins thought he ought to add his opinion to the discussion. "Why would it matter if she was 'ere or not? You'd still be able to do yer part."

The cook snorted derisively. "With Elberta hangin' about and puttin' her oar in it every time I was entertaining one of my sources? You must be daft, boy."

The cook had a veritable army of sources trooping through her kitchen. Chimney-sweeps, costermongers, laundrymen, street urchins, bakers' boys, delivery men and even the men from the gas works if necessary. She plied them with hot tea, sticky buns, Madeira cake and trifle while pumping them ruthlessly for every single morsel of gossip to be had. Her help on the inspector's previous cases had been important, and on several occasions, it had been a tidbit of gossip she'd learned that had been paramount in solving the case. She was most proud of her contribution to the cause of justice. Despite the fact that she never left the kitchen, the cook knew everything there was to know about everyone who was anybody in the city of London.

"I'm afraid you've left it a bit late," Mrs. Jeffries said kindly. "Even if Wiggins goes out tonight to the telegraph office, I doubt a message would reach your aunt before she left in the morning. You did say she lives quite a ways out in the country."

Mrs. Goodge thought about it for a moment and then gave a sigh of defeat. "Oh, bother. You're right. Besides, Elberta would just ignore it anyway. But it's inconvenient, her coming now. Ruddy inconvenient."

Mrs. Jeffries understood why the cook was so upset, but there was nothing they could do about it. "It'll all work out," she said cheerfully. "Besides, if she doesn't come tomorrow, Inspector Witherspoon will be most disappointed. He's so looking forward to meeting her." She could think of no other household in the city in which an employer not only allowed, but positively delighted in the staff's relatives coming to visit.

But then again, Gerald Witherspoon was an exceptional man. He'd not been born to wealth. He'd acquired a fortune and this huge house when his Aunt Euphemia had died. He'd also acquired Smythe and Wiggins at the same time. Mrs. Jeffries, Mrs. Goodge and Betsy had been later additions.

They were all devoted to the inspector and they were equally devoted to his cases. Murder investigations. Not that he knew about their efforts on his behalf. That would never do. But they contributed greatly to his success. As a matter of fact, Mrs. Jeffries thought smugly, if it hadn't been for them, Inspector Witherspoon would still be a clerk in the Records room at Scotland Yard and not one of its best homicide detectives.

"Has the inspector decided who he wants to invite to his dinner party?" Betsy asked.

Mrs. Jeffries frowned. "Yes, I'm afraid it's worse than we feared."

There was a collective groan around the table.

"She's really comin', then?" Smythe asked.

The housekeeper nodded. "Unfortunately, yes. She's going to be in London buying her trousseau . . ."

"You mean that man's really goin' to marry 'er?" Wiggins asked incredulously.

"As far as I know, yes," Mrs. Jeffries replied. "Otherwise, she wouldn't be coming to London. Since she is going to be in the city, the inspector can hardly ignore her."

"But that's not fair," Wiggins yelped. "Isn't this bloomin' party supposed to be for Lady Cannonberry?"

"Well, yes," Mrs. Jeffries said quickly. "She is the guest of honor." Lady Cannonberry was their neighbor, the widow of a peer and a thoroughly delightful friend to all of them. She was also a bit of a political radical, an enthusiastic helper on some of their investigations and very, very enamored of their dear employer. "I'm sure she'll not mind in the least that the inspector's cousin is invited as well."

"But she's only comin' for the dinner party, right?" Smythe asked anxiously. "She's not stayin'?"

"She's not staying," Mrs. Jeffries assured him. "We'll only have to put up with the woman for a couple of hours." She deliberately didn't tell them who else would be on the guest list for the evening. It would only depress them. Gracious, when Inspector Witherspoon asked her to send out *that* particular invitation, she'd been sorely tempted to rip it to shreds rather than pop it in the post-box. But good sense and integrity had prevailed against her personal prejudices and so she'd invited the odious man. But there was no need to share that information yet. "And it's only for a dinner party. We probably won't see her at all, except when we're serving. I hardly think she'll be coming down to the kitchen for a chat.''

Betsy giggled. ''I can't wait to see Luty's face when she hears. Maybe we ought to seat them next to each other.''

''Oh no, lass,'' Smythe said. ''That's not fair. That's no way to treat a friend. To be honest, I'd not stick Miss Edwina Livingston-Graves on my worst enemy.''

''This isn't a toss,'' Chief Inspector Jonathan Barrows said quietly to the constable standing at his elbow. ''This is murder. Cold-blooded, premeditated murder.''

''Yes, sir,'' the constable, a young man who'd only been on the force two months, replied quickly. He glanced around the room and wondered what the Chief saw that he didn't. It sure looked as if the place had been burgled to him. There was a broken pane of glass in the window of the French door. Looked to him like that was how the thief had gotten into the house, but he wasn't about to argue with the Chief Inspector. No sir, not him. He knew what was what. Frowning, he stared through the open bedroom door on the other side of the room. The top drawers in the dresser were open and bits of clothing were sticking out, a silver hairbrush and a bottle of scent were lying on the carpet amidst the tangle of the lace runner and a lamp had been knocked over. He shook his head. Looked like a toss to him. He glanced quickly at the woman crumpled on the floor. She had a knife sticking out of her back. Seemed to Constable Jesse Sayers, the poor lady had had the bad luck to walk in on a thief.

Barrows looked down at the body and grimaced. "Stabbed." He grunted sympathetically. "Not a nice way to die. But hopefully, it was quick."

Constable Sayers cleared his throat. "Uh, sir, P.C. Meadows has already sent for Inspector Nivens. He should be here any minute now."

Barrows's mouth tightened. He didn't like Inspector Nivens. Few people did. But in all fairness, he didn't blame P.C. Meadows for sending for him. Nivens was a good enough man when it came to burglaries, but he knew sod-all about murder. "He'll not be any use to us, will he? I don't want him mucking up the evidence until Witherspoon sees it." Barrows, who normally would have been at home with his feet up and reading a good book instead of standing over a corpse, had just attended a dinner party next door to the Cameron house when the alarm was raised.

He and Mrs. Barrows had just come out to hail a hansom when they'd heard the Cameron butler shouting for the constable from up at the corner. He'd put Mrs. Barrows into a hansom and taken charge.

"I assure you, sir," a harsh voice said from the doorway, "I am properly trained enough not to 'muck up the evidence.'"

Barrows whirled around. "Ah, Nivens. Sorry, I didn't know you were there. But this isn't really your balliwick."

"I understood there'd been a murder and robbery here," Nivens said, stepping farther into the room. He nodded toward the body. "Is that the victim?"

Barrows sighed. That was the sort of question he expected from Nivens. Never could stick the man. Too much of a bootlicker to the politicians, he was. "Of course it's the victim. Not many people nap on their sitting-room floors with knives sticking out of their backs."

Nivens ignored the sarcasm and walked toward the bedroom. "The place has been tossed," he commented.

"No, it hasn't," Barrows said testily. Much as he disliked Inspector Nivens, he'd best be careful. All that bootlicking had paid off. Nivens had powerful friends. "Someone's tried to make it look like a toss. But if a pro did that"—he jerked his chin toward the tallboys—"I'll eat my hat."

"Not every toss is done by a pro." Nivens gave his superior a thin smile. "Did I hear you say you were calling Inspector Witherspoon in for this one?"

"I am," he replied firmly. Nivens might be right, but Barrows didn't think it likely. "I know full well that not all burglaries are done by pros, but someone went to a great deal of trouble to convince us that this one was. This isn't a burglary gone bad, it's murder." He nodded toward the victim. "Someone wanted that woman dead."

"Are you absolutely certain of that?" Nivens asked.

Barrows hesitated. In his heart, he knew he was right. He could smell a sham when he was standing in it. But he'd worked himself up from the ranks with good, honest police work and he wasn't a fool.

Anyone with half a brain could tell that Nivens wanted this case. Scotland Yard was as riddled with politics and pressure as any department in Whitehall. Much as he disliked Nivens, he couldn't honestly say with one hundred percent certainty that this wasn't a burglary. Blasted inconvenient that one of the police constables had taken it upon himself to send for Nivens. "Well, it certainly looks that way to me and I have had a number of years of experience."

Nivens said nothing. He walked over to stand in the doorway between the two rooms, his gaze darting back and forth between them. "No professional would do the drawers like that," he admitted, "and there's plenty of valuables about that should have been grabbed first, but I don't think you can state with any absolute certainty that this is simply a case of murder."

Barrows said nothing.

"In which case," Nivens continued, "I'd venture to say that I'm far more experienced in this kind of case than Inspector Witherspoon is." He walked across the room and knelt down by the body.

Barrows watched him for a moment. Scotland Yard was organized quite rigidly, at least on paper. If he was really following regulations, he'd have called in whatever inspector was on duty and assigned to this district. But no organization was independent of politics or the latest headlines in the *Times*. The police were under constant pressure to solve crimes quickly, efficiently and with some assurance of actually catching the real culprits. Especially now. So organization or not, every chief inspector had his own way of making sure he got his fair share of collars. It was common knowledge that when a good copper was needed to sort out a burglary, Nivens, sod that he was, was the one who got it. By the same token, if one wanted a killer caught, the odds were that Gerald Witherspoon would catch the killer. And Barrows wanted a killer caught. But he didn't dare step too hard on Nivens's toes.

"You're right." Barrows grinned. "Oh, by the way, I shouldn't touch that body if I were you."

Surprised, Nivens looked up. "Why ever not?"

"Because I want Witherspoon to examine the victim."

Niven's eyes narrowed angrily but Barrows continued before he could protest. "I've decided to have you both on this one."

Niven's jaw dropped. "That's highly irregular, sir."

"Of course it is," Barrows said cheerfully, "but after the beating the force has taken over this wretched Ripper case, I'm not going to risk someone else getting away with murder." He turned to Constable Sayers. "Get a lad over to Witherspoon's straight away. Tell him to get here quickly. He and Inspector Nivens will be working together on this one."

"It ought to be a fine day tomorrow," Smythe ventured softly.

Betsy looked up from the apron she was mending and smiled. Smythe was staring over her shoulder, at a spot on the far wall rather than at her. She knew what that meant. The poor man was working up the courage to ask her to go out with him again. She thought it was sweet the way the cocky, sometimes arrogant coachman could be as shy as a schoolboy. "Should be nice," she commented, putting the last stitch through the stiff cotton. "But it'll be cold."

"True," he said quickly, "but it's goin' to be sunny." He cleared his throat. "I'm takin' Bow and Arrow for a good run tomorrow with the carriage, and seein' as it's yer day out, I was wonderin' if you'd like to come along?"

"I would," Wiggins volunteered from the doorway. Blissfully unaware of the scowl the coachman directed toward him, Wiggins and Fred, the household's mongrel dog, advanced into the warm, cozy kitchen. "I've not been out in ages. Where we goin' then?"

Betsy stifled a grin as she caught a quick peek at the thunderous expression on Smythe's face. "*We're* not going anywhere," she said tartly, taking pity on the coachman. "It's my day out, remember? Not yours. You've got to be here to help Mrs. Goodge get her Aunt Elberta settled in."

Wiggins opened his mouth to protest, but just then, Mrs. Goodge, a brown bottle in her hand, came bustling through the kitchen door. "This ruddy cap's stuck again," she cried, charging toward Smythe and thrusting the bottle under his nose. "See if you can get it unstuck. I don't know why they make them like that. Silly bottle makers, don't they know that people with rheumatism in their joints can't undo those wretched tops? If we could, we wouldn't need the ruddy stuff in the first place."

Smythe, wondering when, if ever, he'd get a chance to be alone with Betsy, took the bottle, gave the top a fast, hard twist and when he felt it give, handed it back to the cook. "There you are, Mrs. Goodge. All nice and open for ya. A good night's sleep and a bit of this on yer 'ands and you'll be right as rain tomorrow."

"Is your rheumatism bothering you again?" Mrs. Jeffries asked as she too stepped into the kitchen.

Blimey, thought Smythe, it's a ruddy train station in here. Doesn't this lot ever go to sleep? Blasted inconvenient it was, never havin' a moment to be alone with the lass.

"It's been actin' up a bit." Mrs. Goodge plopped down in the chair next to Betsy. Wiggins sat down next to her.

Smythe sighed inwardly. Maybe they'd all go to bed soon.

"Can we have some cocoa?" Wiggins asked.

Smythe shot the footman a savage frown, but Wiggins didn't see it. He was too busy scratching Fred's ears.

"It's gettin' kinda late," Smythe said quickly. "And with Mrs. Goodge's 'ands actin' up, I don't think we ought to be botherin' her with makin' a 'ot drink."

"Oh, I'll make it," Mrs. Jeffries said airily as she bustled toward the wet larder in the hall. "I've nothing else to do. The inspector's gone up already . . ." she broke off and cocked her head, listening.

From outside the kitchen window, the sound of heavy footsteps running up the stairs to the front door could be heard. A second later, they all heard the loud banging of the knocker.

"I wonder who that could be?" Mrs. Jeffries started for the stairs.

But fast as she was, Smythe headed her off. "I'll go up and see who it is," he said. "It's too late for you to be openin' that front door without knowin' who's doin' the knockin'."

Together, they went up and started down the hall. Inspector Witherspoon, dressed in only his trousers and an unbuttoned white shirt was just reaching for the handle.

"Let me, sir," Smythe called, charging past the housekeeper and making a mad dash for the front door. Blimey, didn't these two realize it weren't safe to be openin' that blooming door at this time of night?

"Oh, that's all right," Witherspoon replied. He slapped the latch back and turned the key. "I am, after all, a policeman."

"But sir." Smythe leapt toward the front door just as the inspector pulled it open. He elbowed his employer to one side and planted his big body directly in front of him. "That's what I'm afraid of, sir. You've put enough killers away to have plenty of enemies out there."

"Uh, excuse me." Constable Sayers blinked at the sight of the huge burly man standing like a mountain on the other side of the door. "But is this the home of Inspector Gerald Witherspoon?"

"It is," Smythe replied as he eased to his left. "And I take it ya want to see 'im?"

"It's a police constable, Smythe," Witherspoon

said cheerfully. "I do believe it's quite safe to let him in."

"Sorry to bother you, sir," Constable Sayers apologized as he came in, keeping a wary eye on Smythe. "But Chief Inspector Barrows sent me round to get you, sir. There's been a murder."

"A murder?" Witherspoon repeated. He hated getting rousted out at all hours for a murder. But then, murderers were not by nature the most thoughtful of people.

"Yes, sir," the young man replied. He noticed that both the woman, who he assumed was a house-keeper, and the big man, who looked more like a thug than a coachman, were still standing beside the inspector. "Chief Inspector Barrows thinks you should come quick, sir. That's why he sent me along to fetch you. A woman's been stabbed, sir."

Witherspoon stared at the young man for a moment. "Chief Inspector Barrows sent you?"

Constable Sayers nodded. "The Chief asked for you, sir, though Inspector Nivens was against it."

Mrs. Jeffries and Smythe looked at each other.

"Inspector Nivens?" the inspector repeated. Gracious, this was most odd. Most odd, indeed.

"Yes, sir. He's on the scene because we thought it was just a burglary. Then the Chief Inspector arrived and said it weren't, that it were murder and we'd best send for you. We've sent along for Constable Barnes as well, sir. He'll meet us there, sir."

"Thank you, Constable." Witherspoon decided to wait till he got to the scene of the crime before asking any more questions. "If you'll have a seat in the drawing room"—he gestured down the hall—"I'll be ready to go back with you in just a few moments."

But Mrs. Jeffries wasn't going to let a golden opportunity like this pass. "Inspector, it's quite cold outside. Why don't I take the constable down to the kitchen for a nice cup of tea or cocoa while you're getting ready?"

"How very thoughtful of you, Mrs. Jeffries," the inspector replied as he headed for the steps. "I'm sure the constable could use something warm to drink."

"Thank you, ma'am, I'd be most obliged," Constable Sayers replied honestly. Truth was, he was frozen to the bone.

"Come this way, then," she said, smiling cheerfully as she took his arm. "We'll have you fixed up in no time."

Smythe, following on their heels, grinned hugely. Mrs. Goodge would really get her apron in a twist now. It looked as if they had them a murder. Even better, if he knew Mrs. Jeffries as well as he thought he did, she'd grill this poor lad until she'd wrung every single little detail out of him.

Barnes was indeed waiting for the inspector when he and Sayers slipped past the police constable, who nodded smartly, and into the back sitting room of the elegant Mayfair home. So was Inspector Nivens.

Feeling a bit awkward, Witherspoon smiled faintly. "Good evening," he said. "I understand Chief Inspector Barrows wanted me to have a look in."

Nivens grunted in reply, so the inspector turned

his attention to the scene of the crime.

The room was small, and in the daylight probably quite a cheerful little place. The floor was covered with a cream colored carpet. Bright yellow-and-white striped wall paper, adorned with colorful prints of pastoral scenes, graced the walls. A small but delicately carved mantel stood guard over the fireplace. A silver pitcher brimming with orange and yellow dried flowers sat atop the buttercup-colored fringed shawl on a table at the far side of the room. Clustered beside it in a nice, cozy circle was a deep brown horsehair settee and two mustard-coloured velvet balloon-backed chairs. On the opposite wall, a door was half open and Constable Barnes leaned against the doorjamb.

Nivens's lip curled when their gazes met. He jerked his head toward the French doors. "We'd best get cracking. The Chief Inspector wants this cleared up as soon as possible."

"Is he still here?" Witherspoon asked, taking care to avoid looking in the direction that Nivens indicated. He wanted to put off looking at the dead woman until the last possible moment. It was quite difficult to ignore her. She did have a rather large knife poking out of her back.

"He's having a quick word with the victim's husband," Nivens replied. "But he'll be back directly. Maybe you'll have this case solved by then." His voice dripped sarcasm but Inspector Witherspoon didn't appear to notice.

Constable Barnes, a craggy-faced man with a shock of iron-gray hair and a ruddy complexion, glared at Nivens's back and stifled a rude remark. Stupid git! He didn't like Inspector Nivens; most of the constables who'd worked with him didn't like him. But he had to tread carefully here; the man was assigned to this case. Thank goodness the Chief had had the good sense to call in Inspector Witherspoon. God knows what kind of muck up Nivens would have made of it.

"You'll want to have a look at the body, sir." Barnes directed his comment to Witherspoon. "The police surgeon should be here any moment now."

Witherspoon smiled briefly and steeled himself. He wished Constable Barnes wasn't so keen on always getting him to examine the corpse. But it was his duty, so he'd best get it over with. He stepped across the room and knelt down by the fallen woman. But he couldn't bring himself to look, not quite yet. He gazed out the window pane to the balcony and beyond that, to the vague outline of skeletal tree limbs and bushes. "Is that a garden?"

"Yes, sir," Barnes replied, "we've had the lads out there having a look round, tramping about in the darkness, but they've found nothing."

"We'll search it again tomorrow morning," Witherspoon said.

"I've already given those instructions," Nivens snapped. He'd come over and stood over them, his pale face set in a scowl, his mouth compressed into a flat, thin line. From the backlighting of the gas lamps on the wall behind him, Witherspoon could make out the sheen of hair oil on his dark blond hair.

"Uh, I say, did you want something?" The inspector didn't mind being a tad squeamish about corpses in front of Barnes, but he didn't wish to make a spectacle of himself in front of Inspector Nivens.

"I want you to tell me what you make of that." Nivens pointed to the body.

"What's the victim's name?"

"Hannah Cameron." Nivens tapped his foot impatiently. "Well, what are you waiting for? Get on with it."

Witherspoon, grateful that his dinner had been several hours ago, forced himself to look down. She lay slumped on her side directly inside of the door. Her hair was a faded blond, going gray at the temples, and her face, now deathly white, was long and narrow. Her eyes, open still, were blue. She'd been wearing a green velvet dress. She did not look like a happy woman. Even in death, there was an air of joylessness about her that filled Witherspoon with regret. But whatever she had been in life, whether harridan or saint, no one had had the right to shove a knife in her back and kill her. "She's dead."

"Of course she's dead," Nivens cried. "That's why you're here. For some odd reason, the Chief Inspector seems to think you're the only person capable of handling a simple homicide."

"I don't think it's simple," Witherpsoon muttered. They never were. He steeled himself and turned her shoulder so that he could see her back. He swallowed heavily and closed his eyes. The handle of the blade stuck out obscenely. The green velvet fabric was soaked with blood. There was more blood on the carpet, directly beneath where she'd lain. He eased her gently back down and stood up. His forehead creased in thought. "Has anyone touched the body?"

"No, sir," Constable Sayers said. "Her husband found her, sir, and he had sense enough not to touch anything."

"It looks as if she were standing looking out onto the garden and was struck from behind," the inspector commented.

"Yes, sir." Barnes had knelt down on the other side of the body. He too stood up. "That's one of the reasons I'm fairly sure it weren't a burglary."

Nivens snorted. "I didn't realize you were such an expert, Constable."

Witherspoon looked at him sharply. "Constable Barnes's observations are always most pertinent. I agree with him."

Barnes smiled, grateful that his superior had stood up for him. "I'm thinkin', sir, that if she were standin' looking out at the garden, the burglar"—he tossed a quick glance at Nivens—"would have already been in the room."

"Of course he would have," Nivens said quickly. "And that's the whole point. She came in and saw the window was broken, walked over to have a look at it and when she had her back turned, the killer, who was probably hiding in that bedroom"—he pointed toward the door on the other side of the room—"stabbed her and then escaped. This is a simple robbery gone bad. There was no reason for the Chief to call you out on this one. With my sources among the thieves of this city, I'll soon find who killed her."

"Do the doors open in or out?"

"In, sir," Barnes replied.

Witherspoon glanced down at the body again and noted that it was lying less than two inches from the door. "If that was the case, Inspector Nivens," he asked softly, "how did the burglar get out?"

Nivens looked confused. "I don't understand your question. Isn't it obvious? He walked out the way he got in."

"Through the French doors?"

"Yes," Nivens said, but his voice wasn't as certain as before.

Witherspoon looked down at the floor again, studying the carpet surrounding the body. He frowned, trying to recall some of the conversations he'd had with his housekeeper. Why, just last week they'd had quite an interesting discussion about blood. What was it she'd said? Then he remembered. "I don't think so. If he'd killed her in a panic, he'd have wanted to get out in a hurry. That means she'd have still been bleeding quite profusely."

"So?" Nivens asked sullenly, his gaze on the doorway in case the Chief Inspector toddled back in just as the brilliant bloody Witherspoon was expounding on one of his ridiculous theories.

"What I'm trying to say"—Witherspoon wasn't sure exactly how to put it. He wished he could remember the precise way Mrs. Jeffries had discussed the matter. "—is that if he tried to get out this door while the poor woman was still bleeding profusely, there'd be blood all over the carpet. He would have had to jostle her and shove her out of the way. As you can see, there's only blood directly beneath the body, which implies that she fell almost directly after she was struck down and that the body hasn't been moved at all. That means the killer couldn't have gone out these doors.''

Nivens stared at him thoughtfully. Then he said, ''That's the most ridiculous thing I've ever heard.''

CHAPTER 2

"I knew it," Mrs. Goodge cried. "I just knew it. Here we finally have us a nice, ripe murder and I'm saddled with my daft old aunt."

"Stop yer frettin', Mrs. Goodge," Smythe said kindly. "It'll not be as bad as ya think. We'll find a way to keep yer auntie occupied."

"Doing what? She's eighty-five if she's a day," Mrs. Goodge muttered disgustedly. "I can hardly shove her into a hansom and send her down to Regent Street to look at the shops."

"Now, now," Mrs. Jeffries soothed. "We'll think of something. If she's that elderly, she'll probably spend a lot of time in her room, resting."

Betsy gave a worried glance at the clock. "Should we send for Luty and Hatchet? You know how Luty gets."

Mrs. Jeffries thought about it. Luty Belle Crookshank and her butler, Hatchet, were dear friends.

They considered themselves almost a part of the inspector's household and as such, they were determined to be in on all of the inspector's cases. They were born snoops. Luty in particular got a bit testy when she wasn't directly informed that they had a killer to catch. "I honestly don't know." She hesitated. "It's awfully late."

"I don't think we ought to bother," Smythe said. "We'll none of us be able to get started until tomorrow. I can always nip out bright and early and bring them back 'ere for breakfast."

"No, you can't," Mrs. Goodge said darkly. "You'll not have time. You've got to help me move Aunt Elberta's bed into that little room next to mine and then you've got to go to Charing Cross to pick her up."

"Can't Wiggins do it?"

"I can't drive the carriage," Wiggins cried. He'd driven the carriage once before and the experience had left him so shaken, he'd sworn he'd never do it again.

"I know," the coachman replied, "and the 'orses know it as well. What I meant was, can't you move the ruddy bed?"

"It's too heavy for him," Mrs. Jeffries said. "As a matter of fact, it'll probably take both of you." She tapped her fingers on the top of the table as she considered a way around their problem. It was imperative they get an early start tomorrow and it was equally imperative that Luty and Hatchet be fully informed. "I'll tell you what," she said, as an idea struck. "The inspector won't be home for hours so there's no reason Smythe and Wiggins can't move the bed tonight. That'll free Smythe up to go fetch Luty and Hatchet early tomorrow morning. We can have our meeting then and we'll bring them up to date on everything we learned from Constable Sayers.''

"He was a nice young man," Betsy murmured, remembering the way the constable's gaze had kept straying to her, even when he was talking to someone else.

"Bit of a nervous Nellie, if you ask me," Smythe grumbled. He too had noticed the way Sayers had been eyeing up Betsy. He hadn't liked it one bit. "Couldn't even hold his cocoa without 'is 'and shakin'.''

"Only because he was cold." Betsy defended him. She'd felt sorry for him. As much as Constable Sayers had tried to hide it, he'd been rattled by seeing the dead woman's body.

"Who's going to fetch Aunt Elberta from the station?" Mrs. Goodge interrupted. She wanted to get this problem sorted out now so she wouldn't have to worry about it all night. "Her train is in early.''

"I will," Mrs. Jeffries volunteered. "I'll pop over in a hansom. We'll bring her back, get her nicely settled in and then start our inquiries.''

"But I wanted to get round to Mayfair early tomorrow," Betsy complained. "You know, before the police start snooping about the neighborhood.''

"They're already snoopin' about," Smythe said. "Your getting there at ten o'clock instead of eight won't make any difference.''

Betsy pursed her lips. "I don't know. We'll have to be really careful on this one. Inspector Nivens would love to catch one of us interfering.''

"We'll just have to make sure he doesn't, won't we?" Mrs. Jeffries said firmly. But despite her bravado, she was concerned. Inspector Nivens had made no secret of the fact that he thought Gerald Witherspoon had help on his cases. If he so much as caught a glimpse of one of them, the jig would be up. What rotten luck that their dear inspector had gotten saddled with that odious man. They'd just have to make doubly sure they didn't get caught.

"Well, at least we found out a few things tonight," Wiggins said cheerfully. "We know who died and where she lived. That's a good start, in'n it?"

The tall, red-haired man with the handlebar mustache sat hunched in a wing-back chair. The collar of his white evening shirt was off and though he was decently dressed in proper black evening trousers and boots, he wore a heavy brown dressing gown over his clothes. His face was buried in his hands. "I can't believe she's dead," he murmured. "I simply can't believe it. Who would want to do such a thing? Why? Why hurt Hannah? Why didn't they just run when they saw her? Why kill her?"

Witherspoon stared at him sympathetically. This was one of the worst aspects of his job, talking to the loved ones of the victim. "I'm terribly sorry for your loss, sir," he said. "But if you're able, we'd like to ask you a few questions."

"Really, Inspector," a woman's voice said harshly, "have you no sense of decency? Mr. Cameron's just lost his wife. He's in shock. Can't this wait until tomorrow?"

Witherspoon raised his gaze and looked at the speaker. She'd been introduced as Fiona Hadleigh, a friend of the victim's who was staying overnight at the Cameron house. She stood next to Brian Cameron's chair, her thin, bony hand on the man's shoulder. A tall woman, she wore an evening dress of sapphire blue velvet fitted at the neck with a double layer of white lace. Matching blue velvet slippers peeked out from beneath the hem of her skirt. Her hair, upswept in an elaborate arrangement on top of her head, was circled with a bandeaux that had a flurry of white ostrich feathers. But despite her beautiful outfit, she was a homely woman, her brown hair streaked with gray at the temples, her face long and horsey and her mouth a thin wedge beneath a rather large nose.

"We're not insensitive to Mr. Cameron's shock," the inspector said softly, "but the sooner we start asking questions, the sooner we can catch the person who committed this foul murder."

"It's all right, Fiona." Brian Cameron raised his head and smiled at her. "The inspector's only doing his job. Please, do go up to bed. There's nothing you can do. Tell the others to go on up as well. There's no need for Kathryn or John to keep the vigil. I'll be all right."

"Nonsense, Brian," Fiona said briskly. "I wouldn't dream of leaving you alone." She walked across the drawing room and yanked at the bell pull. "I'll ring for some tea."

Witherspoon glanced at Barnes, who'd taken out his notebook and was busily scribbling away. Inspector Nivens had gone off to the Yard, no doubt to complain about the situation. Inspector Witherspoon didn't much blame the fellow. It was going to be decidedly awkward for both of them. But he had a duty to perform and, uncomfortable or not, he'd make the best of the situation. "Mr. Cameron, I understand your household is very upset and that it's getting very late. Your servants and your other guests can go up to their rooms as soon as they've made a statement to the police constable."

"P.C. Sayers and P.C. Meadows have taken statements from the staff. I've taken Kathryn Ellingsley's and John Ripton's statements," Barnes told Witherspoon. "The servants have all gone back to bed. But Miss Ellingsley and Mr. Ripton insisted on waiting up for Mr. Cameron. They're in the library if you'd like a word with them."

"Do you think that's necessary tonight?" Witherspoon asked him. He wondered if Nivens had bothered to talk to anyone.

"I think you could question them tomorrow, sir," Barnes replied. "Neither of them saw or heard anything."

Fiona finished giving instructions to the maid and stomped back to take up her post next to Brian Cameron. "Well," she snapped, "get on with it. We don't wish to stand about here all night."

"Then I suggest you have a seat, Fiona," Brian said, softening his words with a smile and a pat on her hand. "Please, Inspector, do sit down and make yourself comfortable. I'm sure you've a number of things you need to ask."

"Thank you, sir," he replied, walking over and sitting down on a hard-backed chair across from the settee. "I'll try to be as brief as possible. First of all, how many people were in the house to-night?''

Cameron thought about it a moment. ''Other than the servants, there was my wife and myself, Fiona, of course, and John Ripton. The four of us had gone to dinner tonight. They'd decided to stay over.''

''Anyone else?''

Cameron shrugged. ''Just Kathryn and the children.''

''Kathryn Ellingsley—she's the governess, I believe.'' Witherspoon stated.

''She's been with us for about six months,'' Cameron replied. ''I've two children, Inspector. Edward and Ellen. Edward's ten and Ellen is eight. This will be very difficult for them to understand.''

Witherspoon clucked his tongue sympathetically. ''How dreadful for them to lose their mother so young.''

''Mrs. Cameron was their stepmother,'' Fiona put in.

''But she's the only mother the children have ever known,'' Brian added. ''We married when they were both babies. My first wife died of influenza right after Ellen was born.''

''So you've been widowed twice, sir,'' Barnes commented quietly.

Fiona Hadleigh glanced at him sharply. ''What's that supposed to mean? The first Mrs. Cameron died of influenza.''

Barnes raised his eyebrows slightly. ''It wasn't a question, Mrs. Hadleigh, just a comment.''

''I'll thank you to keep your comments to yourself.''

Witherspoon cleared his throat. "Can you tell me what happened this evening, sir?"

Cameron sighed wearily. "As I told you, the four of us had dinner together . . ."

"At a restaurant?" Witherspoon interrupted. He hated to be rude, but he'd found that if he didn't get a question out when he thought of it, he sometimes forgot it altogether.

Cameron nodded. "At Simpsons. We were to dine at eight, but the restaurant was crowded so it took quite a while to get served and have our meal. By the time we got home, it was so late that we invited Mrs. Hadleigh and Mr. Ripton to spend the night. They accepted the invitation. John and I had a glass of port before retiring and Fiona and Hannah kept us company. About eleven-thirty, we all went to bed. I read for a while and then just as I started to get undressed, Miriam, my wife's maid, knocked on the door. She asked if I'd seen Mrs. Cameron. She couldn't find her."

"So it was the maid who alerted you to the fact that Mrs. Cameron wasn't in her room?" Witherspoon said. He wanted to get the sequence of events clear in his own mind.

"That's correct."

The inspector thought about it for a moment. "How long was it from the time you went up until the maid came and knocked on your door?"

He shrugged. "Twenty minutes or so, perhaps a bit more, perhaps a bit less. I've really no idea. It's my habit to read before I retire. I remember I'd just put down my book when the maid knocked. But I didn't think to look at the clock."

"And then what happened?" Witherspoon prompted gently.

"Then I went back downstairs thinking that perhaps Hannah had forgotten something and gone to fetch it. But she wasn't in the drawing room or the library, so I had a look in the small back sitting room and . . . and . . ." His voice broke and he looked down at the floor.

"It's quite all right, sir," Witherspoon interrrupted. "You needn't go on about that part of it. We know what you found."

"Had the maid searched for Mrs. Cameron?" Barnes asked.

"I don't know," he replied, shaking his head. "I assume not."

"Why?" the constable persisted. From what he knew of rich people, they didn't get off their backsides and hunt for someone if they had a servant to do it for them.

Brian Cameron seemed surprised by the question. "Why what? Why didn't the maid search? I've no idea. You'll have to ask her."

"Was there any reason that you can think of why your wife went into that room tonight?" Witherspoon asked.

Cameron closed his eyes and shook his head. "Not that I know about. I've no idea why she went downstairs at all. The only thing I can think of is that she'd forgotten something and gone back downstairs to fetch it."

"But if she'd forgotten something, wouldn't she have sent her maid to get it?"

"Usually, yes."

"But this time, she went down herself," Witherspoon mused. He thought back to how the body had been situated in the room. "Is it possible she could have heard something out in the garden and gone down on her own to see what it was?"

"It's possible," Cameron replied. "Quite honestly, Inspector, I've no idea why my wife came downstairs. She only uses that sitting room in the mornings. But as it was, she did go down and it cost her dearly. She obviously surprised a thief and the cur murdered her."

Witherspoon knew he had to tread cautiously here. Apparently, Chief Inspector Barrows hadn't informed the master of the house that his wife's murder might not be as simple as that. "Were any of the windows or doors opened when you came downstairs?"

"I don't know. I didn't think to look. As soon as I realized that Hannah was dead, I sent the butler out for help."

"The front door was open," Fiona Hadleigh volunteered. "I saw it standing wide open when I came downstairs to see what all the commotion was about."

"It was only open because Hatfield was so rattled he dashed out into the street shouting his lungs out for the police," Cameron replied. "It wasn't opened before that. It was locked. I checked that when I came down looking for Hannah." He looked up at Witherspoon. "The police searched the house earlier. They didn't find any windows open and the bolt was still on the back door when they looked. Why are you asking about the doors and windows?"

"If your wife surprised a burglar," Witherspoon

replied, "I'm wondering how he got in and out?"

"Well, surely that's obvious. The French doors in the study. The glass was broken in one of them. That's how he must have gotten in."

Witherspoon thought about the position of the body again, about the way Hannah Cameron had been crumbled in a heap less than two inches from the door frame.

"Mr. Cameron," he began hesitantly, "I'm afraid there's a possibility your wife didn't surprise a thief."

Cameron's brows drew together. "But that's nonsense. She must have. Who else could have killed her?"

Witherspoon thought it prudent not to share all his information with someone who might be a suspect in this case. He was sorry now that he'd said anything. But if Hannah Cameron had surprised a thief, he'd eat his hat for breakfast. "I'm afraid, sir, that we can't rule out any possibilities. I'll have to ask everyone, including your servants, to make yourselves available for further questioning."

Mrs. Jeffries was at her wit's end. Getting Aunt Elberta safely ensconced in the household while at the same time trying to pry a bit of information out of a dreadfully tired Inspector Witherspoon had greatly taxed her resources, not to mention her stamina. But by ten o'clock the next morning, Aunt Elberta was resting comfortably in her room upstairs and they were grouped around the kitchen table. Inspector Witherspoon, having come home very late, had gone to bed with only a weary smile

at his housekeeper and then been up and out with
only a cup of tea for his breakfast.

But Mrs. Jeffries had gotten some basic facts out
of the man. Facts she was eager to share with the
others, all of whom were chomping at the bit to
get cracking.

"What's takin' Luty and Hatchet so long?"
Wiggins asked. "Smythe left to get 'em 'ours
ago."

"It's not been hours," Betsy corrected, but she
too frowned at the clock.

At that moment, they heard the back door opening and the sound of voices.

"Howdy, everyone," Luty called as she dashed
into the kitchen. "I'm sorry it took us so long to
git here, but I had to get shut of some business
before I could come." Luty Belle Crookshank was
white-haired, dark-eyed and sharp as a razor despite her advanced years. She wore a bright blue
bonnet with a plume of peacock feathers on the
crest and carried a large mink muff. Her small
frame was swathed in a heavy black coat which
she shedded as she crossed the room. Tossing it on
the coat tree, she smoothed the skirt of her outra-
geously bright green-and-blue striped day gown
and hurried over to the others.

"I'd hardly call Sir William Marlin 'business to
get shut of,' " Hatchet reproved his employer
stiffly. He was a tall, distinguished looking man
with a full shock of white hair, a carriage straighter
than the Kaiser's and a ready smile that belied his
always correct manner. "Good morning, everyone," he said formally as he pulled out a chair for
his employer. "I must say, I was utterly delighted

when your good man Smythe came round this morning and told us our services were needed.''

''Glad you finally got here,'' Mrs. Goodge said testily. She whipped a quick glance over her shoulder toward the hall and the backstairs. No doubt she was still worried that Aunt Elberta would come bursting in on them.

''We got 'ere as quick as we could,'' Smythe said, dropping into the chair next to Betsy. ''But Luty had some important business . . .''

''Piddle.'' Luty snorted. ''Bill Marlin only wanted to badger me about givin' my money away. I told him it weren't none of his business who I give my cash to and sent him along. Stupid men, always tryin' to stick their noses in other people's business.''

''You didn't have to be so rude to him.'' Hatchet sniffed disapprovingly. ''Honestly, madam, you practically threatened to shoot the poor fellow.''

''I never threatened him,'' Luty protested. ''Can I help it if he turned tail and skedaddled just because I got my gun out?'' Luty liked to carry a Colt .45 in her fur muff when they were on a case.

''Oh dear.'' Mrs. Jeffries cast a worried glance at the muff that lay innocently on the table in front of Luty. ''I thought we'd agreed that perhaps carrying a loaded weapon in London wasn't such a good idea.''

''Don't fret, Hepzibah.'' Luty laughed. ''I only got the gun out to have a look at it. I'm not carryin' it. Hatchet claims it makes him nervous.''

''It would make anyone nervous,'' Hatchet replied. ''And you got the weapon out to terrorize Sir William . . .''

"It worked, didn't it?" Luty shot back. "Bill took one look at my peacemaker and suddenly remembered another appointment."

Hatchet harrumphed loudly. "*Bill* indeed! All he was doing was his proper job, madam. Your late husband did specifically request that Sir William act as your financial advisor."

"Let's argue about it later," Luty replied. "I want to hear what we've got on our plates." She turned to Mrs. Jeffries. "What do we know about this here killing?"

"We've learned enough to get started," Mrs. Jeffries said. "The inspector was too tired to talk when he came home and he was in a hurry this morning. But luckily, one of the constables on the scene was here last night and we got quite a bit out of him. The victim is a woman named Hannah Cameron. Whoever killed her tried to make it look as though she'd interrupted a burglary. She was stabbed in the back. Chief Inspector Barrows of Scotland Yard happened to be leaving the house next door when the alarm was raised and he took charge. The moment he saw the room the woman was found in, he knew it was a case of willful murder."

"Then I take it that someone, presumably the killer, deliberately tried to make it look as though the victim had surprised a burglar?" Hatchet ventured.

"Indeed." Mrs. Jeffries picked up her tea cup. "They went to a great deal of effort. There was a broken window in the pane of the French doors, some drawers were left open and a number of items were found on the floor. But apparently, whoever did it didn't know the first thing about how a real burglar would have behaved. It was the top drawers that were opened, you see," she explained. "And there were a number of small, expensive items in the bedroom that hadn't been touched. A true professional would have nabbed those before he'd even touched the drawers looking for valuables."

Luty's brows drew together. "I ain't followin' ya. What difference does it make which drawers were open?"

"A professional burglar would have started from the bottom up," Hatchet answered. "It's much faster that way. If you start from the top and work down, you have to take the time to close the drawer before you can properly see what's in the one below it. Oh, excuse me, Mrs. Jeffries, I didn't mean to interrupt."

She smiled in amusement. "That's quite all right, Hatchet. You are correct." She went on to tell them the rest of what they'd learned. "So you see," she concluded, "we must be extra careful. Not only is this case extremely puzzling, but we've got to contend with Inspector Nivens being very involved in it."

There was a collective moan from the others. Mrs. Jeffries smiled briefly and went on, "But we do have a list of suspects. Inspector Witherspoon thinks that the killer must have already been in the house. As there was no sign of a door or window being open, he's assuming that the killer either was already in the house or had a key."

"But didn't you just say that this Hadleigh woman noticed the front door standing wide open?" Betsy asked.

"I did," Mrs. Jeffries nodded. "And that's one of the things we'll need to confirm. Brian Cameron claims it was only opened when the butler dashed out to get a policeman."

"Was Cameron watchin' the door the whole time?" Smythe asked. "I mean, a lot of thieves are quick on their feet. If the burglar couldn't have gotten out the French doors in the sittin' room before the alarm was raised, he could have been hidin' and waitin' for a chance to slip out the front door."

"At this point," the housekeeper explained, "we simply don't know enough one way or the other. But if Chief Inspector Barrow and our inspector both think this wasn't a burglary, I believe we ought to go along with that assumption. At least until we have some facts in our possession which indicate differently."

"Who else was in the 'ouse?" Wiggins asked.

"A number of servants were there," Mrs. Jeffries replied, "but most of them were asleep, of course. Then there's the governess, Kathryn Ellingsley; the two guests, Fiona Hadleigh and a Mr. John Ripton; and, of course, Brian Cameron."

"What kind of knife was it?" Hatchet asked.

"Just a simple butcher knife," Mrs. Jeffries frowned. "According to Constable Sayers, there's no way to trace it. There's a lot we don't know, but there's plenty enough for us to get started."

Betsy got to her feet. "I'll get over to Mayfair straight away and start asking questions. By this time, the news of the murder will be all over the place."

"Excellent, Betsy." Mrs. Jeffries smiled in approval. "Concentrate on the shopkeepers and find out what you can about the victim and her family."

"Do you want me to try and make contact with a servant?" Betsy asked.

"Only if you can do so without running into Inspector Nivens," Mrs. Jeffries warned. "Remember, we've all got to keep a sharp eye out. He's actually helping the inspector with this case. They've both been assigned to it and I don't want him catching so much as a glimpse of any of us."

" 'Old up, Betsy," Smythe called to the maid as he too got up. "We might as well go together. If it's all right with Mrs. J., I'll head over that way and begin talking to the cabbies and seein' what I can pick up at the pubs."

"That's a good idea," the housekeeper said. She watched in approval as the two of them put on their hats and coats and started for the back door. Both of them knew precisely what to do, precisely how to begin this investigation.

"I reckon you want me to start buzzin' my sources about information on Brian Cameron," Luty said.

"If you would, please. That would be most helpful," Mrs. Jeffries replied. Luty was rich. She knew a lot of bankers and financial people. Using charm, grace, tact, diplomacy, intimidation and stubborness, she could find out how much a person was worth down to his last penny.

"I'll get the word out too," Mrs. Goodge said. She openly glared toward the hall. "With any luck, Aunt Elberta will sleep a few hours and leave me in peace. I've got a fair number of people stopping by today. Once I tell 'em about the murder, I might be able to learn all sorts of things.''

"What do you want me to do?" Wiggins asked. "With Inspector Nivens hanging about and gummin' up the works, it'll not be easy for me to meet up with a servant from the Cameron 'ousehold.''

Mrs. Jeffries had already considered that problem. "I know. I think that this time instead of trying to talk with one of them at the Cameron house in Mayfair, perhaps you ought to see if anyone leaves the household.''

"You want me to follow 'em?" Wiggins's eyes widened. "You mean you want me to 'ang about waiting for someone to come out? But that could take all day. Besides, what if a copper spots me 'angin' about the place? They'll be combing the neighborhood asking questions.''

"I know, Wiggins," Mrs. Jeffries said sympathetically. "Your task isn't going to be easy. Just do the best you can.''

Wiggins looked doubtful. "Don't be surprised if I'm back 'ere pretty fast. We can't risk my gettin' caught.''

"Use your noggin, boy." Luty reached over and patted his hand. "A clever lad like you ought to be able to give a few policemen the slip.''

Hatchet put his elbow on the table and leaned forward. "I've heard the name Ripton before. I can't remember where. You say the man staying as a houseguest was named John. John Ripton?''

"That's right, though I don't know as yet what connection he has to the Camerons.''

"Probably a pretty close one if he was spendin' the night there," Luty put in.

"Perhaps I'll start my inquiries with this gentleman," Hatchet said.

"Good. That'll keep you out of my hair," Luty rose to her feet. "I'm goin' to git started then. What time should we meet back here?"

"Four o'clock," Mrs. Jeffries replied. "That should give everyone time to learn something."

Inspector Witherspoon wished that Inspector Nivens would stop pacing. Just watching the man was making him tired. He stifled a yawn and promised himself that unless another corpse landed at his feet, tonight he was going to get a decent night's sleep. He wasn't used to trying to think on so little rest.

"Really, Witherspoon," Nivens said testily, "must you keep yawning?"

Constable Barnes, who was standing in the corner of the Cameron drawing room, shot Nivens a quick glare. "The inspector didn't get much sleep last night, sir," he said flatly. "Unlike you, sir, he was here at the crime scene until well after three o'clock."

"Don't be impertinent," Nivens snapped. His mouth clamped shut as the door opened and a young woman stepped inside.

Witherspoon smiled at her kindly. She was quite a lovely woman. Dark auburn hair neatly tucked up in a modest fashion, pale white skin and strikingly beautiful brown eyes. She was dressed in a black skirt and a high-necked gray blouse.

"I'm Kathryn Ellingsley," she said. "I understand you want to ask me a few questions."

Inspector Witherspoon introduced himself and

the others. "Please sit down, Miss Ellingsley."

Her skirt rustled faintly as she walked to the settee and sat down. "I don't know what I can tell
you about this dreadful thing," she began. "I was
asleep. I generally go to bed right after the children."

"We understand that," Witherspoon replied.
"But it's always helpful in a case like this to question everyone in the household."

"I've already been questioned," she said, but
she sounded more confused than angry. "I don't
understand."

"You don't really need to understand," Inspector Nivens said. "Just answer our questions. What
exactly do you do here?" He stalked over and
stood directly over the young woman. His posture,
like his tone, was meant to be intimidating.

Kathryn shrank back against the cushions. "I'm
the governess."

"How long have you worked for the Camerons?" Nivens demanded.

"Almost six months," Kathryn answered.

"What are your duties?" Nivens stared at her
stonily, deliberately giving her the impression he
didn't believe a word she said.

But she'd regained her composure. She straightened her spine and looked him directly in the eye.
"I've already told you I'm the governess. I should
think my duties would be obvious even to someone
like . . ."

Infuriated by her tone, Nivens interrupted.
"Don't be impertinent with me, girl."

"And I'm Brian Cameron's cousin," she finished.

Nivens was taken aback. It was one thing to browbeat the servant of a wealthy household; it was quite another to do it to a blood relation. Even a poor one. He stepped back, his expression softening. "I see," he said, giving her a quick smile. "Well, then, if you were asleep, we shan't bother you with any more questions. You may go, Miss Ellingsley."

Witherspoon, who didn't believe in browbeating anyone, gaped at Nivens. "Excuse me," he said. "But I do have a few questions for Miss Ellingsley."

"Don't be ridiculous, Witherspoon." Nivens waved at him dismissively. "Miss Ellingsley said she was asleep. What could she possibly tell us?"

"We'll never know if we don't ask," the inspector said. He turned and smiled at her. "I'm sorry to intrude on you at what must be a very difficult time, Miss Ellingsley, but if you wouldn't mind . . ."

Kathryn Ellingsley smiled and deliberately turned toward the Inspector. "Ask what you like, Inspector. I want you to catch the person who did this terrible thing."

"Do you know if Mrs. Cameron had any enemies? Anyone who wished her ill?"

Kathryn shook her head. "Hannah hadn't any enemies that I know about. There were people who didn't like her very much, but that's to be expected, isn't it? No one is well liked by everyone."

"Who didn't care for her?" Witherspoon pressed.

"Oh, you know, some of the neighbors weren't

all that friendly to her, and she wasn't particularly popular with the servants.''

"Was she a hard mistress, then?'' Nivens put in. ''Given to sacking people, was she?''

Kathryn turned and gave him a long, steady stare before answering. ''Certainly not. But she was strict with the staff. It was her way.''

"Could you be a bit more specific?'' Witherspoon urged her.

Kathryn Ellingsley hesitated briefly and then looked quickly toward the door. ''I shouldn't have said anything, Inspector. Mrs. Cameron was liked and respected by the entire household.''

Witherspoon smiled faintly, appreciating the fact that the girl didn't wish to cause her cousin distress by being candid about his late wife. ''Miss Ellingsley, you've just admitted she wasn't universally popular. Please, do tell us what you meant. I assure you that nothing you say in this room will get back to Mr. Cameron.''

"I don't want to cause him any more grief,'' Kathryn said quickly. ''He's enough to bear now and I don't think I ought to speak ill of the dead. It doesn't feel right.''

"Of course it doesn't,'' the inspector agreed. ''But murder victims can't be considered in that light. If we're going to catch the person responsible for taking Mrs. Cameron's life, we need to know as much about the victim as possible.''

Kathryn looked down at her clasped hands. ''I didn't mean to imply that Mrs. Cameron was unduly harsh or unfair. She wasn't. She was just strict. But no stricter than many other households.''

Witherspoon leaned forward eagerly. "In what way was she strict?"

"She made the maids account for their day out, made them tell her where they were going and who they were going with," Kathryn said. "If Mrs. Cameron didn't approve, she wouldn't let them go out. She was very strict about morning prayers. None of us were allowed to be absent. But she was always there herself, so she never asked more from the staff than she asked of herself."

Witherspoon nodded slowly. "I see," he said. He wasn't sure what he saw, except he had the feeling that this young woman wasn't being all that truthful with him. He sensed she was holding something back.

"When was the last time you saw Mrs. Cameron alive?" Nivens suddenly asked.

"I guess it must have been about six o'clock. Yes, that's right. She came up to the nursery to say goodnight to the children after they had their tea."

"How was her manner?" Witherspoon asked.

Kathryn stared at him blankly. "Her manner?"

"Was she upset or did she seem worried about anything?"

"No, she was quite ordinary," Kathryn replied. "She inspected the nursery, checked behind the children's ears and then sent them off to bed."

"What did she do then?" Barnes asked.

Nivens frowned at the constable, but for once had the sense to keep his mouth shut.

"She said goodnight and went out." The governess shrugged. "She was already dressed in her evening clothes. I didn't see her after that. I assumed she and Mr. Cameron had left for their engagement. I don't know what else I can tell you. As soon as the children were in bed, I had my supper and then went to my room.''

"Thank you, Miss Ellingsley," Witherspoon said. "You've been most helpful."

She stood up. "I hope you find whoever did this to Hannah. She wasn't the most lovable person in the world, but she didn't deserve to die like that."

"We'll do our very best, Miss Ellingsley," the inspector promised her. "Would you be so kind as to ask Mr. Ripton to step in, please? We'd like a word with him."

"Of course, Inspector." She gave him a dazzling smile and exited gracefully from the room.

"We ought to keep an eye on that one," Nivens said softly, as soon as the door had closed behind Kathryn Ellingsley. "Too pretty for her own good, if you know what I mean."

Witherspoon didn't. "I'm afraid I don't."

Nivens stared at him in disbelief. "Good Lord, man, you've got eyes in your head." He jerked his chin in the direction the woman had gone. "Would you pay much attention to your wife if you had a bit of fluff like that about to play with?"

Witherspoon's jaw dropped. He was shocked to his core. He'd never in his entire life considered women "fluff" and he certainly didn't assume that a pretty woman in a man's household would turn a decent man away from his marriage vows. Nor did he have any reason to believe that Miss Ellingsley was anything less than an honorable woman. He knew there were some at the Yard who considered him a bit naive, but really, Nivens was being decidedly crass. It was only in the interests of interdepartmental cooperation that the inspector didn't speak sharply to the man.

CHAPTER 3

Mrs. Goodge eyed her victim carefully through the back door. Tommy Mullins, the butcher's boy, stood there grinning at her foolishly, him and his chipped teeth. "Do you want me to leave it out here?" he asked, jerking his chin at the brown-wrapped package in his arms, "or should I bring it in and put it in the wet larder?"

Tommy was a skinny, runty fellow with stringy yellow hair sticking out of a stained porkpie hat. His shirt was dirty, his apron even dirtier and his shoes were speckled with clumps of a congealed brown-and-red substance that made the cook shudder. But this was a murder she was investigating, so filthy shoes or not, she'd have him in her kitchen. But she promised herself that arthritic fingers or not, she'd have a good go at the floor with a bottle of Condy's disinfectant as soon as he'd gone. Even though the stuff wasn't supposed to be used for anything but the pipes, if it could kill off the smell in the drains, it could certainly kill off whatever this boy tracked in on his wretched shoes. She hesitated for a fraction of a second and then took a deep breath. Tommy Mullins might look like something the cat dragged in on a particularly awful wet night, but he'd talk the head off a cabbage. More important, he had a twin who worked for a butcher in Mayfair. If Tommy's brother was anything like Tommy, he'd have already wagged his tongue about the Cameron murder.

Mrs. Goodge wasn't one to let a good opportunity slip through her fingers. "Bring it in to the wet larder for me, Tommy." She beamed at him. "And then come on in to the kitchen. I expect you could use a cuppa, couldn't you?"

He stared at her suspiciously as he stepped inside. Mrs. Goodge had a bit of the tartar about her oftentimes. He wondered what had her grinning like a cat which had just got the cream. But he did as she asked, carefully placing the bundle of wrapped meat on the larder shelf and then hurrying into the kitchen. His eyes widened as he saw the table. "Blimey, Mrs. Goodge, that's fit fer a king."

Mrs. Goodge smiled encouragingly as she patted the chair beside her. "It's only a few buns and a bit of cake. Come on, sit down and I'll pour you some tea. It's awfully cold outside."

Mouth watering, Tommy slipped into a seat and gratefully accepted the mug she handed him. He licked his lips as she filled a plate with a slice of cake, a mince tart and a hot cross bun and slid that across to him as well. "This is very nice of you," he said, stuffing a piece of cake in his mouth.

"You're a hard workin' lad," Mrs. Goodge said cheerfully. "Not like some I've known. How's your brother doin'?" It never hurt to prime the pump. Hector, the rag and bones man, was due soon and she wanted to get as much as she could out of Tommy before Hector's cart trundled up the road.

"Oh, you wouldn't believe it, Mrs. Goodge, but 'e got sacked last week."

Mrs. Goodge resisted the urge to snatch the plate out from under Tommy's nose. Tommy's brother sacked! Blast! Fat lot of good it would do her to pump Tommy for information now! Silly boy probably wouldn't know a ruddy thing.

"But 'e's ever so lucky, Tim is. Always was the lucky one in the family, not like me. If I got sacked it'd take me ages to find another position, but not Tim. Oh no, he got himself taken on as an under-gardener right round the corner from where 'e worked." Tommy picked up the mince tart and demolished it in one bite. "Mind you, 'c didn't think 'e'd be doin' much work today, not with the police trampin' about the gardens and makin' a nuisance of themselves."

Mrs. Goodge's heart leapt into her throat. Goodness, was it possible? Could the boy have actually had the good sense to get a job right there at the scene of the crime, so to speak? "Police?" she echoed. "What were the police doin' there?"

"Didn't ya hear? There was this awful murder over where Tim works. A Mrs. Cameron. She got done in last night."

"Who got done in?" a reedy voice asked from the door.

Tommy, his mouth full of mince tart, gaped at the figure stalking toward them. The woman was the oldest person he'd ever seen. Her hair was white and thin enough so that he could see her scalp, her face was a crisscross of wrinkles and she wore a high-necked black dress that had probably been new at Queen Victoria's christening. Bent over her cane, she thumped her way across the floor toward them.

"Aunt Elberta." Mrs. Goodge gasped. "You're supposed to be resting."

"Don't need to rest," Elberta said pleasantly, giving the lad a happy, if somewhat toothless grin. "Be plenty of rest waitin' fer me in the grave. Now, who's this fine boy?"

"He's the butcher's lad," Mrs. Goodge muttered.

"Huh." Elberta cupped a hand behind her ear as she sat down. "Speak up. I don't hear as well as I used to."

"I said, he's the butcher's boy. He brings the meat."

"I thought I heard him talkin' about murder. Who'd he do in?" She pointed a long, spindly finger at him. "He doesn't look like a killer. Mind you," she continued chattily, "you can't always tell by looking at someone. That Hiram McNally that murdered both his sons-in-laws and the housemaid looked like a nice man too."

"I'm not a killer," Tommy protested. He stuffed the last of the bun in his mouth and got to his feet. "I didn't do anyone in."

"Of course you didn't. Don't mind my auntie; sometimes her mind wanders." Mrs. Goodge said soothingly. "Now sit back down and finish your tea." She shoved the platter of food towards him. "Have another bun."

"I'll thank you to keep a civil tongue in your head," Elberta said tartly, giving her niece a good glare. "Tinkers wander, my mind does not."

"I've got to go." Tommy snatched the bun the cook had just put on his plate. "Thanks for the tea, Mrs. Goodge."

John Ripton pushed a hand through his thinning brown hair and sighed deeply. He was a man of medium height and build. Pale-skinned, with light brown eyes, he was one of those men who had a permanent beard shadow on their faces no matter how often they shaved. "This has been the most dreadful experience of my life, Inspector. Absolutely dreadful. Last night was a nightmare. Even after all the police left, I didn't sleep a wink."

Inspector Witherspoon thought it had been a bit more dreadful for Hannah Cameron, but he did feel some sympathy for this man. It couldn't be pleasant to be someone's houseguest and then find that one's hostess has been murdered. "I'm sure it has, sir," he murmured. "And we'll try to make our inquiries as easy for you as possible. But you do realize we must ask you a few questions."

"But I don't understand why." Ripton complained. "I thought Hannah was killed by a burglar. What's that got to do with me?"

"We don't know who killed Mrs. Cameron," Witherspoon said patiently. "But we're doing our best to find out. Now, could you tell me how long you've known Mrs. Cameron?"

Ripton's brows drew together. "What on earth has that got to do with anything?"

"Absolutely nothing." The inspector smiled pleasantly, trying to put the man at ease. "However, I've found the more I know about the victim, the easier it is for me to investigate the circumstances of the crime."

Ripton stared at him for a moment, his expression clearly indicating his view of such a nonsensical notion. "I've known Hannah my entire life. She's my half-sister. Older half-sister," he explained quickly.

"I see," the inspector replied. He wondered why Brian Cameron hadn't mentioned this, stored the fact in the back of his mind and went on with his questioning. He might as well get the basic facts out of the way. "What is your profession, Mr. Ripton?"

"I work for Stoddard and Hart. Commerical builders. I'm the general manager."

"I've heard of them. They're quite a large firm, aren't they? Property redevelopment and that sort of thing." Witherspoon nodded. "Where do you live, sir?"

"In Pinner," he replied. "Moss Lane to be exact. That's one of the reasons I stayed over last night. By the time we got back here, it was too late to get a train home and I knew a hansom would take hours. So when Mr. Cameron—"

"Mr. Cameron invited you to spend the night," Barnes interrupted softly. "Not your sister?"

Ripton looked surprised by the question. "Brian asked me to stay," he said. "But I'm sure Hannah didn't mind. She seconded the invitation. As a matter of fact, she insisted.''

Witherspoon surreptiously stuck his hand in his coat pocket. The house was very cold. There was no fire in the fireplace and he wished he'd had the sense to hang on to his overcoat when he'd arrived today. John Ripton must have felt the cold as well; his neck was muffled in a heavy red scarf, an incongrous note against the somber black evening clothes he wore.

''Could you tell me what happened?'' the inspector asked.

''You mean last night?''

At the inspector's nod, Ripton continued. ''Nothing unusual, if that's what you mean. I'd been invited out to dinner with the Camerons and Mrs. Hadleigh. We met at eight o'clock at Simpsons, had dinner and then came back here for a glass of port. As I said, by the time we'd finished our drinks, it was so late they invited me to stay the night.''

''What time did you retire?'' Witherspoon wondered whether it would be proper to move the questioning into the kitchen. His feet were positively chilled.

''About half past eleven,'' Ripton replied.

''Did all of you go upstairs at the same time?''

Ripton thought for a moment. ''As far as I can recall, Mrs. Hadleigh and Mrs. Cameron went upstairs first. Brian checked to make sure the front door was locked and then he and I followed the ladies.''

''Where was your room, sir?'' Witherspoon

asked. Perhaps it would help to know where everyone was at the time of the murder.

"I stayed in one of the guest rooms on the second floor," he said.

"Where was your room in relation to Mr. and Mrs. Cameron's private quarters?" Witherspoon asked.

"At the opposite end of the hall." Ripton sighed. "Mrs. Hadleigh had the room next to Mrs. Cameron's. Brian's room is beside hers."

"Were the servants still awake when you went up?" Barnes asked.

Ripton frowned, as though it were a difficult question. "I don't know. I don't recall seeing any of them, so I suppose they'd been dismissed for the night."

"Mr. Cameron locked up, not the butler?" the inspector prodded. He'd learned in the past that details could be terribly important.

"Yes, I've already told you that." Ripton's voice rose slightly. "Look, Inspector, I've had a terrible shock and I'm dreadfully tired. Do you think you can hurry this along? I'd like to go home."

"Just a few more questions, sir," the inspector said kindly. But he noticed that the man seemed more annoyed than grieved over the loss of his sister. "Did you hear anything unusual after you went upstairs?"

He shook his head. "Nothing. I went straight to bed and was just falling asleep when the alarm was raised and the police were sent for. After that, it was bloody impossible to get any rest. The police were tramping all over the place, Fiona was having hysterics and well, after all, Brian is my brother-in-law. I felt I ought to stay up and help if I could."

"Did anything unusual happen while you were at the restaurant?" Barnes asked.

"The roast beef was tough," he replied casually, "and Hannah sent hers back to the kitchen. But I hardly think the chef followed us home to murder a complaining customer."

Witherspoon stifled a sigh. "Did you see anyone at the restaurant or on the way home that made you uneasy or suspicious? Any ruffians or odd-looking characters?"

"No, Inspector. There was nothing."

"And you're absolutely certain you heard nothing after you went upstairs?" he pressed. Surely someone must have heard something. If the glass in the window pane had been broken before Hannah Cameron entered the room, she'd have summoned a servant or her husband. Therefore, Witherspoon was fairly certain it had been smashed after she was killed. Gracious, were these people all deaf? This was a large house, but at that time of night, the streets would have been quiet and the sound of glass shattering should have carried quite a distance. "You didn't hear the sound of the glass being broken?"

"No, Inspector. I did not." Ripton rubbed his eyes.

But the inspector wasn't ready to give up. Even if one couldn't hear glass breaking from the second floor, surely someone must have heard a door open or the stairs squeaking when Mrs. Cameron came back downstairs. "How about someone walking about the house? Did you hear anything like that?"

"I heard nothing," Ripton said impatiently, "and I saw nothing. Now, may I please be allowed to get about my business?"

"Excuse me." Betsy smiled at the young man with more enthusiasm than was proper. "But I think you dropped this." She held a shilling in the center of her hand.

He was hardly more than a schoolboy, sixteen at most, and when he saw her dazzling smile, he blushed all the way to the roots of his wheat-colored hair. "That's not mine," he said, but he looked at the coin with longing. "My master didn't give me no money, only told me to come down and book the ticket."

They were standing in the center of the Albert Gate booking office of the Great Northern Railway on William Street. Betsy had spotted the young man leaving the house next door to the Cameron house and had followed him. When he'd gone into the booking office, she'd hesitated for a split second and then pulled open the heavy doors and stepped inside herself. She'd hovered on the far side of the room, pretending to be studying a time-table while he worked his way to the front of the queue. The moment he'd finished his business she'd waylaid him.

"I'm sorry to have bothered you, then." She gave him another dazzling smile. "But I could have swore I saw you drop it." Sighing, she turned to leave. The lad was after her like a shot.

"Uh, excuse me, miss," he said. He leapt in front of her and opened the door. "I din't thank you properly for taking the trouble to ask if the money were mine. Most people woulda just kept it.''

"Not me. I'm an honest girl and it was no trouble at all.'' She stepped out the door, confident that he would follow. He did. She watched him from the corner of her eye as she pulled her coat tighter against the chill air. "I was happy to do it.''

"Uh, my name's Bill Tincher,'' he said, hurrying to keep pace with her as she headed past the newstand towards Knightsbridge. "If I may be so bold as to inquire, what's yours?''

"My name's Elizabeth''—she giggled—"but everyone calls me Betsy. Have you finished with your business then?''

Surprised by her boldness and thanking his lucky stars, he nodded eagerly. "Oh yes, I've booked Mrs. Loudon's ticket.''

"Would you like to walk me to the omnibus stop on the Brompton Road, then? I could do with the company,'' she said briskly. "A girl feels better walking about with a strapping young man such as yourself beside her.'' She was shamelessly flirting with him. But it couldn't be helped. She'd spent half the day chatting up butchers, bakers and green grocers and she didn't have a bit of information about the Camerons to show for her efforts. So she wasn't above using what resources were available. So far, this lad was the best she could do. Blast, she hoped he knew something about the murder.

Beneath the gray material of his footman's jacket, his chest swelled. "I'd be right pleased,'' he replied. "And you're right to be careful. These days you can never tell what's goin' to happen.

Why, just last night there was a horrible murder right next door.''

"Really?" Betsy pretended to be shocked. "How awful. Who got killed?" Deliberately, she slowed her pace. Brompton Road wasn't all that far and she wanted to get as much information out of Bill Tincher as possible.

"Mrs. Cameron. She were murdered right in her own home," he replied, taking her elbow politely as they stepped off the pavement and started across Sloane Street. "It were terrible, just terrible."

"The poor woman." Betsy clucked sympathetically. "How was she killed?"

Bill gently pulled her back as a hansom clip-clopped past. "Stabbed, she was."

"You seem to know an awful lot about it."

" 'Course I do," he bragged. "Chief Inspector Barrows was havin' dinner with Mr. and Mrs. Loudon last night. He were right there when the alarm was raised, went straight round, he did. Then he come back and told the Loudons what had happened. Warned them to be careful and all."

Betsy widened her eyes and tried to look impressed. "What did happen?"

"Seems some think Mrs. Cameron interrupted a thief that were burgling the place," he said eagerly, "but the Chief Inspector don't think that. He's called in some famous detective, some feller the Yard uses when they've got a real hard one to solve."

"Have the police been round to see you then?" Betsy asked.

"What could I tell them?" Bill grinned sheepishly. "I was sound asleep when it happened. No one, not even the Chief Inspector, heard a thing. Mind you, there's some that say there's plenty of strange goin'-ons at the Cameron house, and truth to tell, I've seen a thing or two.''

"What kind of things?" she asked eagerly.

"Well, I really shouldn't be speakin' ill of the dead"—he dropped his voice to just above a whisper—"but there was some funny stories about Mrs. Cameron."

Betsy strained toward him to hear him over the roar of the traffic. "Stories," she repeated. "Oh, do tell me. It's ever so excitin', me meetin' you like this. Nothing ever happens where I live." The moment the words left her lips, she knew from the eager, pleased expression that flitted across his face that she'd made a tactical error.

"And where do you live, then?" he asked, patting her elbow in a proprietory fashion. "Close by, I hope."

She wanted his attention back on the murder, not on her. Perhaps she ought to tone down the flirting just a bit. Bill Tincher seemed like the sort to like the sound of his own voice. "Oh, that's not important." She waved her hand dismissively. "I'm just a housemaid to a gentleman who lives in Holland Park. But do go on with what you were sayin'. It's ever so interesting."

He hesitated a moment, his expression confused, then he shrugged his thin shoulders and continued. "Well, like I was sayin', there's plenty of gossip about the Camerons . . ."

"About both of them?"

"Oh yes," he said, "they've had some awful rows. This summer, when all the windows was

open because of the heat, we could hear them shoutin' at each other something fierce. When I first
heard she'd been murdered, I thought he'd done her
in. Mind you, they hadn't been carrying on as much
as they used to, at least not loud enough for us to
hear.''

Betsy was disappointed. During the heat wave in
August, every temper in London had been frayed
and strained. People had snapped, snarled and generally made themselves utterly miserable. Even she
and Smythe had had a few harsh words. ''Is that
all? Most people get a bit het up when it's hot. I
don't expect Mr. and Mrs. Cameron were any different from anyone else.''

''That wasn't the only time they argued,'' he replied defensively. ''I've heard 'em myself when
they was goin' at it out in their back garden and I
was outside cleaning the brasses on the back gate.
Mrs. Cameron was havin' a real go at Mr. Cameron. Claimed he'd wasted all her money and they
was goin' to be ruined because he didn't have no
head for business.''

''Really?'' Betsy could tell her earlier comment
had offended him and as they were quickly approaching the ominibus stop, she had to make
amends in short order. ''Gracious, you are a sly
one, aren't you? You ought to go to work for the
police. Seems to me you're a real clever lad.''

He grinned proudly. ''Well, there's a few things
I could tell the police, not that they're likely to
listen to me. But I know what I've seen.''

She smiled coyly. ''Are you going to tell me?''

''Are you goin' to tell me where you live?'' He
rocked back on his heels and stared at her boldly.

Betsy felt trapped. Over his shoulder, she could see the ominibus pulling around the corner. She didn't want to tell him, of course. Smythe would make mincemeat of this lad if he came around to Upper Edmonton Gardens. On the other hand, she wanted to know what he knew. It could be important. She supposed she could lie to the boy, but that seemed so wrong. Her conscience would torment her for days.

The omnibus drew closer, the horses' hooves stomping hard against the pavement as they clomped toward the Brompton Road. Betsy tried to think of what to do.

"Well," he demanded, "where do you live, then?"

"You haven't told me where you live." she shot back, stalling for time. Perhaps she shouldn't take this ominibus. Maybe if she was clever enough, she could keep him here and talking until the next one came by.

"Mayfair," he said quickly. "I work for Mr. James Loudon. Now, it's your turn."

Betsy quickly made a decision. "Number twenty-two, Upper Edmonton Gardens."

"Is that in Holland Park, then?" he clarified.

She nodded.

"And who do you work for?"

She gave him an innocent smile. "Inspector Gerald Witherspoon of Scotland Yard."

Fiona Hadleigh glared at the inspector. "Really, sir, I hardly think this is decent. Poor Hannah isn't even buried yet." She flounced across the room and plopped down on the settee. Crossing her hands in her lap, she continued to frown at all three of the policemen.

"I'm terribly sorry to intrude on your grief," Witherspoon began, though to be perfectly honest, the woman didn't look a bit grieved, merely irritated. "But we must ask questions. It's our duty."

"We could have waited until after the inquest, Witherspoon," Nivens said tartly. "I hardly think another twenty-four hours would make all that much difference to this investigation."

Fiona smiled at Nivens. He smiled back at her. Witherspoon glanced at Barnes and shrugged. Today had been most difficult. Most difficult, indeed. But Chief Inspector Barrows had assigned both men to this investigation, so he'd try his best to cooperate. "We've found that in murder cases . . ."

"This is hardly a murder case," Nivens interrupted. "It's a homicide in the course of a burglary. Your usual methods"—he almost sneered as he said the words—"won't find out the identity of the culprit. My methods will. I don't know why the Chief Inspector insisted on your coming in. If he'd let me take charge of everything, we'd have this case cleared up in no time."

"Of course Hannah was killed by a burglar," Fiona Hadleigh echoed. "And as I'm not a thief, I don't know why I have to be subjected to this ridiculous questioning. Nor do I think you ought to be bothering poor Brian."

Witherspoon wished he didn't have to question any of them. But duty was duty and he knew that Nivens was wrong. "Miss Hadleigh," he began.

"Mrs. Hadleigh," she snapped. "I'm a widow. My husband died two years ago."

"Mrs. Hadleigh," he corrected, "could you please tell us what happened last night?"

She looked as though she wasn't going to reply for a moment, then she straightened her spine and took a deep breath. "We went out to dinner..."

"Did anything odd happen while you were at the restaurant?" Witherspoon interrupted.

Nivens sighed loudly.

"Nothing, Inspector. We had our meal and took a hansom back here so the gentlemen could share a glass of port."

"Did you notice if there was anything unusual or different about Mrs. Cameron's manner?" Witherspoon knew he was clutching at straws. But he honestly didn't know what else to ask.

Fiona hesitated briefly. "No, not really."

"Are you sure?" Witherspoon pressed.

"Well," she frowned. "Hannah was a bit preoccupied last night. I will grant you that."

"Preoccupied how?" Witherspoon surreptitiously rubbed his hands together to keep them warm.

"Oh, it was nothing, really." Fiona dismissed the matter. "I shouldn't have said anything."

"No, please," the inspector insisted, "you obviously noticed something odd in her behaviour."

"Really, Witherspoon," Niven scolded, "don't put words in the witness's mouth."

"I'm not," the inspector protested. "But Mrs. Hadleigh strikes me as being a most intelligent and perceptive woman. Witnesses like her are quite extraordinary. I'd like to hear what she has to say." He, of course, didn't believe anything of the sort, but he'd just remembered how his housekeeper had once told him that people would believe the most blatant lies about themselves as long as they were flattering. A happy person was frequently a chatty person. The inspector wanted Mrs. Hadleigh to be very happy. It might be the only way he could get the woman to talk.

"Why thank you, Inspector," Fiona said pleasantly. Her whole demeanour suddenly changed. She relaxed back against the settee and smiled. "How very astute of you to notice. Hannah was definitely preoccupied last night. She kept asking John for the time. It drove us all mad."

"Do you have any idea why?" Witherspoon asked.

"No, not really. But I had the impression she wanted to be home by a certain time. On the way back, she refused to let the hansom driver take the route through the park. When Brian protested, she claimed she was cold and wanted to get home. But I think there was more to it than that. Of course, it could be she merely wanted to annoy John."

"Why would Mrs. Cameron have wanted to irritate her half-brother?"

Fiona laughed. "Simply to be difficult. They've never gotten along very well. I think Hannah knew that John wanted to stay the night, and just to be contrary, she wanted to hurry them home so he'd have plenty of time to catch the train."

"Is there a particular reason she wouldn't want her brother to stay?" Witherspoon asked. He'd gotten the impression from Ripton that Mrs. Cameron had insisted he stay the night.

Fiona's thin shoulders moved in the barest hint of a shrug. "Not really. As I said, they didn't really get on that well. John is actually closer to Brian than he was to her. For some reason, she was a bit out of sorts with him last night. She'd snapped at him twice during dinner. I think she was tired of his company. He can be a most annoying man.''

Barnes looked up from his notebook. ''In what way?''

''He kept trying to bring up business at dinner,'' Fiona replied, looking disgusted by the memory. ''It was revolting. How is one expected to enjoy one's food when every few minutes John would start badgering Hannah about some property she owns over near the Commercial Docks?''

''What was the nature of his . . . er . . . 'badgering'?'' the inspector inquired eagerly. Now they were getting somewhere.

Fiona smiled cattily. ''He wanted her to sell to him. I must say, Brian didn't help matters either. He kept encouraging John every time he brought up the subject. But the property belonged to Hannah, and she was adamant about keeping it herself.'' She laughed harshly. ''Ironic, isn't it? Now that Hannah's dead, John will inherit it anyway.''

''Mr. Ripton will inherit the property?'' Witherspoon asked. ''Not her husband?''

''Oh no, those two buildings have been in Hannah's family for generations. They were left to her with the provision that in the event of her death, they were to stay in the family. As she's no children of her own, they'll go to John. Now that she's dead, he's the only one left.'' She sighed. ''Poor Hannah. She was in such a hurry to get home last night and look what happened.''

Witherspoon's mind was reeling with new possibilities. Hannah Cameron had had words with her

half-brother over dinner. She'd also been preoccupied and eager to get home. Why? Was it only
because she found John Ripton annoying or was
there another reason? She'd been found in a room
by herself, stabbed as she'd stood at the doors leading to a balcony. Maybe she had an appointment
with someone. Someone she let into the room and
who then consequently killed her. The moment the
thought entered his mind, hc knew he was right.
"Mrs. Hadleigh, in your opinion did Mrs. Cameron's wish to get home quickly have anything to
do with her brother?"

"I don't know, Inspector," Fiona replied. "It's
possible, of course. Sometimes she delighted in tor-
menting John." She paused, and her expression
grew thoughtful. "But I don't think that was the
case last night. She was too distracted to take any
real pleasure in annoying him. Or perhaps she
wanted to check on the children or wanted to make
sure the servants had locked the house up." She
shrugged. "I don't know. But I do know I thought
it strange."

"According to what the servants have told us,"
Witherspoon said, "all of the servants, with the ex-
ception of Mrs. Cameron's maid, were in bed."

"That couldn't possibly be true." Fiona shook
her head. "They're lying. Hannah never allowed
all the servants to go to bed when the master and
mistress were out. The butler and a kitchen maid
were always to be up when they got home, in case
Hannah wanted a hot drink from the kitchen."

"Yet last night, she specifically told them they
could all retire." Witherspoon was sure about that
point. He and Constable Barnes had questioned all

the servants when they'd arrived that morning. The housemaids, the footman, the butler and the cook had said the same thing. They couldn't all be lying.

Fiona looked confused for a moment. "That certainly wasn't Hannah's habit."

Nivens had wandered over to stand in front of the fireplace. Witherspoon was aware of his eyes on him. It was making him slightly nervous. It was most inconvenient having the man hanging about while he tried to investigate. Most inconvenient, indeed. "After you retired last night, did you hear anything unusual?"

She thought about it for a moment. "No, I was very tired. I went right to sleep."

"You didn't hear Mrs. Cameron go back downstairs?" he pressed. He'd trod those stairs himself earlier today and the two top ones definitely creaked. Quite loudly. The only way anyone could have gone down them without making a racket was if they deliberately avoided them.

"No, Inspector. I did not."

Witherspoon smiled happily. He was right. He knew it. Hannah Cameron hadn't wanted anyone to hear her going downstairs so she'd been as quiet as a mouse. That could only mean one thing. She didn't want anyone knowing she was leaving her room. But why would she have let her maid stay up? That question bothered him. She'd told everyone else to go to bed, but her maid had still been awake and waiting for her. He glanced at Barnes, hoping the constable would have a question or two of his own. But Barnes was scribbling madly in his notebook. "Thank you, Mrs. Hadleigh. I appreciate your cooperation. Could you ask the butler to send in Miriam?''

''Of course.'' She dismissed them with a nod as she left.

''Why do you want to question the maid?'' Nivens barked. ''I've already spoken to the girl and she's as thick as two short planks.''

Barnes looked up from his scribbling, an expression of mild disgust on his face as he flicked a glance at Inspector Nivens.

Witherspoon, not wanting to offend his colleague, quickly said, ''After speaking with Mrs. Hadleigh, I've thought of another question or two. I'm sure you questioned the girl most thoroughly, Inspector. Most thoroughly, indeed.'' He hoped Nivens hadn't been rude to the maid. He'd noticed the inspector was a bit brusque with servants and hansom drivers and others of that ilk. It rather annoyed Witherspoon. But he didn't wish to make a fuss.

''You wanted to see me, sir?'' a timid voice said from the doorway.

Witherspoon smiled at the dark-haired young woman and waved her into the drawing room. ''Come in, miss,'' he invited, gesturing to the settee. ''Please have a seat. I'd like to ask you a question.''

She looked hesitantly at the settee and then shook her head. ''It wouldn't do for me to sit, sir. If it's all the same to you, I'll stand.''

Though her voice was timid, she carried herself proudly as she advanced into the room. A slender girl, she was quite pretty, with dark brown eyes, full lips and a slightly turned up nose.

"As you wish, miss." Unwilling to sit while a lady stood, Witherspoon rose to his feet. "How long have you been ladies' maid to Mrs. Cameron?"

"A year, sir," she replied. She shot Nivens a malevolent glance.

"Did you like her?"

Miriam hesitated before answering. "She was as good a mistress as some," she replied honestly. "But no, I didn't like her. She was very demanding and most particular about how things was to be done."

"Did she specifically ask you to wait up for her last night?" Witherspoon asked.

Miriam looked surprised by the question. "No. As a matter of fact, she told me I could go to bed as soon as I finished tidying up her toilette."

"Then why did you wait up for her?" He was quite curious now. The maid had admitted she didn't like the woman, and from what Witherspoon had seen of this household, he'd have thought any of the servants would have taken any chance for a bit of extra rest when they could get it.

"I did go to bed, sir," Miriam explained. "But I came back down when I heard her moving about her bedroom, sir. My room's right above hers, sir. I knew she was in her room because I heard the door to her dressin' room squeakin'. I was afraid if I didn't come down and help her get undressed, she'd be a real tartar in the morning."

"Why would you think that?" Barnes asked softly. "She'd said you could go to bed."

Miriam's lips twisted in a bitter smile. "I didn't trust her. She might have said we could go to bed, but I knew if I didn't come down, it'd be the worse for me in the mornin'."

"When you went downstairs, did you find Mrs. Cameron in her room?" Witherspoon didn't even look in Nivens's direction. This was important information and the inspector hadn't mentioned a word of it.

Miriam shook her head. "No sir, I didn't, and I thought it odd, because I knew I'd heard her moving about. That dressin' room door squeaks something fierce."

"What did you do, then?" he asked.

"I looked about for her," Miriam replied. "Glanced in her dressin' room and checked the bath down the hall, but I couldn't find her. I thought she might have gone downstairs, so I decided to wait. I waited and waited but she never come up. That's when I went to Mr. Cameron."

"Why didn't you go downstairs and look for her?" Barnes asked.

Miriam shrugged. "Because I was in my night clothes, sir. Mrs. Cameron would have had a fit if she'd caught me movin' about the house like that."

CHAPTER 4

Smythe reached into his pocket, pulled out a shilling and slapped it on the counter of The Three Stags pub. "What'll you 'ave?" he asked, turning to the young man standing next to him. Smythe kept his voice casual; the bloke was really no more than a lad. Dark blond hair combed back haphazardly over a longish face, deep-set hazel eyes and a slightly protruding mouth.

"A pint of bitter, please." The young man grinned, revealing front teeth that stuck out. But despite the smile, his eyes were puzzled. Smythe knew he was wondering why a perfect stranger had befriended him and hustled him into the nearest pub.

"Two pints of bitter," Smythe called to the barman. He turned back to his companion. "You worked round 'ere long?"

"Two years."

"Got a name?"

"Harry Comstock. What's yours?"

"Joe Bolan," Smythe lied quickly. With Inspector Nivens sniffing around this neighborhood, it wouldn't do to use his own name when he was snooping about. "Well, 'arry, 'ow do you like the area? I'm thinkin' about tryin' to find work 'ereabouts."

"Neighborhood's posh, but the wages ain't. The rich are a tight-fisted lot with their money. Don't much like to share with a workin' man. But there's always a few jobs goin'."

"Where do you work?" Smythe knew very well where Harry Comstock worked. That's why he'd befriended the man.

"Communal garden for a block of Mayfair houses. I'm the gardener and the caretaker. Don't pay a lot, but it keeps the rent paid for the missus." Harry moved his bony shoulders in a shrug. "What kinda work you lookin' for?"

"I've been a coachman most of my life," Smythe said. He wondered how to get around to the subject of the murder. It was so long since he hadn't paid for information, he hoped he hadn't forgotten how to get someone talking. He shouldn't have used Blimpey Groggins so much on the last few cases. Cor blimey, he was getting as tongue-tied as a schoolboy. But that's what came of having money. Made you soft and dulled your wits. The thought of his money momentarily depressed him. Determinedly, Smythe pushed that problem to the back of his mind and concentrated on why he was here. Getting information from Harry Comstock. "But I was thinkin' about lookin' about for somethin' else. Not much call for private coachmen these days. I've done a bit of diggin' in my time. Any jobs goin' where you work?'' He nodded to the publican as their drinks were shoved under their noses.

"Nah." Harry took a long swig from his mug. "The gardens ain't that big and they've just taken on another boy to help me. The residents'll not pay for three when they can get by on two."

"Give you a lot of grief, do they?" Smythe took a sip from his own mug.

"Just some of 'em." Harry suddenly laughed. "Odd thing is the worst one of the lot up and got herself murdered." He sobered just as suddenly when he realized what he'd said. "I don't mean to be disrespectful of the dead."

"Don't fret, 'arry," Smythe said easily. "I'm a workin' man myself. I know what puttin' up with the gentry is like. But tell me about this murder. Who got done in?"

"Well." Harry eagerly began to tell all he knew, which wasn't much. But he had a wonderful imagination and those facts that he didn't know, he easily made up.

Dutifully, Smythe listened to the bloke. Harry, interspersing his tale with quick sips of beer, got happier and happier the longer he talked. Perhaps it was the beer or perhaps it was just that the lad hadn't had anyone to talk to but a privet hedge or an elm tree in a while, but within moments, his tongue was moving faster than a steam engine. "And like I said, I'm not surprised she got herself killed. She's not got many friends."

"Uh . . ." Smythe tried to interrupt with a question, but Harry appeared to be deaf.

"No one likes that woman. Not even her husband. Mind you"—Harry took another quick swig of bitter—"he's not a particularly nice man, either. But at least he doesn't scream like a scalded cat just because I trimmed the hedges a bit too short." He paused to take a breath, and Smythe leapt at his chance, but he was too late. Harry's lungs apparently didn't need much air. "Mind you, I'm sure with these coppers trampin' all over the gardens lookin' for God knows what, I'll hear from Mrs. Masters about them ruddy summer roses." Harry shook his head.

"Who do they think did it?" Smythe asked quickly.

"Some say it was a burglar," Harry replied. He looked pointedly at his now empty mug. Smythe quickly nodded to the barman and Harry resumed talking. "But others say it were probably her husband. Or her half-brother, or even that woman who's always hangin' about moonin' over Mr. Cameron. Not that he's all that bad a bloke, not as tight-fisted as she was, that's for sure. Pay you a bob or two to do a few things for him, Mr. Cameron does. Give me a few bits when I run over to the post office for him last week."

Smythe's interest had perked up at the mention of "husband," "half-brother" and especially at "that woman who's always hangin' about." "What woman is this then, 'angin' about?" he asked.

"Mrs. Hadleigh." Harry snorted. "Claims to be Mrs. Cameron's friend and all that, but she didn't like Mrs. Cameron any more than I did."

"How do you know?"

"Any fool with eyes could see that Mrs. Hadleigh hated Mrs. Cameron. Pulled all sorts of ugly, sour faces at the woman's back whenever Mrs. Cameron wasn't lookin'. But then everyone in the 'ousehold did that exceptin' for Miss Ellingsley . . ." He broke off and sighed. "Now there's a lovely woman. Too bad she had to go to work for the Camerons. But that's what comes of bein' a poor relation. Mind you, I expect that Mrs. Hadleigh will do her best to get Miss Ellingsley sacked now that Mrs. Cameron is gone. She'll not want the master gettin' any fancy ideas in his head about a younger woman. Not that Miss Ellingsley is interested in Mr. Cameron. Good Lord, no. She's got other fish to fry, that one does."

Smythe's ears were ringing. Harry Comstock was like a blocked drainpipe; one good clean-up and words gushed out like backed-up water. There were dozens of questions that he could ask, but he wouldn't be able to ask a single one of them if he couldn't get this fellow to slow up a bit.

"Uh, look," he interrupted sharply. Harry blinked owlishly. Smythe forced himself to smile. "Why don't we go and 'ave us a nice sit down." He jerked his head toward the table near the hearth. "I'll get us a couple of whiskies."

Betsy arrived back at Upper Edmonton Gardens before the others. She found Mrs. Goodge pacing the kitchen floor and muttering. "Silly old thing is going to ruin everything . . ."

"Who's ruining everything?" Betsy asked. She

took her hat and coat off and hung them up.

"Aunt Elberta, that's who." Mrs. Goodge, her face flushed and her eyes flashing behind her glasses, stomped over to put the kettle on. "She's been here all day. You'd think someone her age would have to rest. But no, she's here hour after hour, interruptin' my sources, asking her silly questions . . ."

"Mrs. Goodge." Mrs. Jeffries's soft voice interrupted the cook's tirade. "Do lower your voice. She'll hear you."

"She's deaf as a post," the cook snapped. She picked a plate of buns up from the sideboard and slapped them down on the table. "I had half a dozen people through here today and I didn't learn a ruddy thing. It's all her fault."

Mrs. Jeffries and Betsy exchanged glances as they came toward the table. Both of them sympathized with Mrs. Goodge's plight, but they felt sorry for poor Aunt Elberta too.

"I had a bit of luck today," Betsy said cheerfully, hoping some good news might distract the cook.

Mrs. Goodge snorted.

Mrs. Jeffries drew her chair back when there was a loud knocking on the front door.

"I'll get it," Betsy said, dashing for the stairs.

Mrs. Goodge kept muttering under her breath as she got tea ready, and Mrs. Jeffries, wisely, held her peace. She'd let the cook fume for a few minutes, get the poison out of her system and then they'd have a nice little chat about the best way to deal with Aunt Elberta. Perhaps the others could take turns taking the old dear out to Holland Park.

Betsy returned clutching an envelope.

"Is that for the inspector?" Mrs. Jeffries asked.

"No, it's for Smythe." Curious, but not wanting to let it show, Betsy carefully placed the envelope at Smythe's usual place at the table. "I wonder who's writing to him? It's an awfully posh envelope . . ." She was interrupted by the sound of the back door opening.

Wiggins, accompanied by Fred, dashed into the room a few minutes later. "Am I late?"

"No, Wiggins," Mrs. Jeffries replied.

"Good." Wiggins slid into his chair and beamed at them. "I found out ever so much today . . ."

"I'm glad someone has," Mrs. Goodge interrupted, and then she too broke off as the back door opened again.

This time it was Smythe. He swaggered into the kitchen, a cocky grin on his face, and tossed off a jaunty salute to the others. " 'Ello, 'ello," he said. "What a day I've 'ad. You'll not believe what all I've found out . . ."

"You'll not believe my day either," Mrs. Goodge complained.

"You've got a letter, Smythe," Betsy interjected hastily, hoping to get him to shut up about how much he'd accomplished before Mrs. Goodge worked herself up into a fit.

Smythe's cocky grin faded. "A letter?" He picked up the envelope. His eyes narrowed as he looked at the neat handwriting and he paled as he realized who it was who'd written him. Blast! He'd told that stupid sod not to contact him here. Conscious they were all staring at him, he slipped the letter into the pocket of his waistcoat, plopped down next to Betsy and busied himself pouring out a mug of tea.

"Is something wrong, Smythe? You've gone a bit white about the mouth," Betsy said. "Are you feeling all right?"

"I'm fine, lass." He tried to smile and knew he was doing a bad job of it. He'd kill that ruddy man when he got his hands on him. "Just a bit winded from gettin' back 'ere so fast."

"Aren't you going to open it?" she asked curiously. It wasn't often one of the staff got a letter, especially one in a posh envelope.

"There's no time to now," he explained quickly. "I saw Luty and Hatchet comin' right behind me. We've probably got a lot to get through, so I'll read it later."

"My turn won't last long," Mrs. Goodge said.

Mrs. Jeffries closed her eyes briefly and hoped they could get through this with a minimum of fuss. The cook was already out of sorts, Betsy was dying of curiosity about Smythe's letter, Wiggins probably wouldn't think to be tactful when he started bragging about what he'd learned and goodness knows what Luty and Hatchet had found out.

By the time Luty and Hatchet arrived a few moments later, the rest of the tea things were on the table, Mrs. Goodge's fury had dulled to a slow simmer and Smythe's color had returned to normal.

"Who would like to go first?" Mrs. Jeffries asked.

Luty waved her hand. "If'n it's all the same to everybody, I'd like to say my piece." She plunged straight ahead when no one objected. "I found out quite a bit about Brian Cameron. Seems he don't have much luck with wives. His first one died off from influenza right after she had a child. Brian up and married the second one less than a year after the first one died. Some said it weren't decent, but the man did have two orphan babies he told everyone they needed a mother.''

"Was your source absolutely sure that the first Mrs. Cameron's death was due to natural causes?'' Hatchet asked.

No one was surprised by the question. The same thought had crossed everyone else's mind.

Luty nodded vigorously. "He was sure. They was visiting one of Mr. Cameron's relatives up in Yorkshire when she took sick. But she weren't the only one to get sick—half the village had the flu. A lot of them died.''

"Did you learn the name of the village?'' Mrs. Jeffries asked. She was from Yorkshire.

"It's a place called Paggleston,'' Luty replied. "Brian Cameron's uncle still lives there.''

Mrs. Jeffries nodded. "I believe it's quite near Scarborough. Yes, now I remember. There was a terrible outbreak of influenza a few years back.''

"The first Mrs. Cameron died from the flu,'' Luty said firmly. "My source was sure about that. But that's not what's important. I found out that Brian Cameron inherited a lot of money from her, somewhere in the neighborhood of twenty thousand pounds. He got his hands on plenty when he married Hannah Cameron too, but—and this is the interesting part—seems ole Brian don't have much of a head for business, not that that keeps him from trying. So far, he's invested in a Malaysian tea plantation that got hit with a typhoon and a cattle ranch in Montana that lost every head of beef to hoof and mouth. He put up the money to have two ships built for the Australian trade and put a big lump of cash out on investin' in South American railroads. But it don't seem to matter what he puts his money in—he loses it sooner or later.''

"What about the ships?'' Wiggins asked.

"Sank. Both of 'em. One of 'em sank before she even left the English Channel and the other made it all the way to Fremantle but got hit by a bad storm on the way home and was lost.''

Smythe whistled softly through his teeth. "Cor, the poor blighter don't 'ave much luck.''

"Not with money or wives,'' Luty said. "But as far as my source knew, he hadn't lost the money he'd put in the South American railroads.''

"Will he inherit a lot of money now that Hannah Cameron's dead?'' Betsy asked eagerly.

"I ain't sure,'' Luty admitted. "My source didn't know but he said he'd check on it for me. That was the first thing I thought of too.''

"Excellent, Luty,'' Mrs. Jeffries said, then she caught herself as she saw Mrs. Goodge's shoulders slump.

"I'll have a go next,'' Betsy said brightly. "What I learned sort of goes along with what Luty told us. It seems that Mr. and Mrs. Cameron didn't get on too well. The footman from the house next door to them told me that he heard them arguing all the time.'' She went on to tell them everything she'd learned from Bill Tincher. "And one of the things they argued about was Mrs. Cameron telling Mr. Cameron he didn't have a head for business.''

"Just because a bloke has a bit of bad luck at business don't mean 'e's a killer,'' Wiggins charged. ''There's plenty others that didn't like Hannah Cameron.''

''True,'' Betsy agreed. ''But someone's been up to something funny at that house. Bill told me that last week he spotted someone slipping out of the house late one night. Whoever it was didn't go anywhere; they just crept into the shadows behind one of the trees and stood there for the longest time.''

''Who's Bill?'' Smythe asked.

''The footman from the house next door,'' she replied. ''He's just a lad, but he's a sharp eye and I don't think he was making it up. He did see someone.''

''Was it a man or a woman?'' Luty asked.

''He couldn't tell,'' Betsy said. ''They were swathed from head to foot in a hooded cloak. But it could have been Mr. Cameron.''

''We don't know that, Betsy,'' Mrs. Jeffries said calmly. ''It could have been anyone. Were any of the other suspects in the house that night?''

''I don't know,'' she said, ''but it was on a Friday evening, not this past Friday, but the one before that.''

''You'd best find out,'' Mrs. Jeffries instructed. The nighttime excursion may have nothing to do with the murder, but then again, it was possible. She turned her attention to the footman. ''Why don't you tell us what you learned?''

''I think I know who it was that this footman saw that night,'' he boasted. ''Kathryn Ellingsley 'as a sweetheart.''

''Is her young man a tree, then?'' Mrs. Goodge sniffed disdainfully.

"'Course 'e isn't,'" Wiggins shot back defensively. "But my source told me that she's been sneakin' out late at night to meet her feller. So it were probably Kathryn Ellingsley this Bill saw." Wiggins wasn't really sure his source could be trusted. He'd not even planned on telling the others what he'd found out, considering who his source was for the information. But the cook had niggled him enough so that he'd told all. He wished he hadn't. It would be shameful if the others knew the only person he managed to get talking today was an ten-year-old boy, and then only after he'd bribed the child with a packet of sweets. He wasn't sure the lad wasn't telling tales.

"Kathryn Ellingsley slips out of the Cameron house at night to see her sweetheart?" Mrs. Jeffries clarified.

"That's what the lad said," Wiggins admitted. "But 'e's just a little fellow and I think 'e was just repeatin' what 'e picked up 'ere and there."

"Who was this child?" Mrs. Goodge demanded.

"He's the son of the housekeeper at one of the 'ouses across the gardens from the Camerons," Wiggins explained. "I couldn't find anyone else to talk to. I was lucky I spotted this lad before the coppers spotted me."

"We understand, Wiggins," Mrs. Jeffries said. "It's going to be difficult for all of us to do our investigating, but we'll do the best we can. I think you've done quite splendidly today. Your source might be young and might well only be repeating gossip, but that doesn't mean it isn't true. Did you learn the name of Miss Ellingsley's sweetheart?"

"No, Davey didn't know the bloke's name." He

shook his head. "But I think I can find out. If everyone on the gardens is gossipin' about it, someone must know the man's name."

Hatchet cleared his throat. "I don't think you'll have to bother your source again, Wiggins," he said. "His name is Connor Reese, Dr. Connor Reese, and he's Hannah Cameron's first cousin." He smiled sheepishly. "It seems, my boy, that you and I found out the very same thing today."

"Well, that's a bit of rotten luck," Betsy said.

"Not necessarily," Mrs. Jeffries interjected smoothly. "Hatchet's information apparently confirms what Wiggins learned."

"That's not all," Hatchet said. "I also found out that Dr. Reese hated Hannah Cameron. Unfortunately, I wasn't able to learn why. But I do know that he wasn't welcome in the Cameron household."

"Who's not welcome?" Aunt Elberta said from the doorway. She peered at the group gathered around the table. "Is it a tea party?" Eagerly, she scuttled toward the others, her cane thumping heavily enough to send Fred wiggling under Wiggins's chair. "I just love parties."

Mrs. Jeffries cornered the inspector the moment he came through the front door. She helped him off with his coat and hat and ushered him into the drawing room where she had a glass of his favorite sherry already poured and waiting for him. "Do sit down, sir. You look very tired."

Witherspoon sighed in satisfaction as he eased himself into his chair. "I have had a tiring day, Mrs. Jeffries, and I'm frozen to boot."

"Frozen, sir?"

"Yes, the Cameron house was very chilly, very chilly, indeed. Of course, I suppose one can't blame Mr. Cameron for not having seen to the fires; he has had a rather bad shock. But you'd think the butler would have taken care of it."

"Perhaps he forgot, sir," she ventured. There were a dozen good reasons why the house might have been cold and Mrs. Jeffries didn't want to discuss any of them. She wanted to find out what the inspector knew. The meeting downstairs had been cut short due to Aunt Elberta's arrival, and Mrs. Jeffries was annoyed about that. Goodness knows it was important that they share information. There were a dozen things she needed to know from the Inspector. "Why don't you tell me about your day, sir? You know how I do love hearing about your methods."

He gave her a brief smile. "I'm not sure my methods are going to work in this case. It's a bit of a muddle, I'm afraid. Inspector Nivens still seems to think it was a burglary gone awry and not murder. It's most awkward having him about while I try to question people. Most awkward, indeed."

"I'm sure it is, sir. But knowing you as I do, I'm sure you discharged your duty perfectly. Furthermore, I've every confidence in your methods. They've never failed you before."

Grateful for her confidence, he relaxed a bit and some of the tension left his face. "I did my best. But it's an odd household, Mrs. Jeffries. Very odd, indeed."

"In what way, sir?"

"In several ways. To begin with, no one seems

to be very grieved by Mrs. Cameron's death. Even her own brother didn't seem overly upset by her murder.'' He leaned back, took a sip of sherry and unburdened himself to his housekeeper.

She was a wonderful audience. She listened carefully, asked questions in all the right places and made him feel ever so much better about his own abilities as a detective. By the time Betsy came in to announce that dinner was ready, he was feeling quite on top of things. There was something about discussing the case with his housekeeper that got his mind moving in the right direction. Yes, first thing tomorrow morning there were a number of inquiries he would make.

Smythe was in front of his bank the next morning before it even opened. He paced back and forth in front of the imposing building, his feet smacking hard against the pavement as he scanned the bustling street. He pulled a heavy gold watch out of his pocket and checked the time. Five minutes to nine. The blighter should be coming any minute now. Smythe leaned back against the gray stone building and crossed his arms over his massive chest and prepared to wait. He didn't have to wait long. Within a few minutes, a tall, white haired man with his nose in the air walked briskly toward the bank. He wore a dark gray greatcoat and an old fashioned black top hat and carried a cane.

Smythe leapt away from the building as the man drew abreast of him. Startled, the fellow stepped back. ''Goodness, you gave me quite a start,'' he said, recovering quickly when he saw who it was who'd accosted him.

"I'm goin' to be givin' you more than that if you don't stop sendin' them fancy letters to me," Smythe snapped. "I told ya never to do that."

Mr. Bartholomew Pike, general manager of Breedlow and Bascombs Bank, wasn't in the least intimidated. "Mr. Smythe," he said calmly, "I realize I was acting against your explicit instructions. However, you left me no choice. As I've told you before, you've a number of important decisions to make. If you'll recall, sir, we were scheduled to have a meeting two days ago. When you did not come and you sent no word, I was forced to communicate with you." He took Smythe's arm and started for the front door. "Now, sir, if you'll come with me, we'll take care of business immediately."

Smythe shook him off and dug in his heels. "I don't have time to meet with you now—" he began, but he was cut off by his banker.

"You always say that, sir," Pike challenged, "and I simply must insist that you make time. We've serious business to discuss, sir. You've made another five thousand pounds on those American investments. You must make some decisions. You don't seem to understand, sir. You can't just leave your money sitting in a deposit account . . ."

"Isn't that what bleedin' banks is for?" Smythe yelped.

"Not when one has as much money as you do, sir," Pike insisted. "We're not simply your bankers, sir, we're your financial advisors as well. In good conscience, I simply cannot allow you to . . ."

"Look, mate." Smythe cut him off. He'd love to poke his banker in the nose, but the truth was, he was ruddy good at his job. In the past year, Pike's advice had fattened Smythe's fortune substantially. "I don't 'ave a lot of time just now. I only come to tell ya to stop sendin' them bloomin' letters . . ."

"Letters? I only sent one, Mr. Smythe," Pike said indignantly.

"That's one too many," Smythe snapped. "You've caused me no end of bother." It was more than just "bother." Smythe couldn't risk anyone else at the household finding out that he had money. At this point, they'd feel as if he'd been deliberately hiding the truth from them. Which, of course, he was.

"That certainly wasn't my intention," Pike countered. "But you must realize you have a responsibility. Money is serious business, sir . . ."

"It's my bleedin' money, is'n it?"

"That's not the point, sir," Pike insisted.

"It is the point," Smythe fired back. "It's for me to decide what to do with it and I'll thank you to just sit on it awhile longer until I've a mind to take care of it." With that, he turned and stalked down the street.

"I'll expect to see you next week, sir," Pike called after him. Smythe ignored him. "Bloomin' fool can wait till 'ell freezes over," he muttered as he stormed around the corner. "Blighter's caused me no end of trouble. I've 'alf a mind to pull my money out of that ruddy bank and bury it in the back garden." But he knew he wouldn't. And even if he did take his money from the hallowed vaults of Breedlow and Bascombs, he knew he'd run into the same problem wherever else he put it. Bankers just couldn't stop themselves from giving advice. It was as if they were personally insulted to see great big heaps of cash sitting in a vault minding its own business. Oh no, they were always saying that money had to earn its keep. Well, his money had brought him nothing but grief. He'd never meant to hide his wealth from the others; it had just happened that way. Euphemia, may she rest in peace, had made him promise to stay on at Upper Edmonton Gardens and keep an eye on her naive nephew, Inspector Witherspoon. Before Smythe knew it, Mrs. Jeffries and Mrs. Goodge had come and then Betsy and soon, they were solving murders and watching out for each other. He'd never told them about his money and now he couldn't. It would change things, make him different from them. Not that *he* felt that way, but that's the way they'd see it. They'd not like it. He couldn't stand the idea of losing the very people who'd come to mean more to him than anyone. Especially one particular person. Betsy.

"What's your 'urry, mate?" A familiar voice hailed him from behind.

Smythe whirled around. "As I live and breathe, Blimpey, what's the likes of you doin' in this neighborhood?"

Blimpey Groggins, a short, fat, red-haired man wearing a rust-colored porkpie hat, a dirty brown-and-white checkered waistcoat and a clean white shirt with a bright red scarf hanging around his neck, hurried toward him. A former petty thief and con man, Blimpey'd mended his ways when he'd discovered that his inordinant love of a good gossip and his phenomenal memory for detail could make him a much fatter profit than lifting the occasional silver candlestick or picking a pocket. He was a professional purveyor of information. If you wanted to find out anything about anyone in London, Blimpey was your man. What he didn't already know, he could find out in the blink of an eye. Smythe had used his services on more than one of the inspector's cases.

"Been to the bank," Blimpey wheezed. He lifted one end of the scarf and wiped his face. "Made a deposit."

Smythe raised his eyebrows. "You? Trustin' a bank?"

Blimpey shrugged. "Got to keep yer money somewheres, don't ya? What you doin' round 'ere?"

Smythe shrugged noncommittally. "A bit of this and that. You got time for a quick one?" He decided to spend a bit of his bloomin' money. It was ten times quicker for Blimpey to get the goods on someone than for him to waste hours trying to find a cabbie or publican who knew anything about the murder. He'd gotten blooming lucky yesterday with that gardener; he didn't think Lady Fortune would smile on him twice.

"You buyin?"

"Aren't I always?" Smythe started across the road. "Come on, there's a pub just over there."

Blimpey kept up a stream of chatter until they were seated in the back of the saloon bar at the Horse and Hound. He raised his glass of beer, took a long sip and then sighed in satisfaction. "That's good, mate. What'da ya need, Smythe? Same as always? Bit of information?"

"That's right."

Blimpey took another long swig of his bitter. "You've come to the right man fer it. What's the particulars?"

"I need to know somethin' about some people." Smythe picked up his whiskey and took a sip. He didn't usually drink spirits, especially in the daytime, but the confrontation with his banker had left a bad taste in his mouth.

Blimpey grinned. "That's my specialty, is'n it? Just give me the names and before you can spin yer granny, I'll find out what there is to know."

"One's a doctor by the name of Connor Reese. The other two are John Ripton and Brian Cameron."

"Cameron?" Blimpey's brows drew together as he concentrated. "He related to that woman that got herself knifed the other night?"

"Her husband," Smythe admitted. He'd given up any pretense of keeping his activities secret from Blimpey. The man knew he worked for Inspector Witherspoon and knew that the inspector had built quite a reputation for solving homicides. Blimpey knew everything, including, he suspected, that Smythe had more money than half the toffs in Mayfair. But Blimpey had a code and he lived by it. He didn't shoot off his mouth unless he was paid for his trouble.

"Papers said it were a burglary," Blimpey said conversationally.

Smythe knew he was fishing. "The papers were wrong. It weren't a burglary." No harm in tellin' him that much.

Satisfied, Blimpey nodded. "Didn't think so. No

one's takin' credit for that toss. Besides, a pro wouldn'a a made such a muck up of it.'' He wiped his mouth with his sleeve. "Anyone else, or just them three men?"

"Just the three names I gave ya." Smythe noticed he didn't ask for addresses or anything else. Blimpey didn't need to. He had his own network of information. For a second, Smythe considered adding Fiona Hadleigh to the list and then decided against it. Betsy was tackling that one.

Right now wasn't the time to go poachin' on Betsy's patch. Her nose was still out of joint over his ruddy letter. She hadn't liked the fact that he'd ignored her hints for him to tell her who'd written to him.

"Anythin' in particular ya want to know?" Blimpey asked casually.

Smythe thought about it for a moment. "Find out if any of 'ems 'ard up for money and then see what ya can dig up in general about 'em."

"Want the gossip or just the facts?" Blimpey asked. He finished his drink and looked pointedly at his empty mug.

Smythe ignored the hint. He was going to be payin' Blimpey plenty for the information; he didn't intend to throw any more money down the man's throat. "Get it all for me," he said, tossing back the last of his whiskey and then getting to his feet. "I'll meet ya at the Dirty Duck tonight. That give ya enough time?"

Blimpey looked affronted. "Does a dog 'ave fleas? 'Course it gives me enough time. I'll be there at ten.''

"I might be a bit late," Smythe said. The household had agreed to have their meeting after Aunt Elberta was safely tucked up for the night.

"That's all right. I'll wait fer ya." Blimpey grinned broadly. "Yer payin' fer me time."

Inspector Witherspoon peeked around the door of the drawing room and then breathed a sigh of relief.

"Inspector Nivens isn't here, sir," Barnes said softly as he and the inspector stepped into the room. "He's questioning the neighbors."

"But the police constables did that yesterday," Witherspoon said. "Inspector Nivens was given a complete report. Why's he doing it again?"

"He wasn't satisfied with the reports. Claimed they weren't done properly. Matter of fact, he had a couple of the lads in front of his desk and was tearin' a strip off 'em last night." Barnes looked disgusted. "There wasn't a ruddy thing wrong with those reports, sir. The lads did a fine job of it."

Witherspoon clamped his mouth shut. It wouldn't do to say anything rude about Inspector Nivens, but really, sometimes he was most undiplomatic. "I'm sure they did, Barnes. Perhaps Inspector Nivens is just being unduly cautious."

Barnes shrugged, turned away and muttered something under his breath that Witherspoon couldn't quite catch. He turned back to his superior and asked, "Exactly who are we questioning today, sir?"

"The servants."

Barnes looked surprised. "But we did that yesterday."

"Yes, I know," Witherspoon smiled brightly. "But after thinking about their statements, I realized there were one or two important things that hadn't been asked.''

''Are you sayin' I left something out?'' Barnes asked, his tone defensive. Good Lord, was Witherspoon turning into Nivens?

''Oh no, no,'' the inspector hastily assured him. ''Your questions were, as always, excellent. But I realized last night that I'd neglected to find out the one thing that might be very important to this case.''

Barnes brightened and was immediately ashamed of himself for thinking, even for a moment, that Inspector Witherspoon was anything like Nivens. ''And what would that be, sir?''

Witherspoon beamed happily. He was rather proud of himself for having thought of it last night. ''Something that can help us a great deal, Barnes. I'm assuming, of course, that the killer was in the house.''

''Yes, sir, I agree.''

''And I do hope you've plenty of paper in that notebook of yours.''

''It's a new one, sir.''

''Excellent, excellent.'' Witherspoon couldn't wait to begin. ''Then let's have a go at the butler, shall we?'' He started for the hallway.

''But sir, I don't understand. Exactly what is it we're doing?''

''Didn't I say? Goodness, I'm getting ahead of myself.'' Witherspoon stopped and turned to his constable. ''We're going to do a timetable, Barnes.''

CHAPTER 5

"A timetable, sir?" Barnes was really confused now. "You mean like the railways use?"

"That's it precisely." Witherspoon continued toward the hallway. "Only instead of trains, we're going to have people on ours. I say, I wonder where the maid's gone?" He stopped at the doorway and peered down the silent hall. "Do you think we ought to ring the bell-pull for someone?"

But then they heard footsteps on the staircase and a moment later, Kathryn Ellingsley appeared. Startled, she drew back a bit when she spotted the two policemen lingering by the drawing room door. She came closer, stopping just in front of a huge potted fern sitting on an elaborate mahogany table by the foot of the staircase. "Good day, Inspector. Are you looking for Mr. Cameron?" she asked.

"Actually, Miss Ellingsley, we were looking for the butler." He thought it best to conduct this area of the inquiry solely among the servants.

"Hatfield's downstairs in the kitchen," she replied, glancing briefly at the front door. "He's supervising the food preparations for after the funeral tomorrow."

"I see," Witherspoon murmured. Drat. He didn't relish the thought of dragging the butler away from his duties, especially that particular kind of task. But he needed to talk to the servants. Every one of them. Individually. Perhaps he ought to speak to Mr. Cameron after all. "Oh dear, this is a bit awkward. I'm afraid I'll have to interrupt the household even further. I suppose we ought to let Mr. Cameron know that we're here."

Kathryn gave him a strained smile. "He's not here. He and Mrs. Hadleigh took the children to her estate in the country. It's just outside Tunbridge Wells."

"You mean he's left London?" Witherspoon didn't like the sound of that. They hadn't instructed any of the household to stay in town, but surely leaving before the victim's funeral was a bit much.

"He'll be back tonight," she said quickly. "As will Mrs. Hadleigh. Brian felt the children would be better off away from here. It's been a rather dreadful experience for them."

"Aren't they going to their stepmother's funeral?" Barnes asked.

"No." Kathryn shook her head. "Brian felt that considering the way she died, it would be better for the children not to go. He's only told them that she died. He didn't tell them how. After the funeral tomorrow, the house will be full of people. Brian doesn't want the children to overhear any of the ugly circumstances of her death.''

The inspector felt a surge of pity for the little ones. Losing a mother, even a stepmother, must be very frightening.

"Were the children fond of Mrs. Cameron?" Barnes asked quietly.

Kathryn hesitated and then shrugged. "I think so. They were both very upset when they heard the news. But she was quite strict with them and though she was their stepmother, she was the only mother they'd really ever known."

"Will you be staying on?" Witherspoon wanted to make sure she wasn't planning on leaving town as well. "I mean, now that the children are gone, perhaps you'll go away for a time as well."

She smiled and shook her head. "I'm staying on, Inspector. My only other relation is in a little village in Yorkshire. I may go up to visit him. He's not been well lately and he's quite elderly. But the children will be coming back as soon as this is over, and Brian's asked me to stay on."

There was a knock on the front door. Kathryn moved quickly toward it as footsteps pounded on the back stairs. "Don't bother to come up," she called to the maid whose head bobbed up from the staircase. "I'll get it." She flung open the door and then stepped back. "Come in, Dr. Reese," she said formally.

"Miss Ellingsley." The man took off his bowler and stepped into the hall. He was about thirty, tall and neatly dressed in a dark gray suit with a white shirt and black tie. His hair was that shade of colour that's somewhere between brown and dark blond. He turned and stared at the two policemen out of cool blue eyes.

"This is Inspector Witherspoon and Constable Barnes." Kathryn introduced them quickly. "They're investigating Hannah's death."

"I'm Connor Reese." He stepped forward and offered his hand, first to the Inspector and then to the constable. "I came by to extend my condolences to Brian."

"Are you a friend of the family?" Witherspoon asked.

"Hardly, Inspector," Reese replied. "I'm Hannah Cameron's cousin."

Wiggins eyed the housemaid warily. She skittered about so quickly down the road, he was having a hard time keeping up with her. But he was determined not to go back to this afternoon's meeting empty-handed, so to speak.

The girl disappeared around the corner, and Wiggins dashed after her. Unfortunately, the maid had stopped smack in the middle of the pavement. Wiggins went flying into her, knocking her flat. "Oi . . ." she screamed.

Horrified by what he'd done, Wiggins quickly reached down to help her up. "I'm ever so sorry, miss," he sputtered.

"You stupid git," she snapped. "Why don't you watch where you're going?" She brushed off his assistance and got up.

"I'm sorry, miss." He tried again. Up close, he could see she was quite a pretty girl. Brown hair, neatly tucked up under her cap, scrubbed pink complexion and rather pretty blue eyes. "Please, miss. It were an accident . . ."

"Oh, bother, now me skirts are dirty." She brushed at the loose dirt on the gray broadcloth. Wiggins reached over and tried to help, but she smacked his hand before his fingers even brushed the fabric. " 'Ere, keep your ruddy paws to yourself."

"I'm sorry." He apologized again. "I'm only tryin' to 'elp."

"You'd help more by takin' yourself off and lettin' me be about me business," she said, but her voice had softened a bit and there was a hint of a smile on her pretty face. She turned and started off.

But Wiggins wasn't about to let her get away. "Please, miss," he said, dogging her heels like Fred did when he was trying to get you to take him on walkies. "I am ever so sorry. Is there something I can do to make it up to you?"

"I'm in a hurry," she answered, taking his measure. "I've got to get this ruddy telegram sent."

"Can I walk with ya?" he asked.

She shrugged. As a maid, she didn't often get a chance to meet a young man. "I don't mind. It's a free country. You can walk where you like."

"A telegram, eh?" he said pleasantly.

She bobbed her head. "Right, like I don't have enough to do round that place. Still, it gets me out of the house and what with the police and then that ruddy butler worryin' himself to death over the funeral reception, I'm glad to 'ave an excuse to get out."

"There's police at your 'ouse?"

"Not my house," she corrected him. "I only

work there. I'm the parlour maid. But there's been murder done where I live. The police think it were burglars. Fat lot they know.''

Wiggins inhaled sharply. The girl was a talker, that was for sure. But he'd best be careful. It wouldn't do to be too nosy too quick. Put people off, that did. ''Burglars? Cor blimey, ain't ya scared to stay in a such a place?''

''Weren't no thieves.'' She snorted derisively. ''Besides, why should I be scared?''

''But you just said there was murder done,'' he said. He watched her carefully. Despite her brave words, he could see a flash of fear in her pretty eyes. ''That'd scare me, all right. I'd be out of that 'ouse fast as I could.''

She shrugged. ''Got no place to go, do I?''

''Who got killed, then?'' Wiggins thought this the strangest conversation he'd ever had.

''The mistress, Mrs. Cameron. She were knifed a couple of nights ago. We've had the house full of coppers ever since. God, they ask a lot of questions.''

''That's their job, is'n it?''

''Bloomin' stupid, the lot of them,'' she charged. ''Especially that smarmy lookin' one with the greased-back hair. Stupid git, don't have enough brains to see what's right under their noses, think that just because we're servants we ain't got eyes in our heads and treat us like dirt, they do.''

Wiggins suddenly realized the girl wasn't particularly talking to him; she was just talking.

''Place was bad enough before the old cow got knifed,'' she continued, ''now it's even worse with that Hadleigh woman flouncing about and givin' everyone orders. No talkin', no laughin', no doin' nothin' but waitin' on her hand and foot.''

Wiggins stared at the girl in amazement. He had the impression that she'd be haranguing a lamppost by now if he hadn't happened along. Some people were like that. They simply had to get it all out. ''Who you on about?''

''That ruddy Mrs. Hadleigh,'' she snapped. ''Got her cap set for the master and the mistress not even buried yet.'' She lifted the hem of her dress and stepped onto the street.

Wiggins took her arm. ''Allow me,'' he said graciously as they crossed the road.

''And the police poppin' in every few minutes with their silly questions . . . It's enough to blind a saint, I tell ya. Especially that one copper that kept on about who we talked to and did we have a feller and all sorts of silly things that weren't none of 'is business.''

''So the police 'ave questioned you, 'ave they?''

''I wouldn't call it questions,'' she answered, ''more like accusations.''

That didn't sound like Inspector Witherspoon. ''Accusations? What they accusin' you of?''

They waited for a dray to pass and then crossed to the other side before she answered. ''Well, he didn't come right out and say it, but he kept on about did I have a feller and that sort of thing and it weren't just me—he asked all the maids the same thing. But none of us do have sweethearts—we'd have not kept our jobs if we did. I tried tellin' this Nivens feller that, but he wouldn't listen.''

''Why did he want to know if you 'ad a young man?'' Wiggins asked curiously.

" 'Cause he's a ruddy copper," she snarled.
"And if there's thievin' done, the first thing they
think of is that it's some maid who's got a thief
for a sweetheart. He practically accused every one
of us of lettin' someone in the house that night."

Wiggins was incredulous. "Not all coppers is
like that, surely?"

"Most of 'em is," she argued. "There's two of
'em seems to be in charge, but I don't think neither
of 'em knows whats what, if you get me meanin'.
'Course the other one's nicer, treats us decent-like.
But even the nice one don't know his arse from a
hole in the ground. He ain't askin' the right questions either. But that's his problem, not mine."

For a housemaid, her language was very rough,
almost crude, but Wiggins would worry about that
later. "Do ya know somethin', then?"

" 'Course I do," she said with a laugh. "Well,
not really. It's just that I know a thing or two about
what the coppers didn't ask and should have."

Wiggins stopped. The girl was so surprised by
his movement she stopped too. He stared at her a
moment, wondering if she was just having him on
or if she really knew something. Her mouth quirked
in a grin, her eyes were sparkling mischieviously
and he thought she might just be paying him back
for his knocking her down. Or she might just be
tryin' to make herself seem important.

"I thought you was goin' to walk with me," she
taunted.

She was teasing him, he was sure of it. But he
couldn't take the risk. Maybe she really did know
something. "Can I buy you a cup of tea?" he asked
politely. "There's a tea house not far from 'ere."

"I've got to send this ruddy telegram off first," she replied, "but now that Mrs. Cameron's dead, I don't have to go rushin' back. God knows Mr. Cameron's not goin' to notice; he's not home. Tell you what, you come with me and then after I've sent it, you can take me fer tea."

At four o'clock, they were assembled around the table in the kitchen of Upper Edmonton Gardens. Mrs. Goodge was actually smiling as she put the teapot on the table.

"Where's Aunt Elberta?" Smythe asked.

"Gone to her room for a nice lay down," the cook replied. "That long walk she went on this morning really took the wind out of her sails. She could barely keep her head up at lunch."

"You let your poor old auntie go out for walk alone?" Wiggins asked.

"Lady Cannonberry kindly volunteered to take her out," Mrs. Jeffries said quickly. She didn't want anyone thinking the cook was derelict in her duty towards her elderly relative. "Ruth was distributing pamphlets for the Women's League for Equality and had to be out anyway. She took Aunt Elberta with her. Said she did a fine job too."

"Did Aunt Elberta know she was handing out pamphlets?" Betsy asked in amusement. Their neighbor, Lady Cannonberry, was a bit of a political radical. Not that they thought any less of her because of her activities. On the contrary, they all admired her for working so hard for her beliefs. At least the women admired her; the men thought she ought to be ashamed of herself, but didn't quite have the courage to bring the subject up anymore.

Mrs. Jeffries smiled. "I don't think so. But she enjoyed the walk and it did keep her out of the kitchen. Now, who'd like to start?"

"I would," Mrs. Goodge stated firmly. "I found out a bit of gossip about the Camerons. It seems that Mr. Cameron is a bit of a ladies' man and Mrs. Cameron suspected him of playing about, if you take my meaning."

"Half the husbands in London are suspected of that," Luty laughed. "But he ain't dead, she is."

Mrs. Goodge leaned forward eagerly. "Yes, but what if he wanted to get rid of her so he could get him a new wife? It wouldn't be the first time a man's done murder for that reason."

"It certainly isn't," Mrs. Jeffries said. "Do go on, Mrs. Goodge, tell us the rest."

"Not much more to tell. But the gossip I heard is that Fiona Hadleigh's rich and Brian Cameron's been seeing her on the sly. According to my sources, he's gone down to her country house more than once lately to see her and he didn't take his wife with him."

Mrs. Jeffries thought that most interesting. "Anything else?"

"Well." The cook dumped a teaspoon of sugar into her tea. "There was no love lost between the late Mrs. Cameron and her half brother, John Ripton. The two of them have never gotten along, and if it wasn't for Mr. Cameron's influence, Hannah Cameron wouldn't have allowed Ripton in the house."

"She didn't seem to like any of 'er family, then, did she?" Wiggins put in. "I found out today that she can't stand her cousin, either."

"Do you mind?" Mrs. Goodge asked archly. "I wasn't finished with my bit."

"Oh, sorry." Chastised, the footman sank back in his chair and waited his turn.

"As I was sayin', Hannah Cameron wouldn't have allowed Ripton in the house. Seems John Ripton spends it faster than he earns it. He's always resented the fact that Hannah inherited the family money and some valuable property and all he got was some poxy little stocks that don't earn more than a few pounds a year." Satisfied that she'd done her fair share, Mrs. Goodge settled back in her chair.

"Is that it, then?" Wiggins asked. "Can I go now?"

"Yes, Wiggins," Mrs. Jeffries said patiently. "Do tell us what you found out."

Wiggins told them about how he'd tracked the Cameron housemaid and pounced upon her when she was well out of range of any police constable that might have recognized him. Naturally, he omitted any reference to knocking the poor girl flat on her backside. "Anyways," he continued, "I couldn't suss out why she was talkin' me 'ead off and me not even askin' any questions." He took a sip from his mug. "But after I took her fer tea, I realized why Helen was rattlin' on so. Seems the 'ousehold is right strict. They 'ad to be quiet as mice when they was workin'. No natterin' in the kitchen in Hannah Cameron's 'ouse, that was fer sure. It was like she'd been savin' up her words and when she 'ad someone to listen to 'er, she couldn't stop."

He didn't tell them the other reason the poor girl

had talked his ear off. It didn't have anything to do with the murder, and it would shame her if he repeated it. But as they'd shared tea and cakes at Lyon's, he'd realized that Helen was lonely. Desperately so. Because of her crude speech and rough ways, the other servants in the Cameron house looked down on her. Wiggins knew all about that. House servants were the biggest snobs in the world. Before he came to work for the inspector's Aunt Euphemia, he'd had plenty look down their noses at him too.

"Well, go on then. What did she tell ya?" Luty prodded.

"Really, madam," Hatchet said, "do let the lad tell it in his own fashion."

"Helen said the police weren't askin' the right questions," Wiggins said. "She said they should 'ave been askin' why people was still dressed in their evening clothes when they shoulda been gettin' ready for bed."

"Why were they dressed in their evening clothes?" Betsy repeated. "What did she mean?"

"That Fiona Hadleigh," Wiggins explained. "Helen said when she stuck her head out to see what all the commotion was about, she saw Mrs. Hadleigh, and the woman was still wearing all her evenin' clothes."

"But from what the inspector said, they'd only retired a half hour or so before the body was discovered," Mrs. Jeffries pointed out. "Why did Helen seem to think Mrs. Hadleigh's attire was important? I frequently have my dress on a good hour after I go up to my room. Perhaps she was reading or saying her prayers."

"She still had that thing in her hair," Wiggins explained.

"What thing?" Betsy asked curiously.

He frowned, trying to remember what Helen had called the blasted thing. "That bandeau or maybe it was a hat . . . I don't know, but Helen said it were funny, that even if she was readin'—'cause I did think to mention that to 'er—she'd 'ave taken that ruddy thing out of her hair at the very least. But she 'adn't. 'Er 'air was still done up. Helen claims there weren't no books in the guest room either, so Mrs. Hadleigh couldn't have been reading."

"That's a good point, Wiggins. This girl sounds right sharp." Luty drummed her fingers on the tabletop. "I like to dress up. But when I'm wearin' fancy duds, I don't keep 'em on a minute more than I have to." She glanced at Mrs. Jeffries. "You wear a plain, sensible dress, Hepzibah. But if you was gussied up in an evening gown and yer head was loaded with baubles, you'd take that get-up off quicker than spit."

"Madam, really," Hatchet hissed. "Do watch your language."

"Oh, don't be such a priss, Hatchet." Luty waved at him dismissively. "I'm tryin' to make a point. It's the kinda detail a woman would notice, not a man. Besides, from what we know, the killin' took place a good twenty mintues or a half hour after they all went up to bed. No woman keeps her corset on that long if she don't have to. So why was this Hadleigh woman still gussied up like the dog's dinner?"

"Why indeed?" Mrs. Jeffries mused. "Had I been in full evening regalia, I would have taken

them off as soon as I got to my room. But she
didn't.''

''That's not all I learned, either,'' Wiggins said
proudly. ''You know 'ow the inspector said the
'ouse was so cold the next day? Well, Helen told
me they found one of the windows on the top floor
wide open. But they didn't say nothin' to the police. Seems that the butler was scared they'd all get
the sack because that must 'ave been 'ow the killer
got out.''

''How big is the house?'' Betsy asked.

''Three floors and an attic.''

''The killer climbed down from a third floor
window?'' Mrs. Goodge snorted delicately. ''I'll
believe that when I see it.''

''It's possible, though,'' Smythe said quietly.
''Some burglars make workin' second and third
stories in a 'ouse their specialty.''

Mrs. Jeffries thought about this new information.
Could it be possible that Inspector Nivens was correct and this murder was a burglary gone wrong?
No, she didn't believe it. Chief Inspector Barrows
had taken one look at the scene of the crime and
he'd known it was cold-blooded murder.

''But surely the police searched the house the
night of the murder and they didn't notice any windows left open?'' Hatchet said.

''Helen said that she doesn't think the constables
looked all that carefully,'' Wiggins replied. ''The
window on the third floor has these right heavy
velvet curtains that go all the way to the floor. The
curtains cover the whole wall. Mrs. Cameron got
'em cheap from some estate sale last year and stuck
them in this top bedroom. The room 'asn't been

used properly in years. Helen said that a body could glance in that room and unless there was a right gale blowin' they wouldn't even notice the window were open.''

"I cannot believe the police would be that negligent." Hatchet shook his head. "It doesn't make sense. The police were specifically looking for that kind of evidence. Is it possible this young woman was pulling your leg?''

Wiggins felt himself blush. "Well," he admitted, "it's possible, but I don't think so. We was gettin' along right good by the time she told me this. And why would she be 'avin' me on? She didn't know I was snoopin' about tryin' to find out about the murder. She's the one that brung the subject up in the first place.''

"It's more likely someone in the household opened the windows the next day and then forgot to mention it to her,'' Betsy guessed.

But Mrs. Jeffries didn't think so. Nor did she think the police had overlooked an open window. Despite the very bad publicity the police had gotten in the last months over this wretched Ripper case, they weren't incompetent fools. But that was a matter she'd have to take up with the inspector. Now, she needed to get this meeting moving along. Time was running short. Aunt Elberta might come trundling in at any moment and she did have her own information to report. "Excellent, Wiggins," she said. "You've done a fine job.''

"Right, my boy." Hatchet echoed her sentiments. "Good work. If you're quite through, I'd like to share what I've learned. I found out something very useful about John Ripton.''

"Of course, Hatchet." Mrs. Jeffries forced a cheerful smile. Her turn would come soon enough.

"It seems Ripton isn't just a bit hard up for money these days," Hatchet began. "According to my sources, he's desperate enough that he swallowed his pride a few days ago and asked his sister for a loan."

"How the dickens did you find that out?" Luty demanded irritably. On their last few cases, her butler had gone positively mute on the subject of his sources.

Hatchet gave her a superior smile. "I have my ways, madam. But I assure you, my information is absolutely trustworthy."

"Did 'e get the money?" Smythe asked, even though he could guess the answer.

"My source wasn't sure," he replied with a faint frown. "But he's working on it for me. I ought to know by tomorrow."

"I'll bet ya she didn't give it to 'im," Wiggins said eagerly. "Accordin' to what Helen told me, Mrs. Cameron weren't the generous sort."

"Is that it, then?" Smythe asked.

Hatchet nodded. Mrs. Jeffries took a deep breath, but before she could get her mouth open to speak, Fred leapt up and started tearing for the staircase. A second later, they heard the front door open and footsteps coming down the hall.

"I'll see who it is," Betsy said, getting to her feet and dashing out of the kitchen. She returned a few moments later, her expression wary. "It's the Inspector," she hissed softly. "He's home for tea."

"Bloomin' inconvenient, that is," Mrs. Goodge mumbled as she got up and headed for the larder.

"We'd best be off." Luty sprang up and tapped Hatchet on the shoulder. "There's someone I want to talk to before it gets too late."

"When shall we meet again?" Hatchet asked politely as he too rose and pulled out Mrs. Jeffries's chair.

"Tomorrow afternoon," the housekeeper replied. She stifled a sigh. She'd so wanted to tell them her informaton. But it could wait a day or two. As a matter of fact, it might be even more effective if she kept this little tidbit to herself for a while.

As the others said their goodbyes, she hurried out of the kitchen and up the stairs. Not finding the inspector in the drawing room or the dining room, she looked into the study.

Inspector Witherspoon was sitting at his desk, his head bent over a sheet of paper. He was scribbling furiously.

"Excuse me, sir." She advanced into the room and stopped in front of his desk. "I didn't hear you come in."

Witherspoon looked up and beamed at her. "I thought I'd nip home and have a spot of tea."

"Mrs. Goodge is preparing a tray," she replied. Curious about what he was writing, she glanced at the paper. "Would you like it served in here?"

"That would be fine," he said.

She was now standing directly opposite him but she could see quite a bit. The paper was filled with straight lines, both vertical and horizontal. Along one edge, a list of names was written and along the top. . . . She cocked her head to one side to get a better view, but his handwriting was so small, she couldn't quite make it out.

"It's a timetable, Mrs. Jeffries," the inspector said.

Startled, she drew back. "Do forgive me, sir. I didn't mean to pry . . ." She let her voice trail off pathetically.

The ploy worked perfectly.

"Of course you weren't prying, Mrs. Jeffries," he said, putting his pen down. "Naturally, you were curious. Anyone would be and I know how interested you are in my methods. Well, I've come up with a new one. I do believe I'm onto something very important here. Very important, indeed."

"You're so understanding, sir," she murmured. "What is it, sir?"

"This is a timetable." He tapped the paper proudly. "I think you'll find this quite fascinating. Do sit down. I'll tell you all about it. I think it'll help me to clarify things in my own mind if I discuss it."

"Thank you, sir." She sat down in the maroon wing-back chair next to his desk and folded her hands in her lap expectantly.

The inspector took a deep breath and then leaned back in his chair. "As I said," he began, "this is a timetable. Only instead of trains or omnibuses, it's got people on it." He leaned forward, picked up the paper and shoved it toward her. "The names on the left are the people who were actually in the Cameron household when the crime took place."

"What's this on the top of the page?" she asked, though she could see perfectly well what it was.

"That's the time frame," he replied. "Quite

clever, I think. As you can see, I've broken the time down into ten-minute increments. I think this is going to work beautifully, don't you?''

She hadn't a clue what he was talking about. All she saw was a list of names down one column and a list of times at the top. The neatly marked-off squares on the paper didn't tell her anything at all. ''I'm afraid I don't quite understand, sir.''

He looked disappointed. ''Oh, really? I thought it quite self-explanatory.'' He jabbed his finger at the list of names. ''It seems to me that if I can locate where everyone was from the time the Camerons and their guests arrived home until when the body was discovered, I'll know who the killer is.'' He sat back and waited for her reaction to his brilliant plan.

Mrs. Jeffries had no idea what to say. Knowing the movements of the suspects was one thing, but she didn't quite see how his timetable was going to tell them that. People lied. Especially someone who'd just shoved a knife in some poor woman's back. But she could hardly say that to the Inspector.

''Of course, sir.'' She smiled reassuringly. ''Why, this is very clever, sir. Naturally, you'll corroborate all the statements of where the suspects were at any specific time with witnesses.''

His bright smile faded. ''Well, that might be a bit difficult . . .''

''Not for you, sir,'' she said bracingly. Actually, now that she thought about it, this timetable of his might be a good idea. ''Now, don't be coy, sir. You know I'm onto you. Really, sir, you are becoming a bit of a tease. I know precisely how you'll verify the facts.''

"You do?"

"Certainly." She broke off and laughed delightedly to give herself time to think. "When Mrs. Cameron was killed, the servants were all in bed, but I'll wager they weren't asleep. Now, sir, if the staff sleeps on the floor above the guest rooms . . ."

"They do," he interrupted eagerly. "All of them except the governess."

"Then they most probably heard the Camerons and their guests moving about. You know, sir, doors squeaking, floorboards moaning, that sort of thing. You've already decided to go back to the Cameron house tomorrow morning and have a word with each and every one of the servants about what they heard and, more importantly, when they heard it. Then, of course, you'll take a new statement from Brian Cameron and his two houseguests to verify what the servants say." It was weak and she knew it. But it was the best she could do on the spur of the moment. The servants probably hadn't heard any noise at all. In most households, the staff was worked so hard they slept like the dead the moment their heads hit the pillows. But his timetable might work with the suspects. Perhaps Cameron or one of his houseguests might let something slip. Furthermore, one never knew what the inspector would come up with when he was trying a new method. It just might work.

Witherspoon nodded happily. "You're onto me, Mrs. Jeffries," he said. "That's precisely what I'm going to do. I should have liked to do it this evening, but the Chief Inspector has called us in for a progress report." He sighed. "It'll be very interesting to see what Inspector Nivens has to say. I'm afraid I don't have much progress to report."

"Nonsense, sir, you've accomplished a great deal." She hesitated. "I mean, sir, look at all you've found out already."

"What have I found out?"

"Well," she hedged, "you've found out that Mr. and Mrs. Cameron weren't on the best of terms and you've learned that Mrs. Cameron was in a hurry to get home that night. And what about John Ripton, sir? You've found out that he wanted her to sell him her property and now that Mrs. Cameron is dead, he'll inherit it."

"Yes." Witherspoon cheered up. "I think you're right. We have learned a great deal." He patted his timetable. "We'll learn even more once I've completed this, too."

"It's all right, Fred." Wiggins reached over and pulled the dog closer against his side. It was as much to keep warm as it was a display of affection. "We'll not be much longer," he crooned. "We shouldna come out at all. But you know, Fred, I didn't want to get stuck with Aunt Elberta, and the way Mrs. Goodge was eyein' us up when her old auntie come thumpin' down them stairs, well, I knew we'd best make tracks."

He and Fred were sitting behind a privet hedge in the gardens behind the Cameron house. His back was up against the cold brick of the garden wall and it was almost dark, but he was well hidden from prying eyes even if it had been broad daylight.

The trees were bare of leaves, the ground was damp and his backside was getting numb. But he didn't want to miss the chance that he could find out something. He'd remembered what Mrs. Jeffries had told them when she'd brought the inspector's empty tea tray downstairs. The master of the house wasn't due home till late tonight. Wiggins had decided that if any of the staff was going to go out and have a bit of time to themselves, they'd do it while Brian Cameron was gone. "Maybe I'll get lucky and Helen will come out for a bit of fresh air," he said aloud. Fred snuffled softly and licked him on the ear. "Silly pup." He chuffed the dog under the chin. "You're a good feller, ain't ya? You know the real reason I'm sittin' 'ere. Not that we're likely to see 'er, but ya never know. She's a bit on the rough, but I liked 'er." He honestly didn't expect to see anyone come out of the house. Most of the windows were dark and the place was as silent as a tomb.

A cold blast of air shook the leaves and Wiggins dug his cold hands into the dog's fur. Fred cuddled closer. "Maybe we ought to pack it in," he mumbled. In truth, he was beginning to get right hungry, not to mention feeling a bit foolish. "No one's comin' out."

But just then, he saw a crack of light appear at the back door. Wiggins sat up and strained in the failing light to see what was going on. The light disappeared and a woman swathed in a long, dark cloak stepped out. She looked to the left and the right, then walked quickly across the gardens toward the small gate at one end.

Fred snuffled and sniffed. "Hush, boy," Wiggins whispered. "We don't want 'er to 'ear us." But the woman was struggling with the latch on the gate and didn't look toward the hedge. She yanked the gate open and went out.

Wiggins got up and motioned to the dog. Silently, they followed her. By the time they were through the gate, he saw her disappearing around the corner. "Let's 'ope she don't grab a 'ansom," Wiggins muttered to Fred.

He hurried after her, his footsteps moving lightly on the pavement. At the top of the road, the traffic both on the pavement and in the road was heavy.

The dark figure was moving more quickly now and he had almost to run to keep up with her. Fred, delighting in the chase, trotted along next to Wiggins as they scampered up the road, taking care to stay far enough back so that they'd not be noticed.

They seemed to walk for ages. She moved fast and soon they were moving toward the park. Wiggins had a moment's panic when she disappeared behind a four wheeler crossing Park Lane, but a second later she emerged in front of Stanhope Gate. She paused at the gate and looked around her. Then she went through the gate and into Hyde Park.

"Come on, Fred, let's not lose 'er." He and the dog made their way carefully through the heavy traffic on Park Lane. They cut through the pedestrians on the pavement and followed their quarry into the park. She was practically running now, and Wiggins had to do the same. Fred, clearly enjoying the game, soon flew ahead of his master. Wiggins whistled him back as they gained on her. Suddenly, she stopped and looked around her again.

Wiggins had no choice but to go past her. Her face was well hidden by the hood of her cloak so he couldn't see what she looked like. Nonchalantly, he wandered toward a bench and sat down on it. Fred jumped up and sat beside him. Pretending he was fixing his shoe buckle, Wiggins bent down and looked back the way he'd just come. The woman had been joined by a man.

"Blast," Wiggins mumbled. Fred woofed softly, sensing his master's distress. "I can't see who it is and I'm too bloomin' far away to get a better look."

But his luck suddenly changed, for the couple turned and started walking toward him. As they drew abreast of him, he pretended to be fixing the buckle of his other shoe. Keeping his head down, he cocked his ear to one side to see if he could suss out what they were saying.

"Don't worry, love," the man said in a soothing voice. "It's almost over now."

They continued on down the path. Wiggins looked up and bit his lip. Blast! He had to know more. He couldn't just let them disappear. He waited till they went a bit farther up the footpath. "Come on, Fred, let's follow 'em."

CHAPTER 6

Betsy frowned at the clock for the tenth time in as many minutes. "Where is he?" she said to the others sitting at the kitchen table. "For goodness' sakes, it's gone on twelve o'clock."

"Now lass," Smythe soothed, "I'm sure 'e's fine. Just lost track of the time is all." He hated seeing Betsy's face all pinched and riddled with fear. Even more he hated the dread clawing at his own belly. It wasn't like the lad to miss a meal. Wiggins wasn't one to stay out and worry the blazes out of the rest of the household either.

"But he's been gone since right after tea," Betsy wailed. "He didn't have his heavy coat with him, only that thin little jacket, so he's probably half frozen by now. And what would 'e be doin' till this time of night, anyway?"

"He might 'ave stopped into a pub," Smythe replied, "to warm 'imself up a bit. You know Wiggins. 'E mighta started chattin' with someone and then walked 'em 'ome and then lost track of what time it was and all.'' But even as he said the words, Smythe knew they sounded hollow. His mind flashed back to the pub he'd been in earlier tonight with Blimpey Groggins.

A right rough place it was too. In his mind's eye, Smythe could still see the ruffians lined up at the bar, pouring four-ale and gin down their throats and just itching for an excuse to put their fists in anyone's face. London was full of men like that. Thugs that would slit your throat for the price of a beer. He hoped Wiggins hadn't run in to anyone like that. He prayed the silly git had gotten lost or was stranded or was chasing Fred. The thought of the dog brought some small measure of comfort to him. ''He's got Fred with 'im and 'e'll go fer anyone that tries to mess about with Wiggins.''

''I'm going to box his ears when he gets here,'' Mrs. Goodge declared. ''Stupid boy, worryin' us like this. He's probably out standing under some silly girl's window and tryin' to write one of those wretched poems of his.''

Mrs. Jeffries didn't wish to add to the tension by voicing her own fears. And she was afraid. Wiggins hadn't ever been this late before. ''I'm sure he'll be home any moment now,'' she said firmly, ''and I'm equally sure he'll have a perfectly valid explanation as to where he's been this evening.''

''I think we ought to tell the inspector he's gone missing.'' Betsy drew a deep, long breath into her lungs. ''Wiggins is a bit silly at times, but he's never, ever done something like this. He knows we'd be worried sick about him. Something's happened to him.''

"Nothing's happened to Wiggins," Mrs. Jeffries said firmly, hoping it was true. She'd never forgive herself if their involvement in the inspector's cases led to one of them getting hurt or worse. Sometimes, when the chase was on, she forgot they were dealing with killers. "He's really quite able to take care of himself. Let's give him a bit longer. If he's not home within the hour, I'll wake the inspector."

"I'm going to have his guts for garters," Mrs. Goodge hissed, but her voice was shaky and behind her spectacles, and her eyes were brimming with unshed tears. "If anything's happened to that silly boy, I'll—I'll . . ."

Her tirade was interrupted by a soft bark from outside the back door.

"That's Fred." Betsy leapt to her feet and flew down the hall toward the back door. The rest of them were right on her heels. Even Mrs. Goodge managed to move with a speed that belied her bulk.

"Let me get it," Smythe ordered as Betsy reached for the lock. He gently eased her aside, slid the bolt and threw the door open.

"Oh? Waited up for me, did ya?" Wiggins grinned at them cheerfully as he and Fred sauntered inside. "That's right nice of ya. Cor, it's right cold out tonight. I could do with a cup of cocoa."

For a long moment, everyone relaxed in intense relief that the lad was safe and home. Then the tongues started wagging.

"Cocoa! You daft boy," Mrs. Goodge snapped. "You've had us worried sick."

"Where have you been?" Betsy cried indignantly. "We were about to rouse the inspector and call out the constables."

"You've a lot to answer for tonight, lad," Smythe warned, "and from the way the ladies was all wringin' their 'ands and 'aving you floatin' face down in the Thames, you'd better 'ave a good story." As the others were quite happily tearing a strip off the lad, he decided to go easy on the boy.

"Come into the kitchen, everyone," Mrs. Jeffries instructed. "And we'll see what Wiggins has to say for himself."

"What's goin' on?" Wiggins asked anxiously, realizing at last that everyone was rather annoyed with him. "I know I'm a bit late, but when I tell ya what I've found out, you'll . . ."

"A bit late," Betsy snapped. "We've been walkin' the ruddy floor for hours worryin' about you." When she lost control of her temper, Betsy frequently lost control of her speech as well. Glaring at the hapless footman, she stalked to the table, yanked a chair out and plopped down. "You'd better have a good reason why you're so bloomin' late."

Wiggins swallowed nervously. Cor blimey, they were really het up. "Er, look," he began, "I didn't mean to be out this long. I didn't mean to worry anyone." But he was secretly pleased that they cared enough to be worried about him. "But I was stuck, ya see, and I couldn't get away."

"Stuck where?" Smythe asked.

Wiggins rubbed his hands together to get them warm and eyed Mrs. Goodge wariy. She'd picked up a wooden spoon from the sideboard and was smacking it hard against her palm. He had a feeling she was pretending it was his backside she was walloping. "Hyde Park. I was 'idin' in some bushes and then when I followed 'em back to the Cameron 'ouse, I got stuck 'idin' in one of them nasty little side passages behind the dustbins because there was coppers all over the street and I didn't want 'em to see me. I only got away when the police constable dashed off to the corner 'cause a hansom 'ad run into a cooper's van . . ." He paused to take a breath.

"Wiggins," Mrs. Jeffries said, "please start at the beginning and tell us everything. Otherwise, we're going to be here all night."

"It's like this, ya see," he said slowly, "I went back to the Cameron 'ouse after tea. I was hopin' to get another go at talkin' to Helen."

"Humph," Mrs. Goodge exclaimed. "Didn't I tell you? He was out moonin' over a girl."

"But Helen never come out," he continued. "But just when I was about to give up and come 'ome, I seen a woman slip out the back door. I weren't sure what to do, but she come out so quiet and sly-like, I were sure she were up to something and I was right. She went to Hyde Park."

"Did she see you following her?" Smythe asked quickly.

Wiggins shook his head. "No, I kept well back and I was careful. Anyways, in the park, she met up with a man. I didn't know who he was at first, so I followed 'em, of course. I heard 'er callin' 'im Connor, so I sussed out it must be Connor Reese."

"Who was the woman?" Betsy asked. "I'll bet it was Kathryn Ellingsley."

"It was," Wiggins replied. "Looks like my

source was right. She has been slippin' out to meet her feller. 'Course I was surprised to find out it were Dr. Reese she was sweet on . . .''

''Do get on with it, Wiggins,'' Mrs. Jeffries said impatiently. ''It's very late and we've got to get up early.''

Chastised, he nodded. ''I couldn't 'ear what they was sayin' at first, but then they sat down on a bench, private like, near some bushes and started talkin' their 'eads of. Fred and me slipped round to one side and crept up real quiet-like so we could 'ear everything.'' He smiled proudly.

''What did they discuss?'' Mrs. Jeffries prompted.

''That's the funny bit. She kept tellin' 'im that they couldn't go on the way they was and I thought maybe 'e were married or somethin', but that weren't it at all. Seems that this Connor Reese mighta been Hannah Cameron's cousin, but 'e didn't dare set foot in the Cameron 'ouse. There was real bad feelin' on 'is part toward Mrs. Cameron. 'E 'ated the woman. I 'eard 'im say so.''

''We know that, Wiggins,'' Betsy said. ''But did you find out why he hated her?''

''No, 'e never said, but I do know that 'e don't 'ave an alibi for the night of the killin','' he replied, ''and 'e's scared the police is goin' to find out about the bad blood between 'im and 'is cousin and come to question 'im.''

''Why would that worry him?'' Mrs. Jeffries mused. ''Many people dislike their relatives. He wasn't in the Cameron house that night. I don't see that his lack of an alibi makes him a real suspect.''

''But that's just it, Mrs. Jeffries,'' Wiggins said

hastily. " 'E was in the 'ouse that night. 'E told Kathryn Ellingsley 'e' left when 'e 'eard the Camerons and their guests come in. Kathryn was supposed to 'ave nipped down and locked the French doors behind 'im. Only one of the children started to cry and she didn't. Reese let 'imself out and when Kathryn did try and get down there to lock the door, she saw Mrs. Cameron going into that room."

"Cor blimey," Smythe muttered, "that puts a different twist on things, don't it?"

"That's not all," Wiggins said. "When they was talkin', I heard somethin' else, too. Seems that the governess 'ad been sneakin' out lots o' times to be with Connor Reese. She'd wait till the children was asleep, slip out the French doors and then slip back in again before the Camerons come 'ome from wherever they was. But that night, she didn't slip out so 'e snuck in to see why she 'adn't come to meet 'im."

Mrs. Goodge leaned forward. "The girl has been sneaking out regularly?"

Mrs. Jeffries wasn't interested in the governess's morals. There was something far more important she needed to know. "Why didn't Kathryn go out that night?"

Wiggins smiled triumphantly. "Because she was sure Mrs. Cameron was on to 'er. I 'eard 'er tellin' 'im—that's why she didn't meet 'im. She was convinced Mrs. Cameron was layin' a trap to catch 'er out. When she saw Mrs. Cameron goin' into that room later, she knew she was right too."

"I wonder how she knew?" Betsy mused. "I mean, surely Mrs. Cameron wouldn't have told her anything, not if she was trying to trap her.''

"She never said 'ow she found out.'' Wiggins shrugged nonchalantly.

"That would explain why Hannah Cameron was in the sitting room that night and why she was in such a hurry to get home from the restaurant,'' Mrs. Jeffries said thoughtfully. There was something about the situation that didn't make sense. "Let me see if I understand precisely what you've said, Wiggins. According to what you overheard tonight, Kathryn Ellingsley and Connor Reese are attached to one another . . .''

"They're in love,'' he corrected. " 'E's wantin' to marry 'er straight away.''

"Yes, yes.'' The housekeeper nodded. "I understand that part. Are you sure about the rest? About what you overheard?''

He looked offended. " 'Course I am,'' he insisted. "Mind you, they didn't say it straight out, but from the way they was talkin', you could tell she'd slipped out to see 'im lots of times and that she was sure Mrs. Cameron were on to 'er.''

"But why didn't she just see Connor Reese on her day out?'' Betsy asked. "Why go to all the bother of sneakin' about? Even if Mrs. Cameron and her cousin disliked each other, that shouldn't have stopped Kathryn from seeing him on her free time.''

"Of course it would,'' Mrs. Goodge declared. "If she did, Hannah Cameron would have tossed her out on her ear.'' She said it so vehemently that everyone turned and stared at her.

"Don't you understand?'' the cook continued. "Hannah Cameron was very, very strict. I've worked in those sorts of households. Let me tell you, if a maid or a governess or a cook so much as thinks about disobeying the mistress's wishes, she's out on her ear. You've all gotten spoiled, the right lot of you. This house isn't like most. Inspector Witherspoon is a kind, decent man that treats us like people. Mrs. Jeffries doesn't go poking her nose into our business, either. I've seen plenty of women like Hannah Cameron and they're all the same. Mean, miserable tyrants, so ruddy wretched with their own lives they can't stand to see anyone happy. Well, bully for Kathryn Ellingsley, that's what I say. If she is in love with this young man, I'm glad she took her chances and kept right on seein' him. I hope neither of them is the killer.''

Mrs. Jeffries was very tired the next morning as she served the inspector his breakfast. Furthermore, she was deeply troubled by the progress on this case. She had a feeling she was missing something important, some clue that was right under her nose but that she hadn't taken notice of because she was too distracted by everything else. The distractions had to cease.

Nothing was going as it should. The household hadn't had a proper meeting about the case since it began; they'd been constantly interrupted by one thing or another. Everyone seemed to be dashing off in his or her own direction and not sharing what they'd learned. This simply wouldn't do. If they were going to catch this murderer, they needed to pool their information. But between Aunt Elberta popping into the kitchen at the most inappropriate moments, Wiggins worrying them to death and the inspector's unexpectedly late hours at the Yard, they weren't progressing well at all. She sighed.

"Are you all right, Mrs. Jeffries?" the inspector asked.

Turning away from the sideboard, she smiled brightly and lifted the pot. "I'm fine, sir. Would you like more tea?"

The inspector popped the last bite of egg into his mouth and shook his head. "I really don't have time. I've too much to do today. It'll probably take hours just to get my timetable filled out properly."

Mrs. Jeffries quickly put the pot down and then took a seat at the table. She didn't want him dashing off just yet. If they were going to get this investigation under proper control, there were one or two things she had to do. There was plenty of information to be had, but unfortunately time enough to sit down and dig it out of people was in short supply. That was going to stop too. Right now.

"You must eat a good breakfast, sir," she said calmly as she shoved the toast rack toward him. "You'll not do yourself nor your investigation any good at all if you don't eat and rest properly."

Witherspoon looked longingly at the two remaining slices. Mrs. Jeffries, seeing him weaken, tempted him further by pushing the marmalade pot next to the toast rack.

"Well"—he hesitated for a split second—"I suppose you're right. I must eat, keep my strength up. Goodness knows this case certainly requires an enormous amount of stamina. Chief Inspector Barrows had us in his office last night until after ten o'clock." He picked up a piece of toast as he spoke and slathered it with butter. "I gave him a full report of my progress and he seemed to think we were making some strides in the case. Then, of course, Inspector Nivens gave his report.'' He dug a spoonful of marmalade from the pot and dumped it onto his plate.

"Was Inspector Nivens able to contribute anything?'' Mrs. Jeffries asked. She might as well find out what that one was up to. She wondered how she could share what they'd learned from Wiggins. And share it she must, because it could completely change the direction of the investigation. Additionally, she had to think of a way to let him know why the Cameron house was so cold the day after the murder. That open window could be important.

"Not really,'' Witherspoon said honestly. "Though perhaps I'm being unfair. He did report that his own inquiries had revealed that none of the criminal underworld knew of any burglars working the area. Even knowing that, he still doubled the police patrols along that street and had several constables doing duty in front of the Cameron house as well. Still, I mustn't be critical. Inspector Nivens is doing what he thinks best.''

"I'm sure he is, sir,'' Mrs. Jeffries replied, deciding to take the bull by the horns. "But you know, sir, it's only to be expected that Inspector Nivens isn't much help on this case. He's nowhere as brilliant or experienced as you are.''

"Dats mos kind of you...'' Witherspoon smiled around a mouthful of toast. "Thank...''

She waved off his garbled attempts at modesty. There wasn't time for pleasantries. "Of course you're brilliant, sir,'' she continued briskly. "You're the only detective at Scotland Yard who realizes the value of a true investigation. I do believe, sir, that after this case is completed, you ought to speak to the Chief Inspector about training others in the force to use your methods."

"Do you really think I should?" he responded, looking both pleased and surprised by the suggestion.

"I do indeed, sir. Your methods get results."

He beamed appreciatively and then his smile vanished as quickly as it had come. "Er, Mrs. Jeffries, precisely which of my methods are we referring to here? I mean, sometimes I rely on my—well, one hates to use the term, but there's really no other to use—my inner voice. That's not the sort of method I could really teach anyone else to use, is it?"

Mrs. Jeffries kept her smile firmly in place. His "inner voice" had caused the staff no end of trouble on one of his previous cases, but she could hardly fault him for that as she was the one who'd invented the wretched idea. "Agreed, sir. Your unique abilities are precisely that—unique. They can't be taught. But you could teach other policemen about your additional methods. You know the sort of thing I'm referring to, sir. Your technique of never taking a first statement at face value."

Witherspoon looked puzzled. Mrs. Jeffries realized she was going to have to be far more specific.

"Take this case, for instance," she continued brightly. "I know good and well you'll take your timetable and go right back to the Cameron house. You'll question the staff again, just as you said you would when we spoke yesterday afternoon. But, sir, you'll not just repeat the same questions you've already asked. You'll get the staff talking freely and you'll do it with such tact, diplomacy and sensitivity, they'll remember a myriad of details about the night of the murder. Then you'll go over all the statements the uniformed lads have gotten from the neighbors, compare the new statements of the servants with what other witnesses say and from there, you'll leap hot-foot into a new direction. That's what you always do, sir. You get people to talk and remember.'' She was laying it on a bit thick, but she didn't think he'd notice.

Witherspoon regarded her thoughtfully for a long moment. ''Yes,'' he agreed slowly, ''I do do that, don't I?''

''It's one of your many talents, sir,'' she replied. She was banking on the fact that if Hannah Cameron knew Kathryn Ellingsley was slipping out to meet her young man, someone else in the household knew it too. She was also hoping a few more chats with the servants would reveal the truth about the open window as well. Additionally, there was the chance that if he did get the servants talking freely, the inspector would learn about Brian Cameron's doomed business ventures, John Ripton's need for money and Connor Reese's hatred of the victim. She had no doubt that some of the servants knew about all these matters. Perhaps even all of them.

The inspector's expression was reflective as he finished his morning meal. Mrs. Jeffries busied herself clearing up the breakfast things. By the time the inspector had gone, she was quite sure in her own mind precisely what they had to do and more important, where the best place to do it would be.

To that end, she put the dirty crockery on a large wooden tray and hurried down to the kitchen.

Aunt Elberta was still at the breakfast table. Betsy was sweeping the floor, Smythe was filling the coal shuttle, Mrs. Goodge was whisking cooking pots into the sink and Wiggins was in the corner, stuffing paper into the toes of his boots.

"Smythe, can you bring the carriage here, please?" she asked.

"I thought the inspector had already left," the coachman replied quizzically. He put down the bucket and brushed his hands together. "Is 'e wantin' me to take 'im somewhere?"

"It's not for the inspector," Mrs. Jeffries said blandly, "it's for us."

Betsy stopped and leaned on the top of the broom. Mrs. Goodge paused, her hands still in the soapy water and Wiggins looked up from his task, his mouth open in surprise. Before any of them could formulate a question, she continued. "We're going to Luty's."

"Who's Luty?" Aunt Elberta croaked. She'd forgotten she'd already met the woman.

"She's a dear friend." Mrs. Jeffries smiled brightly at the old lady. "You're coming with us. Betsy, go to Aunt Elberta's room and get her warmest wrap. Wiggins, pop upstairs and get my notepaper."

"How long are we going to be gone?" Mrs. Goodge asked darkly. She hated being away from her kitchen. The thought of missing one of her sources caused her genuine pain.

"Just for a couple of hours this morning," she assured the cook, "but don't fret. We're leaving a note on the back door telling anyone who comes calling to come back early this afternoon."

Smythe grinned hugely, as though he'd figured out what the housekeeper was up to. "Right, then, I'll get the carriage."

Betsy bustled back in with Aunt Elberta's coat, almost bumping into Smythe. He grabbed her arms to steady her. "Want to come with me, lass?"

"I've got to finish my chores—" she began but Mrs. Jeffries interrupted her.

"Nonsense. I'll finish the sweeping and Wiggins can help Mrs. Goodge with the pots and pans. You go with Smythe. By the time you get back, we'll be ready."

Wiggins tossed his boots down and stood up. "Why're we goin' to Luty's, then? I thought she was comin' 'ere."

Mrs. Jeffries refused to tell him. She'd wait till they got there. It was time to get cracking on this case.

"Do please sit down, miss," Witherspoon said kindly to the young maid. He was aware that two sets of eyes watched his every move and that one set thought he was a fool. But he was equally aware that Mrs. Jeffries was right; he was a very good detective and he'd become so because of his methods. He was just going to ignore Inspector Nivens's sneering expression and carry on with his investigation. "If I remember correctly, you're named Helen Moore."

The girl bobbed her head politely, but her eyes swept the small sitting room, her gaze taking in Nivens, who was standing next to the fireplace with his arms crossed over his chest and a scornful look on his face. Barnes was sitting quietly in a chair with his notebook on his lap.

"Yes, sir, I am."

"Do you mind if I call you Helen?"

Her chin jerked up in surprise. "No," she replied, her expression confused. It wasn't like the gentry or the coppers to ask your permission to do anything. But Helen decided she liked this man. He had a kind face. She'd noticed he seemed to treat everyone, gentry and servant, like they were important, not like they were dirt. Not like that other one. She gave Nivens a quick, disdainful glance and then looked back at Witherspoon. "You can call me what ya like, Inspector."

"Good. Now, Helen," the inspector began, "you seem to be a very bright young woman."

Nivens harrumphed in disbelief.

Witherspoon ignored him and carried on. "And I'm going to ask for your help with this dreadful murder."

"I'll do what I can, sir."

"Excellent," the inspector replied. "Would you like a cup of tea?"

Taken aback, Helen blinked and then nodded. The inspector smiled politely at Nivens. "Inspector Nivens, would you be so kind as to go to the kitchen and ask for a pot of tea?"

Nivens's mouth dropped open in shock. A funny cough emerged from Barnes's throat. It sounded suspiciously like a laugh. But before Nivens could gather his wits to protest the indignity of the request, Witherspoon carried on. "I do hate to ask," he said blandly, "but I've a lot of questions for this young woman and for the rest of the staff. I really don't want them coming in and out while I'm speaking with Helen. Nor do I want any other member of the household to interrupt us.''

"Now see, here," Nivens sputtered.

"I would send the constable," Witherspoon said conversationally, "but I need Barnes to take notes. He's so very good at it, never misses a word. Most important, that. And as you so kindly told Chief Inspector Barrows last night, I know you're eager to do everything you can to help this investigation.''

Nivens's nostrils flared with rage, but the mention of Barrows's name kept his mouth firmly shut. With one last, contemptuous glance at Witherspoon, he stomped out toward the back stairs.

"Now," the inspector said softly to Helen. "Let's talk about the night of the murder, shall we?''

"What are we doin' 'ere?" Wiggins asked as he opened the carriage door and helped Aunt Elberta out.

Mrs. Jeffries smiled serenely as she got out of the carriage and then turned to help Mrs. Goodge down the tiny metal step. "Don't worry, Wiggins, all will be revealed in a few moments.''

Everyone got out and Smythe turned the carriage over to one of Luty's manservants, who'd come running when he saw them pulling up.

Luty Belle Crookshank lived in a three-story mansion in Knightsbridge. She was standing in the open front door as the household of Upper Edmonton Gardens descended upon her en masse. "Lands sakes, we was just fixin' to come over to your place,'' she said, ushering them inside.

The house was exquisite, with a parquet inlaid floor in the foyer, a mammoth crystal chandelier on the ceiling and a wide staircase sweeping up to the second story. No one took any notice of their surroundings; they'd all, save Aunt Elberta, who was gawking like a schoolgirl, been there before.

"Do forgive us for barging in like this," Mrs. Jeffries began, "but"—she glanced meaningfully at Elberta—"we have certain requirements that only you can fulfill."

Luty grinned. "I think I know what ya mean. Come on in to the drawin' room and we'll have us a nice sit-down."

"Where's Hatchet?" Betsy inquired. It was rare to see Luty without the butler hovering somewhere close.

"I'm right here, Miss Betsy," Hatchet said from the door of the library. "And, of course, like madam, I'm delighted to see you." But he looked as puzzled as the rest of them.

"Luty," Mrs. Jeffries said, "do you think Effie Beals could take Aunt Elberta out to the gardens? They're quite spectacular, even this time of the year. When she's finished with showing her the gardens, do you think she might take her down to the kitchen for some tea and cakes?"

Aunt Elberta was whisked away in very short measure, and soon they were all seated in Luty's sumptuous drawing room. Before the questions could start, Mrs. Jeffries began issuing orders like a general.

"We're going to need a lot of help, Luty," she

said. "This case has gotten completely away from us. Between Aunt Elberta's visit and our constant interruptions, we've not even had time to have a good meeting to share our information or our ideas. Today, that's going to change."

"Tell me what ya need," Luty declared, "and I'll see that ya git it."

"First of all, I want you to ask your cook to whip us up something to take back for lunch and possibly dinner tonight. Mrs. Goodge may not have time to cook when we get home."

"But the inspector doesn't like fancy food," Mrs. Goodge protested. In truth, though, she was delighted at the thought of having the whole day to pump her sources.

Luty reached over and patted her arm. "Don't worry, I'll have him fix somethin' simple like roast beef or steak and kidney pie. He'll squawk like a scalded rooster, but he'll do it."

"Could 'e fix us some of them fancy cream cakes?" Wiggins asked eagerly.

"Wiggins," Mrs. Jeffries objected, "we mustn't take advantage of Luty's hospitality."

"Piffle, Hepzibah," Luty said stoutly, "it's no trouble. That lazy cook of mine spends half his time sittin' on his backside. He'll enjoy fixin' up something special for you all to take home."

"Thank you, Luty," Mrs. Jeffries replied gratefully.

"What else do you need, madam?" Hatchet asked.

"Well, if you could spare one of your maids or footmen, I'd like someone to take Aunt Elberta out during the days."

"Effie can keep her occupied," Luty answered. "She likes gettin' out and about. You want me to send her home with you today?"

"That would be fine," Mrs. Jeffries said. "And lastly, I want us to finally, finally, have a decent meeting about this case."

"It's about time, I'd say." Luty stood up. "Fer the last couple of days, we've been runnin' around like a bunch of chickens with their heads cut off. I'll ring fer tea and we can find out what's what about this killin'."

"A pity Inspector Nivens didn't stay," Barnes said quietly to Inspector Witherspoon as soon as Helen had left to fetch Mrs. Cameron's maid. "He might have discovered something useful."

"I expect he's his own inquiries to take care of," the inspector replied, but he was sorry Nivens hadn't stayed as well. He was quite pleased with the inquiries so far. He'd be even more pleased when he had a moment to fill in his timetable— especially with the information he'd just received from Helen. But the timetable could wait until he was finished.

"Excuse me, Inspector." Brian Cameron stood in the doorway, a quizzical expression on his face. "If you've a moment, I'd like to speak to you."

"Certainly, sir," Witherspoon replied.

Cameron smiled fleetingly and stepped into the room. "I don't want to tell you your business, but I fail to understand what you're doing here. For God's sake, man. My wife's funeral is this afternoon."

"We're investigating your wife's murder," he

answered, somewhat taken aback. "I do assure you, we won't be intruding upon you or your household while you're paying your last respects to your wife. We only wish to have a few words with your staff."

"My servants know nothing of this matter," Cameron exclaimed. "Why are you wasting time here? Shouldn't you be out trying to apprehend the monster that did this?"

Witherspoon didn't know what to say. What did the man expect him to do, ask people in the street if they'd recently stabbed some poor woman to death? But on the other hand, he could understand Cameron's point of view. "We're doing our best, Mr. Cameron. But these things take time."

"How much time?" Cameron whispered, his face a mask of anguish. "I've had to send my children away, I'm worried about my staff and if it wasn't for the support of my friends, I believe I'd go out of my mind."

"I'm sorry if we're upsetting your household routine, especially at a terrible time like this," the inspector said apologetically, "but it really can't be helped."

Cameron gestured impatiently. "I'm not concerned about our routine, Inspector. Under the circumstances it would hardly be normal in any case. I suppose what I'm really asking is if you've made any real progress. I'm sorry, I know I must sound half-demented. But when the butler told me you were here, I'd hoped you might have some good news for me. I don't think I'll be able to rest until Hannah's killer is brought to justice."

"Oh, give it to me." Fiona Hadleigh's voice

sounded from outside the room. "I'll see that Mr. Cameron gets it."

She flounced in carrying an envelope. "This telegram just came for you," she said, ignoring the policemen.

"Thank you, Fiona." He took it and tore it open.

"Good day, Mrs. Hadleigh," Witherspoon said politely. Barnes merely bobbed his head at the woman.

"Back again," she said archly, but she was watching Cameron out of the corner of her eye. "I should have thought you'd be finished here."

It was Barnes who answered her. "We've a number of questions still to ask, Mrs. Hadleigh. As a matter of fact, now that you and Mr. Cameron are both here, would you mind going over a few things with us?"

Witherspoon blinked in surprise. Though he encouraged Constable Barnes to participate fully in their investigations, he was a bit startled by his boldness. He hadn't planned on asking either of them anything until after he'd filled in his timetable.

Then again, Barnes was a most intelligent man. The inspector decided that if he had some questions to ask, they were probably very good ones.

CHAPTER 7

"This room's much cozier," Luty said as she ushered them into a smaller sitting room down the hall from the drawing room. "The fire's already lit."

"This one's my favorite," Betsy said, smiling as she turned in a slow circle. The walls were painted the colour of thick cream, an exquisite Persian carpet was on the floor and the windows were hung with cheerful blue-and-cream flowered print drapes.

At one end of the room next to the cheerful fire, there was a round mahogany table and six chairs. Luty pointed. "You all have a seat," she instructed. "Tea'll be ready in a minute."

While they were taking their places, Hatchet arrived pushing a heavy silver cart loaded with a china rose teapot with matching cups, a tray of tea cakes and a Battenburg cake.

Wiggins licked his lips at the sight. "Cor blimey, this is right nice."

"You just help yerself," Luty ordered. She sat down next to the housekeeper and for a few moments, everyone busied themselves pouring tea and filling their plates with sweets.

"If no one has any objection," Mrs. Jeffries began, "I'd like to begin." This time she wasn't taking any chances, so she plunged straight ahead. "Actually, I've been trying to tell everyone this information for two days now and I haven't had much success. I'm not sure it's important, but it may be."

"What is it, then?" Betsy asked. "Have you figured out who the killer is already?"

"Not quite, my dear." The housekeeper smiled ruefully. "But I think I've found out something that eliminates one of our chief suspects. I don't think Brian Cameron's the murderer."

"Why not?" Luty demanded. "Seems to me he's the one with the strongest motive. Accordin' to what Mrs. Goodge heard, he's a real ladies' man. Lots of men like to rid themselves of an inconvenient wife so's they can be free to git another one. Besides, look at some of the other cases we've worked on. Husbands can't ever be ruled out. Not unless there's an eyewitness that saw 'em someplace else when the killin' was done." Luty, though she professed to have had a happy marriage to the late Mr. Crookshank, frequently took a dim view of the marital state.

"I don't think we ought to knock 'im out of the runnin' yet," Smythe added. "I found out that Cameron's already gone through all of his wife's

money. My sources told me there was a fine set-
tlement from her family when they got married and
he's spent just about every bloomin' cent. What's
more, that Mrs. Hadleigh is sweet on the man and
she's got plenty of lolly.''

"That may be true—'' Mrs. Jeffries began
again, only this time she was interrupted by
Hatchet, of all people.

"Really, Mrs. Jeffries,'' he chided, ''I do think
it's a bit premature to start eliminating anyone as
a suspect. Unless, as madam colorfully puts it,
you've got an eyewitness that clears him.''

"There's no eyewitness.'' Mrs. Jeffries took a
deep breath. Really, sometimes they were most im-
patient. ''But there is something just as good.''

"And what's that, then?'' Mrs. Goodge asked.

"A motive. Brian Cameron didn't have a motive
to kill his wife,'' she said. ''Unless, of course,
you're willing to accept the premise that he murdered the woman on the off chance that he could
find another wealthy woman to marry him.
Namely, Mrs. Hadleigh.''

"But she probably is fixin' to marry the bloke,''
Smythe protested. ''She's got 'er cap set for the
man and 'e probably knows it.''

"That may be true,'' she replied calmly. ''In
which case, I'd be more likely to think Mrs. Hadleigh was the killer than Mr. Cameron. With Mrs.
Cameron dead, Brian Cameron stands to lose
everything, including the very house he lives in.''

"You mean the 'ouse belonged to Mrs. Cameron?'' Wiggins asked.

She nodded. ''Not quite. The house belongs to
Mrs. Cameron's *family*. She has a lifetime use of

it, but upon her death, the actual property goes to John Ripton. So you see why I was inclined to eliminate her husband. Now, that doesn't mean he didn't do it, but it seems to me he's got less of a motive than some of the others that were there that night.''

"John Ripton for one," Mrs. Goodge said thoughtfully. "Seems to me that he's goin' to do quite nicely. He not only gets his hands on those dockside properties but he gets the house as well."

"And the income that comes with the house," Mrs. Jeffries added. "The maintenance and upkeep on the property and the servants wages are paid out of a trust established by Mrs. Cameron's family before she married."

"And Ripton didn't much like his sister," Luty commented.

"But that don't mean 'e killed 'er." Wiggins hated the thought that a man could murder his own kin in cold blood. "And what about Kathryn Ellingsley and Dr. Reese? Seems to me that they didn't much like 'er either. Especially Dr. Reese. 'E's Mrs. Cameron's cousin. Does 'e inherit as well?"

"Hold yer horses, there," Luty said. "Just what about this Ellingsley woman and this here Reese feller?"

Mrs. Jeffries realized they hadn't brought Luty and Hatchet up to date on the latest developments in the case. She quickly filled them in on Wiggins's adventure of the night before.

Luty shook her head slowly. "All right, I'll give ya that the girl might not a liked Mrs. Cameron, but if she's in love with this feller Reese and fixin' to marry him, why would she kill the woman? Why not just marry Reese and get out of there?''

"Because she couldn't," Smythe replied. He smiled apologetically for stealing Mrs. Jeffries's thunder, but he'd learned quite a bit from Blimpey Groggins the other night. "Not yet, anyway. My sources give me some information about Reese. He's been studyin' to be a doctor, just got 'is degree from the Edinburgh Medical School a few months back. But 'e don't 'ave much in the way of a practise. 'E spends most of 'is time workin' with the poor over in the East End and that don't give 'im much of a wage to support a wife on." He hoped the killer wasn't Reese. From what Blimpey had told him, the good doctor sounded a right decent sort of bloke.

"If 'e can't support 'er," Wiggins asked curiously, "why's 'e trying so 'ard to talk 'er into marryin' 'im now? And I know 'e is. I 'eard it with my own ears."

Smythe shrugged. "I don't know, maybe 'e's got expectations of an inheritance or somethin'. But I do know that right now, Reese hasn't got two farthings to rub together."

"Perhaps that's something we ought to find out," Mrs. Jeffries murmured thoughtfully. "We've concentrated our efforts on finding out what we could about what Ripton stands to inherit. But as Wiggins pointed out, Dr. Reese was a relation as well."

"I think I can find out," Smythe volunteered. He already had Blimpey working on that very problem. "It may take a day or two, though. The family fortune seems to be muddled up with trusts and all sorts of complicated bits and pieces.''

Mrs. Jeffries nodded. She was a bit disappointed that the others didn't agree with her reasoning about Brian Cameron. But then again, she told herself briskly, other points of view are most important. Besides, she had a few other things to tell them, but that could wait for a few moments. ''Were your sources able to give you any other information?''

''Not really,'' Smythe admitted. ''Just 'eard more about what we already knew, you know, that Ripton was 'ard up for cash and that Cameron was a bit of a ladies' man.''

''You've done better than I have,'' Betsy said morosely. ''All I found out was that the Cameron household's been sending a lot of telegrams to Yorkshire, but that's just because of his uncle being so ill.''

''At least you found that out,'' Mrs. Goodge said. ''With Aunt Elberta hovering around the kitchen like the Angel of Death, I haven't found out a ruddy thing.''

''There's something I don't understand,'' Hatchet said with a frown. ''If Hannah Cameron's money was all gone, why did John Ripton ask her for a loan?''

Mrs. Jeffries brightened and silently patted herself on the back for having had the foresight to learn that particular fact. ''Her own capital might have been gone,'' she replied, ''but she could borrow from the trust. As a matter of fact, from what I can tell, the trust was set up specifically to keep most of the family money out of her husband's hands. She can borrow from it whenever she pleases and, of course, it never has to be paid back.''

''But is'n that the same as 'avin' the money?'' Wiggins asked. ''I mean, couldn't Mr. Cameron just get 'er to give 'im some whenever 'e needed it?''

''Of course,'' Mrs. Jeffries replied. ''For the first few years of their marriage, that's precisely what she did. But as the marriage deteriorated, so did Hannah's willingness to dip into her money.''

Hatchet nodded in satisfacton. ''Yes, it makes sense now.''

''What makes sense?'' Luty asked irritably. ''You're gettin' as tight-lipped as one of them mummys at the British Museum. Come on, tell us what ya mean.''

''I was going to tell what I've learned, madam,'' Hatchet answered. ''I was merely waiting my turn.''

''All right, all right,'' Luty waved impatiently and looked around at the rest of them. ''Everyone finished?'' As they nodded in assent, she shot her butler a scathing glare. ''There, happy now? It's your turn.''

''Thank you, madam.'' Hatchet reached for a napoleon and laid it daintily on his saucer. ''As I told you at our last meeting, I'd decided to look more closely at John Ripton. In doing so, I not only found out that he was hard-pressed for money, but that he'd asked his half-sister for a loan. Well, my sources confirmed yesterday that Ripton had gotten the loan from Mrs. Cameron. As a matter of fact, he and Mrs. Cameron had an appointment at her bank for the day after the lady was murdered.

That's the real reason he stayed the night at the Cameron house. Mrs. Cameron was going to loan him two thousand pounds from the family trust.''

"Cor blimey," Wiggins exclaimed. "I guess Ripton was right narked when she were killed."

"Bloomin' Ada," Smythe muttered. "That lets 'im out as the killer."

"Not so danged fast," Luty charged. She hated it when Hatchet got the goods before she did. "If Ripton's gonna inherit the family trust, then seems to me he'd have the best motive for killin' the woman. With her dead, he gits it all."

"No, he doesn't, Luty," Mrs. Jeffries said. "The trust was set up by Mrs. Cameron's family specifically for her. When she died, the ability to borrow from the trust died with her. All Ripton gets is the property and the means of upkeep for the house."

"So that means Ripton was better off with her alive than dead?" Betsy murmured.

"Correct, Miss Betsy." Hatchet grinned. "For all their dislike of one another, my sources confirmed that Mrs. Cameron frequently helped her half-brother financially."

"But them properties must be worth something," Luty charged.

"They are," Hatchet said. "No doubt Ripton will make a handsome profit off them."

"More than two thousand quid?" Wiggins asked.

"Probably," Hatchet answered. "There's rumors in the city that the area over by the Commercial Docks is scheduled for redevelopment . . ." His voice trailed off and he frowned thoughtfully. "Which means that Ripton could stand to gain a lot more than what his half-sister was going to loan him.''

"Then that gives 'im a motive to kill Mrs. Cameron,'' Wiggins exclaimed.

"Now, Mrs. Hadleigh, do you think you could be more specific as to the exact time you went upstairs on the night of the murder?'' Barnes asked. He'd decided that if the inspector's timetable was going to be of any use at all, they ought to get another quick statement out of the houseguests before they questioned the servants again. He hoped the inspector didn't mind, but he hadn't had a chance to ask for permission.

"No, Constable,'' she said coldly. "I cannot. I wasn't all that aware of the time when I went upstairs, merely that it was late. The best I can tell you is what I've already said. I *think* it was close to half past eleven.'' She started for the door. "Now, if you don't mind, I must get ready to leave. The funeral's in less than an hour.''

"Yes, Inspector,'' Brian Cameron added. "Your questions will have to wait. We simply don't have time to spare.'' With that, he joined Mrs. Hadleigh at the door, nodded brusquely and the two of them left.

"Sorry, sir,'' Barnes said hastily. "Didn't mean to overstep my authority . . .''

"It's quite all right, Constable.'' Witherspoon sighed. "I understand what you were doing and if I do say so myself, it was a jolly good idea. You were trying to pinpoint their movements before I spoke to the staff, weren't you?''

Pleased, Barnes nodded eagerly. "I thought it

would be easier that way"—he glanced glumly at the closed door —"but it looks like they flummoxed us."

"Not to worry, Barnes," the inspector said kindly. "While they're gone, we'll have a nice chat with the staff. That'll give me a chance to fill out our timetable. By the time they're back from the funeral and the house is quiet, I'll have all sorts of questions for the lot of them. By the way, I wonder where Inspector Nivens is today? Do you think he's going to the funeral?"

"I shouldn't think so, sir." Barnes was in a quandry. Nivens wasn't planning on paying his respects to the dead today. The constable knew that for a fact. He had his sources of gossip at the Yard, and what he'd heard this morning when he'd run into Constable Griffith had confirmed his worst suspicions about Nivens. That's why he'd been so eager to ask his questions. But he didn't want to say anything to the Inspector. He could be wrong. There might be a perfectly good reason why Inspector Nigel Nivens had gone over everyone's head and gone off first thing today for a visit to the home office.

"Does everyone understand what they're to do?" Mrs. Jeffries asked.

"I'm to keep on digging about all of them," Mrs. Goodge said.

"And I'm to find out what I can about Fiona Hadleigh," Betsy clarified. "But, Mrs. Jeffries, her house is in the country."

"She spends a lot of time with the Camerons," Luty pointed out. "We already know that. Seems to me a resourceful gal like you ought to be able to get someone's tongue waggin' about the woman."

Betsy looked doubtful. "Well, I'll do my best . . ."

"You'll do fine." Smythe patted her on the shoulder and was rewarded with one of her beautiful smiles. If he had to, he could always set Blimpey on the problem of the Hadleigh woman. Of course, he'd have to figure a way to get the information to Betsy without her knowing what he'd done.

"You still want me to keep my eye on Connor Reese?" Wiggins asked. "Wouldn't you rather I try findin' out what I can about John Ripton?"

"I'm taking Ripton," Hatchet answered. "I've already got my sources digging further into the man's life. I fear changing at this late date will only delay our investigation."

"Is there some reason you're not interested in Reese?" Mrs. Jeffries asked. "I know it's a bit of a bother, having to go over to the East End . . ."

"It's not that I don't like the East End," Wiggins interrupted. Actually it was, only he didn't want the others to think him a coward. The police had never caught this Ripper fellow that had done in all those poor women. The bloke might still be about and maybe by now, he'd decided to start slicing up young men as well.

"I don't like the East End," Betsy said cheerfully, "and no one else who'd ever spent much time there would like it either." She'd grown up in that district and thanked her lucky stars daily that she'd managed to get out.

"It is a long ways for the lad," Smythe said thoughtfully. "Why don't I take Reese and let Wiggins have Brian Cameron? Cameron's 'ouse is close by and I can always use the carriage to get over to that part of town if I 'ave to."

"As long as the two of you think that's a good idea," Mrs. Jeffries said, "then I don't see why any of us should object. Luty, are you all right with your task?"

Luty nodded. "If there's anything to know about Kathryn Ellingsley, I'll find it. She's a suspect too, though it seems to me that exceptin' fer havin' to sneak out to meet Dr. Reese, she'd have no reason to want the woman dead."

"Oh, I don't think she could be the killer," Wiggins objected.

"You never think a pretty woman's capable of murder." Hatchet sighed, as though he couldn't remember what it was like to be taken in by a pretty face. "Despite much evidence to the contrary. The female of the species is frequently deadlier than the male."

Luty chuckled. "Too bad so many of you men keep forgettin' that."

"Excellent." Mrs. Jeffries smiled in satisfaction. "We all know what we're going to be doing. I'll keep prodding the inspector and in general picking up what I can, and all of you will be out there gathering clues."

Mrs. Goodge shifted in her seat. "Don't you think it's time we got back? That butcher's boy is due round and I'd like to have another go at him." She was going to get some information out of Tommy Mullins if she had to shake it out of him.

"Goodness," Mrs. Jeffries said, "you're right. We really ought to get going. We've a lot to do today. But before we go our separate ways, I just want to say that for the first time since this case began, I've a very good feeling about it. I just know we're going to be successful in bringing this killer to justice."

"Mrs. Hadleigh, I do realize you're tired," the inspector said politely, "but we really must trouble you to answer our questions. It'll only take a few moments."

They'd buried Hannah Cameron and the funeral reception was over and done with. Witherspoon and Barnes had spent the day questioning servants and generally trying not to make a nuisance of themselves while the family paid their last respects to the dear departed.

"Really, Inspector," Fiona Hadleigh snapped. "This is ridiculous. I don't see what it is you're trying to prove . . ."

"I've just another simple question or two," Witherspoon said quickly. "Do you think it would be accurate to say that you were in your room by eleven thirty-three?"

According to Miriam, Mrs. Cameron's maid, she was sure she heard movement in the Hadleigh guest room when she went looking for Mrs. Cameron. Miriam's estimate of the time had been just after eleven thirty, and if one correlated her statement with the butler's, who claimed he heard the guest room door close at approximately eleven thirty-five, then eleven thirty-three was a fair guess.

"You can say whatever you like, but that won't

make it a fact.'' She jerked her chin toward the paper in his hand. ''What is that thing?''

''A timetable,'' the inspector said proudly. ''It's quite useful in ascertaining where everyone was at specific times during the evening of the murder.'' Unfortunately, so far it hadn't given him a clue as to who the killer might be, but he was a patient man. He'd keep right on digging.

Fiona Hadleigh said nothing. She simply stared at him for a moment and then she shook her head. ''If you think that one of us murdered Hannah, you're very much mistaken. It was a burglar who killed her.''

''We don't really know that, Mrs. Hadleigh,'' Witherspoon began, but he broke off as the door opened and Inspector Nivens came inside. ''Good day, madam.''

''Inspector.'' Her voice was frosty but Nivens didn't appear to care. He gave Witherspoon a smile and a nod.

''Good day, Inspector Nivens.'' The inspector wondered why the man looked so pleased with himself. ''Have you come to lend us some assistance?'' Perhaps Nivens wouldn't mind doing a quick round of the neighbors to see if any of them had anything to add to the timetable. One never knew what one would find out until one asked. It was quite possible some neighbor had seen a light go on in one of the rooms and had noted the time. That could be quite helpful, quite helpful indeed.

''No, Witherspoon, I haven't.''

The inspector thought he heard Barnes groan softly.

''I've just had a chat with Chief Inspector Barrows," Nivens announced. "And after I told him about a certain fact that's come into my possession, he quite agrees with my previous assessment about the way this case should be handled."

"Fact?" Witherspoon queried. "What fact?"

"There was an open window on the third floor the night Hannah Cameron was killed," Nivens replied.

"What window?" Fiona demanded. "What are you talking about?"

Nivens's smile grew positively smug. "The window in one of the guest rooms was open that night. That's how the thief got out of the house. It seems our uniformed lads were in a bit of a hurry when they searched. They didn't take the time to properly examine the whole house. It happens sometimes. Especially when there's a great deal of confusion."

"That doesn't sound right, sir," Barnes protested. His expression was angry but his voice was calm. "Those lads aren't careless, especially when there's been murder done."

"Are you saying it wasn't open?" Nivens inquired mildly.

Barnes hesitated. He and Witherspoon had heard about the window being left open today. Curious, he'd nipped up to have a look for himself. The awful thing was, with those floor to ceiling curtains, the window really could have been overlooked. But still, it seemed wrong somehow. "No, sir. But it's a straight drop down."

"Don't be naïve." Nivens laughed. "There's a solid drain pipe less than a foot away from the thing. A good snakesman or second-story man could get down and out of the gardens in less than a minute.''

Witherspoon couldn't argue with his colleague. Facts were facts and it was possible a burglar could have shimmied down that drainpipe. But even with the evidence of the open window, he was sure that murder, not burglary, had been done in this house. ''I do agree that the evidence of the window is quite strong,'' he began.

Nivens cut him off. ''Your agreement isn't necessary, Inspector,'' he said. ''Chief Inspector Barrows's is. As of right now, this isn't going to be investigated solely as a homicide, but as a burglary. My balliwick''—he grinned—''wouldn't you agree?''

''Well, of course you've quite a bit of experience in burglary,'' the inspector answered, ''but nonetheless, a woman was murdered.''

''But not deliberately, Witherspoon,'' Nivens shot back. ''Her death is the result of her being in the wrong place at the wrong time. The thief panicked. But don't worry. I'll catch the blighter.''

''You'll catch him, sir,'' Barnes said softly, his heart sinking by the minute.

Nivens flashed them a broad smile. ''Of course. Who else? I'm taking over this case. You're welcome to lend a hand, Witherspoon, but considering you haven't any experience, I don't really see that you'll be all that useful.''

''I don't believe it, sir.'' Constable Barnes shook his head as he and Witherspoon trudged down the front stairs of the Cameron house. ''The lads wouldn't have overlooked an open window. For goodness' sakes, that's exactly what they were looking for that night—the way the thieves—or killer, if you ask me—might have gotten out.''

Witherspoon couldn't believe it either, but he wasn't one to question his Chief's orders. ''Perhaps they made a mistake,'' he suggested glumly. ''It's possible. You said yourself that with those curtains it was jolly difficult to even realize that room had windows.'' But he didn't think the constables had overlooked anything. He thought that for some odd reason, Chief Inspector Barrows was giving way to pressure. ''But it is peculiar,'' he muttered. ''Very peculiar, indeed.''

''What is, sir?'' Barnes asked as they turned onto the road and started walking toward the corner. ''The fact that Inspector Nivens has now gotten charge of the case?''

''Well, yes . . .''

''Nothing odd about that, sir.'' Barnes snorted in disgust. ''Nivens just called in some favors and had a bit of pressure applied to the Chief.''

Witherspoon wished he could be shocked by such a statement, but the sad fact was that he wasn't. He knew he was a bit naive about such things, but one would have to have lived in a cave not to know that Scotland Yard was as subject to political pressure as any other social institution. It was clear, even to him, that Nivens had pulled his political strings and used the excuse of one open window to get the case classified as a burglary instead of a homicide. Murder, had, of course, been done, but once the powers that be decided it was done in the course of a break-in, then Nivens, not himself, was clearly the officer to put in charge.

He still didn't understand what was motivating the Chief Inspector. "Why, Barnes?" Witherspoon shook his head. "I don't understand why. Inspector Nivens knows that this isn't a burglary . . ."

"Of course he does, sir," Barnes interrupted angrily. "But he doesn't care. He wants you off the case, sir, for one reason and one reason only. He wants all the glory of solvin' this one. He don't want to have to share it with you. Let's face it, sir. His name will be on the front pages of every paper in the country if he brings someone in for this crime. The public isn't all that happy with the police these days, not after all that horror in Whitechapel. They haven't caught the Ripper yet, and from the gossip I hear, they're not likely to either. Nivens knows that. He knows the home office doesn't want another unsolved murder on their hands. The Ripper case has already cost Sir Charles Warren his job. There's more than a few more at the top that are worried about theirs too. Nivens is no fool. He knew what he was about and let's face it, sir, an unsolved burglary, even with a killing, is a sight better in the public's eye than a cold-blooded murder."

Barnes's analysis did shock the inspector. He didn't want to believe that even Inspector Nivens was so brutally ambitious. "Surely not . . ."

"I'm as sure of it as I am that my missus'll have Lancashire Hot Pot waiting on the dinner table on Thursday nights," Barnes cried, "and I'm just as sure that Nivens has as much chance of solvin' this one as I do of havin' dinner with the Prince and Princess of Wales. But that doesn't mean that he won't arrest someone for it. He'll find some poor sod to parade in front of Fleet Street.''

Witherspoon wanted to protest but found that he couldn't. He feared Barnes could well be right. He hated the thought that justice might not be done in this case, that Hannah Cameron's killer might get away with it. There was nothing more abhorent to him than the unlawful taking of human life. For that matter, though he was careful to keep his thoughts on the subject to himself, he didn't really believe that anyone, even lawfully constituted authorities like courts and judges, had the right to take a life. That was God's place, not man's. But the Inspector refused to give up hope. ''Perhaps we do the man an injustice,'' he murmured. ''Perhaps he will find the killer.''

''Not in our lifetime, sir,'' Barnes said glumly. ''The only chance Hannah Cameron had at justice disappeared when they took you off the case, sir, and that's a fact.''

''Git out of my way,'' Luty hissed at Hatchet. She tried poking him with her parasol, but he wedged himself in the doorway of her elegant carriage and wouldn't budge.

''I'm not moving, madam,'' he shot back, ''not until you come to your senses.''

''There ain't a danged thing wrong with my reason, Hatchet,'' she snapped, ''and the last time I looked, I was able to take care of myself. I've done it fer a number of years now.''

''That isn't the point, madam,'' he said acidly. ''It's ridiculous and foolhardy for you to go traipsing off to the East End of London on your own this time of the day.'' Hatchet wouldn't have liked her going to that part of town at any time of the day, but he was especially aggrieved that she'd taken it into her head to go now. It would be dark shortly.

She glared at him. "Well, I'm sorry that you're so het up over it, but my sources told me that Kathryn Ellingsley is goin' over that way to meet this Reese feller and I want to find out what she's up to."

"She's probably not up to anything except wanting to visit her sweetheart," he replied. He didn't know how the woman managed to find out so much information in so little time. They'd only finished their meeting with the others a few hours ago. If he were of a suspicious nature, he'd think the madam was bribing someone at the Cameron house for information. The moment his back was turned, the madam had taken it into her head to go careening off after her quarry. Luckily, John had tipped him as to madam's plans. Undignified as it was, he'd dashed out and leapt for the carriage just before she took off. "And all you'll do is waste your time and endanger yourself. In case you've forgotten, they haven't caught the Ripper."

"I've got my peacemaker." Luty dumped the parasol on the seat and patted her fur muff. "And Dickory's with me."

Hatchet rolled his eyes. Dickory, the coachman, was an excellent driver. But he, like most of Luty's household, was a stray she'd taken in when she found him cowering in a back alley after he'd been tossed out of a pub by a couple of sailors. "Dickory would be useless if you got into difficulties, madam," he said through clenched teeth. "You know I've an appointment so I cannot go with you." His own appointment involved one of his sources of information and he didn't want to miss it. On the other hand, he didn't trust the madam not to take off on her own the minute his back was turned. Dickory, unlike most of the others in the household, was totally cowed by her.

"Then you'll just have to take me with you." Luty grinned. "I figure we've got just about enough time fer you to talk to your source and then by the time you're done, we ought to be able to find Kathryn and her sweetheart." She pulled a man's gold watch out of the folds of her coat, flipped open the case and nodded. "It's just gone on four. If'n you can git a move on, we ought to be able to do what you need to and then git to the East End just about the time this Dr. Reese finishes fer the day."

Hatchet's eyes narrowed as he studied his employer. She settled back on the seat and smiled at him innocently. He didn't trust her for a moment. She was being too reasonable. That meant one thing. She was up to something.

"Well, you comin' or not?"

"Oh yes, madam," he replied. He eased his left side out of the carriage door and stuck his hand in his pocket. Taking care so that she wouldn't see, he pulled out a small metal object. "I'm coming."

"Good, I'll wait while you go git yer coat and hat."

She'd be off the moment he got out of the carriage.

"That won't be necessary, madam." He lifted the object to his lips and blew. The shrill blast of

the whistle had the back door opening and John, a
lanky twelve-year-old who was allegedly training
to be a footman in the household but was really
another stray that Luty was housing and educating,
came bursting out. In his hands he carried the butler's cane, heavy greatcoat and formal black top
hat. "Here ya are, Mr. Hatchet." He handed them
to Hatchet inside the carriage. "I told ya she was
up to somethin'." He bobbed his head at his employer and benefactress.

"You little traitor," Luty yelped. "See if I ever
trust ya again."

"Sorry, madam." John's smile made it apparent
he was anything but contrite. "But I couldn't let
ya go off on yer own, not to the East End."

"Thank you, John," Hatchet said formally.
"Your help has been most invaluable."

John waved and went back inside. Luty turned
on her butler. "Where the dickens did ya get that?"
she asked, glaring at his whistle.

"Never you mind, madam," Hatchet put it back
in his pocket and then picked up his cane and
rapped on the top of the carriage. "I always knew
it would come in useful."

She snorted. "Where we goin'?"

"To the West End," he said.

"That where your source is?"

Hatchet was loathe to share this with her, but he
really had no choice. "Yes. To be precise, madam,
we're going to visit a man I used to work for."

Luty realized he'd said "man" and not "gentleman." "What's his name?" She was quite curious
now.

"Newlon Goff." He sighed. "He was my first employer."

Luty cocked her head to one side and studied him. Hatchet's expression was sour enough to curdle cream. "What's wrong? Don't ya want to see this Goff feller?"

"Not particularly, madam." Hatchet coughed slightly. "However, I've found him to be a most enlightening source of information about some of the less than honest citizens of our fair city."

"He some kind of policeman?" Luty asked curiously. She couldn't imagine that her butler had ever worked for a lawman; he'd have told her.

"Hardly, madam." Hatchet tried to keep his face straight but failed. It had been most difficult to get just the right expression on his face when the madam had started asking her question, but the strain was worth it. But he honestly didn't know how long he could keep the pretense up. This was too delicious. In another moment, he'd be grinning from ear to ear.

Hatchet leaned closer to Luty. "But he's quite well known to the police force. One could say the inside of the Old Bailey is almost a second home to him."

Luty was getting suspicious now. Despite his expression, Hatchet's eyes were sparkling. "He a lawyer?"

"Oh no, madam, but he knows quite a number of them very well."

"Well, then what in the blazes is the man?" she demanded.

Hatchet broke into a wide smile. "A felon, madam."

"You mean a criminal . . ." Luty sputtered. She couldn't imagine that Hatchet even knew, let alone had been employed, by a crook. "a . . . a . . ."

"A thief, madam. He was only released from Pentonville a few months ago."

"You worked for a thief!" She was affronted that her boring, staid, impeccably correct butler had kept this interesting tidbit from her. "And you never told me!"

"Not just any old thief, madam." Hatchet was enjoying himself enormously. "But one of the best in the business."

CHAPTER 8

———◦◦◦———

Mrs. Goodge hummed as she cleared up the last of the tea things. Without Aunt Elberta underfoot, Tommy Mullins's second visit to her kitchen had been quite a success, if she did say so herself. She couldn't wait to tell the others what all she'd learned. Pity that everyone, including Mrs. Jeffries, was still out.

She glanced out the window, noted that it was getting darker by the minute and decided to lay the table. Yet she wasn't rushed this evening. It was a godsend, not having to actually cook for the household when they were on a case. Thanks to Antoine, Luty's toff-nosed French cook, there was a casserole in the oven, fresh baked rolls and a lovely sponge and cream cake that would have Wiggins moaning in pleasure.

They should be in soon. Mrs. Goodge ceased humming and broke into the first verse of *Christ, the Lord, is Risen Today.* She'd gotten to the first Hallelujah when there was a soft cough from behind her. Startled, she dropped a spoon and whirled around. "Gracious, Inspector," she gasped, "you did give me a fright. We didn't expect you home so early."

"I'm dreadfully sorry, Mrs. Goodge," Witherspoon replied. "I didn't mean to scare you. But there was no one upstairs when I came in." His tone was vaguely curious.

Mrs. Goodge thought quickly. She could hardly announce that the rest of the staff was out investigating his murder. "No, sir, they're all out. Smythe's gone over to coddle those horses of yours," she lied and crossed her fingers behind her back. "Betsy's run a pound of sugar over to Lady Cannonberry's, Wiggins is out giving Fred a walk and Mrs. Jeffries is . . . is . . ." she broke off as her mind went blank.

"Mrs. Jeffries is where?" the inspector prompted.

"Right here, sir," the housekeeper, still in her coat and hat, stepped into the kitchen, a calm smile on her face. "I'm sorry I wasn't home when you arrived, sir, but I had to dash over to the butcher's shop. The beef he sent over today wasn't what we ordered. But not to worry, sir, it's all straightened out now."

Witherspoon nodded distractedly. He was still somewhat depressed. The interview with his Chief Inspector had been very tedious. "That's nice," he murmured. "Ah, when's dinner to be served?"

"Whenever you like, sir." Mrs. Goodge spoke quickly. "It's in the oven."

"I'll bring it up to the dining room when you're ready, sir," Mrs. Jeffries said as popped her bonnet on the coatrack and removed her coat. She could tell he was upset. "But wouldn't you like to have a glass of sherry first?"

Witherspoon glanced at the tea kettle. "I'd like a cup of tea more," he said. The kitchen, with its cheerful warmth, was comforting. "If you don't mind, I'll just have a quick cup down here." He sat down at the head of the table.

Mrs. Jeffries and the cook exchanged quick, surreptitious glances.

"Tea'll be ready in two shakes of a lamb's tail. Would you like a cup, Mrs. Jeffries?" Mrs. Goodge asked as she put the kettle on to boil.

"Yes, thank you." The housekeeper took a seat next to Witherspoon. "Is there something wrong, sir?"

"Wrong." He sighed and smiled wearily. "Not really. I mean, not officially."

"So the case is progressing," she prodded.

"Actually, well, I suppose one could say that. The truth is, Mrs. Jeffries, there isn't a case to progress. At least, not a murder case. Not for me."

Mrs. Jeffries went absolutely still. Surely, surely, she'd misunderstood him. "What do you mean, sir?"

"Chief Inspector Barrows and his superiors have decided that the case is to be investigated as a burglary, not a homicide. I've been taken off it. Inspector Nivens is now in charge."

Newlon Goff lived in some rented rooms off Drury Lane in the tawdry section of the West End.

Hatchet kept a firm hand on Luty's elbow as they went inside the shabby two-story house and climbed the rickety stairs to the second floor. He rapped firmly on the door. From inside, a muffled voice yelled, "Look, I've already told you, you'll get your rent tomorrow."

"It's Hatchet," he called. "Not your landlord. Open up, Goff. We've business to discuss."

The door cracked open an inch and then widened further. "So it is you," said a tall, gaunt man with thinning iron-gray hair and piercing brown eyes. He wore a clean white shirt, dark tie and freshly pressed trousers. "Come in," he offered, his eyes sweeping them and lighting in amusement when he saw Luty. "I see you've brought a visitor."

"This is my er . . . associate, Mrs. Crookshank." Hatchet introduced them.

Goff bowed formally. "Newlon Goff, at your service, madam."

Luty grinned. "Pleased to meet you, Mr. Goff."

They stepped inside and Luty was surprised by how clean and well kept the place was, considering the house itself was one step above a tenement. The paint might have been cracked and peeling, but the day bed was neatly made; there were books stacked along the walls; a table and two chairs, both with missing spokes in the backrest, sat next to a lumpy green settee that had seen better days. But the oil-cloth on the table, though faded, was clean, and the chairs, though delapidated, were free of dust.

"Do sit down, Mrs. Crookshank." Goff gestured to the settee. "And you too Hatchet. Welcome to my home, such as it is."

"Thank you." Luty dropped onto the worn cushion and made herself comfortable.

"May I offer you some refreshment?" Goff asked as he sat down on one of the chairs.

"No, thank you," Hatchet said quickly, sitting down and then leaning forward, balancing part of his weight on his walking stick as the chair groaned in protest. "We don't have much time." He wanted to get this over and done with. He could tell by the glint in madam's eyes that she was enjoying herself far too much.

Goff raised his hand. "Of course, I quite understand. I'll get right to the point. I was able to find the information you requested." He stopped abruptly and smiled.

Hatchet sighed and dug out some notes from his pocket. He placed them on the table. Goff picked them up and started to count them.

"It's all there," Luty said testily. It was one thing for her to annoy her butler, but she wasn't going to stand for anyone else thinking he was a cheat. Though she would taunt him nicely for having to use bribery to get his information. That was too good a chance to pass up. "You jus' get on with it and tell us what ya know."

Goff grinned. "I didn't mean to be offensive, madam."

"None taken," Hatchet said quickly. The last thing he wanted was madam getting into a character debate with Newlon Goff. Both of them were far too fond of the sound of their own voices for that.

"As you surmised, Hatchet," Goff began, "if the Cameron house was burgled, it wasn't done by pros. Nobody, and I do mean nobody, is owning to that toss.''

"Could it have been an amateur?''

"It would have had to have been. A pro wouldn't have stabbed that woman. They'd have just gotten out.''

From the corner of his eyes, Hatchet noticed Luty nodding and looking very satisfied with herself. So far, Goff had only told them what they already knew. "Yes, we were very much aware of that fact.''

Goff looked amused. "I'm sure you were, but isn't it nice to have it confirmed? But I'll bet you didn't know that this isn't the first break-in for the Cameron family.''

"Are you sayin' they was robbed before?'' Luty asked. She wondered why Mrs. Jeffries hadn't found that out from the inspector.

"Not directly,'' Goff said. "But Brian Cameron has an uncle. A Yorkshire man by the name of Neville Parrington. Six months ago, his London town house was burgled.''

"Was someone killed?'' Hatchet asked.

Goff shook his head. "No, no one was even there the night it happened. But I got curious about it and asked a few questions. What do you think? No one owns up to that toss either.''

"How much was stolen?'' Hatchet's chair creaked and he tightened his grip on the cane.

"As a matter of fact, the only thing taken from the townhouse was some papers.''

"What kind of papers?'' Luty demanded.

"No one really knows,'' Goff answered. "They were kept in a strong box in Parrington's study.

The thieves took the box. My guess is they were after something inside it.''

"Maybe the burglars were interrupted," Hatchet mused. He couldn't think why this would have anything to do with the Cameron case, but nevertheless, it was interesting.

"It's possible, I suppose," Goff said doubtfully. "But a pro wouldn't have walked out with just a box full of papers unless it contained the deed to Buckingham Palace. The place was ripe for picking. There were lots of silver trinkets laying about, not to mention a wad of notes stuffed in the bottom of the old man's desk."

"That's most curious," Hatchet said.

"Curious." Goff hooted with laughter. "Don't be stupid, Hatchet, it's more than that. It means whoever broke in was after something, and it wasn't a silver candlestick. The place was completely empty. Old man Parrington had gone to the theatre and given his servants the night off.''

"What did the police think?" Hatchet asked.

Goff grinned slyly. "They didn't think anything. Parrington never reported the break-in. He just shut up the house and left."

"Then how the dickens did you find out?" Luty demanded.

"Oh, madam," Goff replied, "that was the easy part. Parrington may not have reported the burglary to the police, but his neighbors did. They were most alarmed and insisted the police patrols in that area be increased. Of course, my contacts are always interested when the peelers show up in any neighborhood in force."

*   *   *

"I can't believe this," Mrs. Goodge moaned. "Just when I'd found out a bit too. It isn't fair, I tell you. Just not fair."

"It's worse for the inspector," Wiggins said loyally. "He was so depressed 'e didn't eat 'ardly any of that nice casserole."

"He should have raised more of a fuss," the cook cried. She was actually quite enraged about the whole situation. For the first time since this case had begun, she'd found out something useful and now it didn't even matter. "He shouldn't have allowed them to toss him off the case. Anybody with half a brain in their heads can see this is a case of cold-blooded murder, not a bungled burglary."

"Of course it is, Mrs. Goodge," Hatchet agreed. "But I hardly think that even if the inspector had 'raised a fuss,' he'd not have been allowed to continue the investigation. As Mrs. Jeffries has already explained, politics is raising its ugly head. The police aren't anxious to have another unsolved murder on their hands. Especially a murder of a wealthy and prominent citizen."

"But murder was done," Betsy argued. "They can't pretend she wasn't stabbed."

"Yes," Hatchet agreed, "but a killing in the course of a burglary has far less of an impact on the public." He sighed. He too was bitterly disappointed.

"Silly fools," Luty muttered. "I can't believe they're so stupid. Besides, they didn't give the inspector time to solve the case."

"They don't want there to be a case to be solved," Mrs. Jeffries added. "That's really the point. I've no doubt that Chief Inspector Barrows was quite willing to continue investigating the case as a homicide, but, unfortunately, he was overruled when the evidence of that open window was found.''

"They was just lookin' for an excuse,'' Smythe murmured. "And Nivens found it for 'em. Sneaky little sod.''

"That woman was killed by someone in that house,'' Betsy said fervently, "and she might not have been a very nice woman, but she didn't deserve to get murdered that way. It makes my blood boil to think some killer's going to get away with it.''

"I agree,'' Mrs. Jeffries said. "But I don't know what we can do about it. It would be difficult, if not impossible, to continue to investigate a case the inspector is no longer involved with.''

"Are you sayin' we ought to give up?'' Wiggins asked incredulously.

"Well,'' the housekeeper said, "I don't see that we can continue . . . .''

"Fiddlesticks,'' Luty interrupted. "Where's it written in stone that just because the inspector's off the case that we can't keep nosin' around?''

"But how could we hope to bring the murderer to justice if the inspector can't make an arrest?'' Mrs. Jeffries pointed out. She didn't want them to be bitterly disappointed when and if they determined who the killer was. With the position the police were taking, unless they had incontrovertible proof of the identity of the murderer, she didn't think Witherspoon could act.

"Who says 'e can't make an arrest?'' Smythe added his voice to the argument. "If'n we can figure out who the killer is, we can find the evidence, and once that 'appens, they'll 'ave no choice but to let the inspector make an arrest.''

Mrs. Jeffries was sorely tempted. But there was one thing stopping her. What if Inspector Nivens was right? What if it really had been a burglary gone bad? They'd spend the next few days or possibly even weeks, running all over London seeking clues and risking exposure of their activities. If it turned out that Nivens did make an arrest on the burglary, they'd not only be disappointed, but they could very well damage the inspector and themselves irreparably. Oh, she wished she'd had time for a good, long think about the situation. But as soon as the inspector had eaten his dinner, he'd gone up to bed. She'd sent Wiggins over to find Luty and Hatchet and then waited for the others to come in.

If Mrs. Jeffries had only had more time to think about the problem, if she'd only been able to stave off saying anything until tomorrow morning, she was sure things would be much clearer in her mind.

"Look," Smythe said reasonably, "what it boils down to is this: are we gonna stop our investigatin' just because the inspector's off the case or are we gonna keep on? I say we keep right on goin'.''

Mrs. Jeffries looked around the table. She suddenly realized she was being rather arrogant. This wasn't just her decision. It belonged to all of them. "How do the rest of you feel?"

"Let's keep at it," Mrs. Goodge declared.

"I don't want to give up," Betsy said.

"Never could stand politicians stickin' their noses in where they don't belong.'' Luty sniffed disdainfully. "And they shoulda had better sense than to stick their noses in murder. I say we keep diggin'."

"I agree," Hatchet echoed.

Mrs. Jeffries folded her hands together in front of her as she looked at the faces around the table. Everyone looked determined to proceed. Everyone, that is, but Wiggins, who was staring down at the tabletop with a sad, almost wistful expression on his face.

"Wiggins," she prodded gently, "what do you think?"

He looked up slowly. "It's a bit 'ard to put into words, but I'm thinkin' we got no right to stop," he said earnestly. "I'm thinkin' that since we started it, we've got to finish it. I mean, like Betsy said, maybe Hannah Cameron weren't a very nice woman, but no one deserves to get a knife shoved into their back in their own 'ome. Besides"—he dropped his gaze again, as though he were embarrassed—"this might sound a bit funny, but I'm thinkin' if we don't do it, who will?"

There was a long moment of respectful silence. Wiggins's words had a most profound effect on them, especially on Mrs. Jeffries. She knew precisely what he was saying and he was absolutely right. Now that they'd started along this path, they had almost a moral obligation to keep going, regardless of what the consequences might be. As he'd said, if they didn't do it, no one would. "Well said, Wiggins," she said firmly. "We'll keep on. But do keep in mind that we'll have to be very, very careful and that even if we find out who the killer is, unless we can get proof, our efforts might be to no avail. Now, let's get cracking. Tomorrow . . ."

"Tomorrow," Mrs. Goodge squealed. "What about now! I've found out somthing and I'm goin' to burst if I don't tell it. It seems that there is some money in the Cameron family. It belongs to Brian Cameron's uncle."

"Neville Parrington," Luty mumbled.

Mrs. Goodge gasped. "How did you know that?"

"We found out he got burgled too," Luty explained. "Only it were six months ago and nothin' was taken exceptin' a box full of papers. Is that what you found out?"

"No. I just found out about Parrington being rich, and I mean very rich. Cameron, who's ignored the old man for the past five years suddenly started cozyin' up to him a year or so ago when his wife stopped handin' it to him. He even went up to Yorkshire to visit him. That's how Kathryn Ellingsley happened to get her position as the Cameron governess. She was living with her uncle until Brian and Hannah Cameron brought her to London. They let their other governess go to give Kathryn the position."

"Why would she want to come down here and be a governess when she could stay in Yorkshire and not have to work?" Betsy asked. That didn't make sense to her at all. If she had a rich uncle, she'd certainly not be minding someone else's children.

"I know why," Wiggins interjected. "She wanted to come to London because she'd met Connor Reese and fallen in love with him." He smiled.

"I 'ad another chat with Helen this afternoon."

" 'Ow'd you manage that?" Smythe asked.

"She had to go and send another telegram," Wiggins replied. "I walked along with 'er. She told me all about 'ow Kathryn Ellingsley met Reese. Seems the girl 'ad come with her uncle to 'is town 'ouse about six months ago and they'd gone to 'ave dinner with the Camerons. Reese showed up to 'ave a go at Hannah Cameron over somethin' and they 'ad a right old dust-up. The next day, Reese went round to the uncle's 'ouse to apologize for disruptin' the dinner party. But Kathryn and the uncle were fixin' to leave for Yorkshire. So 'e wrote 'er a letter and she wrote 'im back." He smiled brightly. "Before you knew it, Kathryn 'ad agreed to come down to London with the Camerons and look after the children. But Helen's sure she only came so she could be near Dr. Reese. They started sneakin' out to be together almost as soon as she got into town."

Mrs. Jeffries's head was spinning. So much information. But did any of it have to do with Hannah Cameron's murder? She simply didn't know. Tonight, as soon as the others left and she could have some time alone in her room, she'd try putting the pieces together to see if any of them fit. "Goodness, you've all found out quite a bit today. Does anyone else have something to contribute?"

"I'm finished," Mrs. Goodge mumbled. She was a bit annoyed that everyone else seemed to have stolen her thunder.

"Madam's told you our news," Hatchet said, "except for one thing." He went on to tell them about Goff's certainty that the burglary at the Cameron house wasn't the work of professionals. Not that anyone was surprised.

"In that case," Mrs. Jeffries said a few moments later, "why don't we see what we can find out tomorrow? Everyone meet back here after supper and we'll see if we've learned any more."

Betsy pulled her heavy cloak tighter, stepped down off the train and onto the platform at Tunbridge Wells. She patted her pocket to make sure the small black purse containing her money was still safely on her person. She wasn't sure how far the Hadleigh house was from the station, and it was good to have money in any case. She swallowed nervously as she realized how far from home she was. A lot of people, one person in particular, would probably be a tad annoyed with her for taking off before breakfast and going off alone. But she was determined to learn what she could. Was it her fault that Fiona Hadleigh lived in Tunbridge Wells and not in London?

The platform had cleared of people and she noticed the conductor staring at her. Clutching her ticket, she hurried toward the small waiting room. Stepping inside, she looked around and spotted the schedule on the far wall next to the door. Betsy dashed over, checked the times of the afternoon trains and smiled. She wouldn't have to rush. There was a late afternoon train at four that would get her back to London before anyone even knew she was gone.

But it took her more than two hours to find the Hadleigh house. It was, indeed, out in the country.

Betsy took refuge in a copse of trees directly across the road from the residence.

Betsy wearily leaned up against a trunk and stared at the large, red brick house through a pair of ugly, black wrought iron gates. The house sat well back from the road. A broad lawn enclosed completely by a high stone fence surrounded the place.

Now that she was here, she wasn't quite sure what to do. This wasn't like London. She glanced at the road. There weren't any houses or other buildings, only a small, narrow, unpaved lane leading toward the town. She looked back at the house. From here, it appeared to be empty. The place was deadly silent and there was no smoke coming from any of the chimneys. Where was everyone? There ought to be groundsmen and gardeners and people moving curtains as they dusted and cleaned. But she hadn't so much as seen a tradesman go up through the gates.

Supposedly, Brian Cameron had brought his children here to stay. But if they were here, she thought dismally, they were kept inside. Probably to keep from freezing to death, she thought morosely. Her feet were so cold she could hardly feel them.

A huge bank of clouds seemed to appear from nowhere, blocking the pale wintry sun. "Blast," she muttered aloud, "it'll probably be pouring soon. This turned out to be a silly idea."

But Betsy wasn't about to give up. Not yet, anyway. She'd come all this way and she was determined that the journey shouldn't be wasted. She kept to her shelter for more than two hours but she saw nothing. She was just about to give up and go back into town when a wagon, loaded with boxes and trunks, pulled around from the back of the house. Curious, she stepped closer. The wagon drew up to the gates and a young man nimbly jumped down, opened the gate and led the horses through.

Betsy knew this was her only chance. She waited till he was closing the gates and had his back to her before dashing out into the road. Taking a deep breath, she started back toward town, taking care to limp slightly as she walked.

Her ruse worked. Five minutes later, she was sitting next to the driver, a nice lad named Michael Hicks.

"It's ever so nice of you to give me a lift," she gushed. "I can't think what happened. I guess the agency must have made a mistake."

"Lucky for you I happened along," Michael Hicks replied. He was a slender young man with dark hair, a narrow face and deep set hazel eyes. He looked about twenty.

"Or you'd have been bangin' on that front door for hours," he continued. "The rest of the staff left this mornin' for London. Only reason I didn't go was because Mrs. Hadleigh needed me to bring her trunks into town."

Betsy smiled charmingly. "Well, I'm going to have a harsh word for the agency. Imagine sending me all the way to Tunbridge Wells to look after two children that aren't even there."

He clucked at the horses. "You lookin' for a position as governess, then?"

"Oh, yes," she replied brightly. "According to

the agency, I was to interview with your Mrs. Hadleigh for the position." She crossed her fingers and hoped that her fibs in the course of justice wouldn't do anyone else any harm.

Michael Hicks looked confused. "That's funny. They've already got a governess. Nice young lady she is too." But then his expression cleared and he laughed. "Mind you, no doubt her nibs will send her packin' as soon as she and Mr. Cameron are married. I can't see Mrs. Hadleigh wantin' a pretty lass like that Ellingsley girl about the place. That's probably why you've had a wild goose chase." He snorted in derision. "Just like her to jump the gun and have you come all the way out here for nothing."

Betsy felt like she'd found pure gold. "I was told the lady of the house was a widow and that there were two children."

"She is, but not for long." He shook his head, his expression disgusted. "And there are two little ones, but they're not hers."

"What? Not her children?"

"They're not here anymore, either," he said. "They went back to London early this morning with their father."

"I don't understand." Betsy frequently found that playing stupid got her lots of information. "The agency specifically said I was to come and interview for a position as a governess. But if she doesn't have any children . . ." she let her voice trail off in confusion.

"Mrs. Hadleigh was only takin' care of the children for a few days. There was a tragedy in the family. Mind you, that won't stop her from usin' it to her own advantage.'' He clucked at the horses again. ''Humph. She already has. Already rented a big house right in the same block as Mr. Cameron's. Don't know how she found the time, what with the funeral and all. But I'll say one thing for the woman—she knows what she wants and don't let no grass grow under her feet while she's gettin' it. She's probably plannin' on bein' Mrs. Cameron before that other poor woman is cold in her grave.''

''Gracious,'' Betsy cried, ''this sounds most curious. Who, pray tell, is being buried?''

''Mrs. Cameron,'' he replied, giving her a quick, sympathetic look. ''The mother of the two children. Well, she was actually their stepmother. She was stabbed to death a few nights back.

''How dreadful.'' Betsy was glad she'd gotten the East End out of her voice and learned the proper way of speaking from Mrs. Jeffries. She could tell that he believed her story, unlikely as it was. ''Someone was killed? Perhaps it is best that I was unable to interview for a position. Though, I must say, it's very inconvenient having come out all this way.''

''Better a bit of inconvenience than a blade in yer back,'' he said darkly. Then he shook his head quickly. ''Forget I said that. It's no business of mine what the gentry get up to.''

She didn't want him to dry up now. ''Oh, please, Mr. Hicks,'' she implored, ''do tell me what you know. I must report this to the agency. If something is amiss with this household, I can't let them send some other poor girl for the position. The agency is most respectable. They'll not like any of this.

No, indeed they will not." She crossed her fingers, hoping he would rise to the bait.

"You can call me Michael," he said, giving her a quick grin. "And as you've come all this way, I reckon you do have a right to know what's what."

"Oh, thank you." She gave him her most dazzling smile. "Now, why don't you start at the beginning. I'm really most confused, and you do have such a nice way of speaking."

"He's well liked in the area," Blimpey Groggins declared. "I'll give 'im that much. Don't charge those that can't pay and won't turn anyone away."

Smythe nodded. He and Blimpey were standing on the steps of the Mile End Chapel staring at a run down building opposite them. The offices of one Dr. Connor Reese were on the ground floor of the structure, which was right next to a police station. The building leaned slightly to one side, the bricks were old and discolored and the neighborhood was rough. " 'Ow's 'e pay his expenses, then?" Smythe asked. "Not many round these parts can afford to pay."

"But there's some that can," Blimpey said. "Not everyone in the East End is skint, you know. Plenty of shopkeepers and such that have a few bob to spare. But like I said, no one would say a word against the man. He's well liked. There's more than a few about this neighborhood that owe the man their lives. I also heard that Reese coulda worked in a practise over on Harley Street, but he chose to come work in this neighborhood. Good thing too. Not many want to take care of people over here."

"Yeah," Smythe muttered. "That's the truth.

Any idea why Reese hated his cousin?''

Blimpey laughed. ''Is that all ya want to know, then?''

''I want to know everything,'' Smythe replied. He watched a blond haired young woman come out of the doctor's front door. She clutched her shawl tightly about her thin shoulders and braced herself against the cold air. He felt sorry for the girl; she was thin and pale. But in her hand he noticed she had a brown bottle. Medicine, probably. Maybe it would do her good. It flashed through his mind that had fate not intervened, Betsy could well be the young woman leaving the doctor's office. He thanked his lucky stars she wasn't. If she had been, he'd never have met her. Then he wondered, for the hundredth time, where she'd gone off to so early this morning. She'd already left when he came down to breakfast. He didn't like it. Much as he respected her independence, he didn't like her goin' off without a word to anyone.

''The family used to be quite friendly, seein' each other at holidays and the like,'' Blimpey began. ''But then Reese's father and Hannah Cameron's mother were killed in a carriage accident and some property that should have been Reese's unexpectedly went to Hannah Cameron. There was some kinda dispute about the death.''

''What do ya mean? Dispute? They was either dead or they wasn't.''

''Nah.'' Blimpey wrinkled his nose. ''It weren't like that. It were somethin' to do with the time . . . Who died first and what have you. I'm checkin' into it, but sussin' out somethin' like that's not so easy. Anyways, when Reese's mother tried to take the Cameron woman to court, sayin' that there was somethin' funny about the whole thing, that the property belonged to her son, Hannah started a lot of vicious talk about the woman . . . and this was before the case was even heard.'' Blimpey stepped further back into the shadowed eaves of the chapel as a policeman from the station across the road stepped outside.

"Mrs. Reese was of a high-strung nature, and when the gossip and such started—and right old rotten gossip it was too," he continued, still keeping an eagle eye on the copper, "she started takin' laudanum for her nerves. A week or so before the case was to be heard, she took too much of it and died. The case was dismissed and Hannah inherited the lot."

"Why didn't the son fight fer the inheritance?" Smythe grinned as Blimpey flattened himself against the wall of the Chapel as the policeman sauntered past.

"He'd just gone away to Edinburgh, to school." Blimpey breathed a loud sigh of relief as the peeler turned the corner and disappeared. "He probably didn't have the lolly. Ruddy soliciters don't work fer free. Ask me, I've paid enough of 'em in my time."

"Do ya 'appen to know what property was in dispute?" Smythe asked. He'd heard about Hannah Cameron's wealth, about the trust set up when her own father died. But that had been eight years ago, before she married Brian Cameron.

"A couple of pieces of property over on the docks," Blimpey replied. "I can get ya the addresses if ya want me to."

"I do." He was curious now. Really curious. That property was also a bone of contention between the victim and her half brother, John. Smythe was becoming increasingly certain that Hannah Cameron was killed because she owned those buildings.

"Fair enough," Blimpey said. "I can get that information fer ya by tonight."

"Can ya get it any sooner?" Maybe he ought to take a quick run over there and have a look at them.

Blimpey looked surprised. "I can do it now, if ya want."

"Good." Smythe gave him a cocky grin. "As a matter of fact, if ya don't mind, I'll come with ya."

"It's gettin' a bit late, isn't it?" Smythe drummed his fingers on the table and tried not to look at the clock for the hundredth time. "Betsy shoulda been back by now."

"I'm sure she'll be here any moment," Mrs. Jeffries replied, but she too was concerned. "She's rarely, if ever, late for the evening meal."

"Should I go ahead and serve?" Mrs. Goodge asked. "I've already taken Aunt Elberta her dinner on a tray. She regrets she'll be unable to eat with us, but she's too tired." She grinned. "Effie took her to Kew Gardens today. Poor old woman's dead on her feet. She's going right to bed as soon as she eats."

"Why don't we wait just a few more minutes?" Mrs. Jeffries replied. "The inspector's gone over to Lady Cannonberry's and Luty and Hatchet aren't due for another hour."

"Maybe I ought to go out and look for her,"

Smythe said. Blast, he was goin' to give her the sharp edge of his tongue when she came home. What was she thinkin', worryin' him like this?

"Where would you go lookin'?" Wiggins asked. "She never said where she were goin'."

Smythe glared at him, not liking the reminder that she was out there with night comin' and not one of them knew where she was.

"She'll be here any moment now," Mrs. Jeffries said. "I'm sure of it."

"Sorry I'm late," Betsy called as she came in the back door and rushed into the kitchen. She skidded to a halt, her smile evaporating as she came face to face with Smythe. He towered over her, his hands on his hips and his face set in a scowl that could strip the polish off the floor. "But it really couldn't be helped."

CHAPTER 9

Betsy swallowed nervously. Smythe looked ready to spit nails. She knew she was a bit late, but she'd figured that the gossip she'd gotten out of Michael Hicks was worth it. Now she wasn't so sure. "Uh, listen," she began, but he cut her off.

"No, you listen," Smythe said, trying hard to keep a lid on his temper. "It's dark. You didn't tell anyone where the blazes you was goin', and you've been gone since before breakfast. We've been worried sick, lass. Remember how it felt when you was worried about Wiggins?"

"But that was different," she protested. "He didn't get home till after midnight."

"It isn't different, Betsy," Mrs. Jeffries said firmly. "We've all been just as concerned about you. Mainly because you left so early and said nothing as to your plans."

In fact, no one but Smythe had really been too

anxious, but the housekeeper had decided to intervene to keep this incident from becoming a full-out spat between the two of them. The last thing the household needed was Betsy and Smythe feuding.

"But you're home now," she continued briskly. "Safe and sound. So let's have our meal and by then, Luty and Hatchet will be here and we can all share what we've learned today."

"That's a good idea," Betsy said as she scurried past Smythe, who was still scowling like a fiend. She took off her coat and hat and quickly took her place at the table.

"Let's talk about something other than the case," Mrs. Jeffries said. "Give ourselves a bit of break from thinking about it all the time. How are the preparations for Inspector Witherspoon's dinner party coming along?" she asked the cook.

Mrs. Goodge looked unconcerned. "It's done. The meat's been ordered and the fishmonger's getting us a nice bit of haddock for the evening."

"The silver's polished and all the linens have been pressed," Betsy put in.

"And I've dusted out them dining room curtains all right and proper," Wiggins added. "And washed the windows inside and out. Seems to me the only fly in our ointment is the inspector's cousin bein' one of the guests."

"She'll only be here for few hours," Mrs. Jeffries said matter-of-factly, "and considering she's only in London to buy her wedding clothes, I don't think she'll be all that interested in us." She sincerely hoped that Edwina Livingston-Graves wouldn't take it into her head to stay for a visit. That would be most unfortunate.

"Let's hope not," Mrs. Goodge said fervently. "Don't relish the thought of her hanging about the place. I don't care if she is the inspector's relation; she's more trouble than she's worth. Most inconvenient woman, she is."

"What did you say?" Mrs. Jeffries asked, putting down her fork.

"I just said she's a most inconvenient woman," Mrs. Goodge repeated, "and I was bein' kind by just callin' her 'inconvenient' and not a few other names I could think of if I wasn't so polite. Why? Is it important?"

The cook's statement niggled something at the back of Mrs. Jeffries's mind, but before she could grasp the notion and wring any sense out it, it was gone. She shook her head, "No, it's nothing," she said, reaching for her fork and slicing a bite off her roast potatoes. But she promised herself she'd think about it later. Tonight, when she was alone.

They finished eating quickly and cleared up. The last of the dishes had just been put into the drying rack when they heard the distinctive sound of the carriage pulling up outside. A few moments later, Luty and Hatchet were sitting at the table with the others.

"I hope you all have somethin' decent to report," Luty began testily. She shot her butler a disgruntled look. "Because I ain't found out nothin'."

"I have something to report." Hatchet smiled smugly.

"Only because you snuck out before I was up this mornin'," she charged.

"He weren't the only one sneakin' out at the crack of dawn." Smythe shot Betsy an evil look. He still wasn't ready to forgive her for causing a few more gray hairs in his head.

"I found out a few things," Wiggins said cheerfully. "And if it's all the same to the rest of ya, I'd like to go first."

"By all means," Mrs. Jeffries said.

"Well, I 'ad another chat with Helen today . . ."

"Another one," Smythe interrupted. "Cor blimey, Wiggins, unless the girl's dafter than a mad dog, she'll know you're up to something if you keep after 'er."

"She likes me," he said defensively. "And she's not mad. Besides, ya told me to keep an eye on Brian Cameron, but 'e don't go nowhere. All 'e does is stay in that 'ouse with that Mrs. Hadleigh fussin' all over 'im. It's not my fault that Helen's the only one I can get at, and what's more, she trusts me. She told me somethin' today she's afraid to tell the police."

Mrs. Jeffries leaned forward eagerly. "What did she tell you?"

"It were somethin' about John Ripton," he said slowly. "Accordin' to Helen, 'e didn't go right up to 'is room when 'e said 'e did. She says she knows 'cause she saw 'im comin' upstairs right before all the shoutin' started."

"Why didn't she tell Inspector Witherspoon?" Betsy demanded.

"Where was she when she saw Ripton?" Smythe challenged. "I thought everyone except Mrs. Cameron's maid 'ad gone to their rooms."

"She were peekin' down the back stairs," Wiggins stated, "and she didn't tell the inspector because she was afraid 'e'd give 'er away to the Camerons and she were scared of losin' 'er position. But she saw Ripton, saw 'im plain as day. Helen 'ad just reached the landing to the third floor, when she 'eard 'is footsteps comin' up the front stairs. You can see the front stairs if you go to the bottom of the servants stairs and peek around the corner. She did and she saw Ripton comin' up as plain as day."

"Why would she be frightened of losing her position?" Hatchet asked. "For goodness' sakes, the Cameron house isn't a prison. People are allowed out of their rooms, I presume."

"But it is a bit like bein' in stir," Wiggins protested. "And she were scared to say anything 'cause she didn't want anyone knowin' what she was doin' roamin' about the house that time of night."

"And what was she doing?" Betsy asked suspiciously.

"She were hungry," he explained. "The other girl she shared the room with 'ad gone to sleep and so she went down to the kitchen to pinch a bit of food. All she took was a sausage and a bit of bread. But she were afraid that if she said anythin' and the Camerons found out, they'd think she was a thief and toss 'er out on 'er ear."

Mrs. Jeffries considered this new information carefully. "Was she absolutely sure about who it was she saw coming up the front stairs?" she asked.

"She saw Ripton as plain as day," he replied.

"Ripton does have a good motive," Hatchet

added. "That property he inherited on the Commercial Docks is going to be redeveloped. Now he can sell it and make an enormous profit."

"How the blazes do you know that?" Luty yelped.

"My sources, madam, aren't all former convicts." He sniffed disdainfully. "Some of them are quite informed about the financial community."

"Former convicts?" Wiggins looked at Hatchet with disbelief. "You? You know someone who's done time?"

Hatchet realized that everyone was staring at him. "It's not quite what you think," he sputtered.

"Oh, fiddlesticks, Hatchet." Luty waved dismissively. "Don't get yer trousers in a twist. It ain't no crime to know someone who's been in jail. But we ain't got time to discuss it now." She turned to the housekeeper. "What are we gonna do now? Seems to me that Ripton's got to go to the top of our suspect list."

"I agree," Mrs. Jeffries replied. "We know that Ripton needed money now. That's why he'd asked his sister for a loan."

"But she was goin' to loan him the money," Betsy charged. "So why would he kill her? Even if he does inherit that property, if it were cash he needed, and he needed it quick, he'd have to wait for all the legal things to be over. I mean, even when you inherit, it takes a bit of time to get things sorted out. You don't just get the deed to a piece of property the next morning."

"I think 'e was scared she'd changed her mind," Wiggins said. "Remember 'ow she acted when they was all at dinner? She were right upset with him because 'e kept badgerin' her to sell to 'im. Maybe he figured she'd changed her mind about loanin' the money, so 'e decided to do 'er in instead and get what was 'is once and for all.''

Mrs. Jeffries thought about that. Wiggins did have a point. From what the inspector had said about the victim's behaviour on the night of the murder, she could well have changed her mind. The problem was, they simply didn't know. "Whether she changed her mind or not is unknown," she said, "but it's important that we figure out a way to get Helen to tell the inspector that she saw John Ripton coming up the stairs that night. If, indeed, she saw him right before 'all the commotion,' then there is a possibility he's the killer. In any case, he can't be counted out.''

" 'Ow we gonna do that?'' the footman asked. "I don't think Helen's goin' to be too eager to say anythin'.''

But Mrs. Jeffries already had an idea. "Wiggins, go up to the inspector's study. You'll find his timetable on his desk. Bring it down and bring down the bottle of India ink and his pen.''

"Back in a tick.'' The footman dashed off. Fred, who was bored, followed right at his heels.

"What are you plannin' on doin?'' Smythe asked her.

"I'm not sure,'' she said. "It will depend.''

Wiggins was true to his word and returned a moment later, the requisite items clutched in his hand. He sat them down in front of Mrs. Jeffries. " 'Ere you are. They was right where you said they'd be.''

No one said anything as Mrs. Jeffries studied the sheet in front of her. She ran her finger down one column while scanning the top with her gaze. "Yes, here it is—Helen. And here's the square for eleven forty-five. We're in luck. It's empty. She claims to have been asleep since half past nine. Now, let's look at the same time square for Ripton. Ah, as I thought, he claimed to have been in his room."

She looked up and smiled. "Is anyone here any good at copying?"

" 'Ow do ya mean, Mrs. J.?" Smythe asked curiously. He thought he knew what she wanted from them. "If ya mean what I think ya do, it's a bit risky."

"It's very risky," she agreed, "but we've really no choice. Not if we're to give the inspector the means to bring the murderer to justice."

"I don't see what Mrs. Jeffries is up to," Wiggins cried.

"It's very simple, Wiggins," Mrs. Jeffries replied. She tapped the empty square under Helen's name. "We've got to fill in this space."

Hatchet leaned over and stared hard at the paper. "The inspector's handwriting is very distinct. It might be difficult to duplicate it."

"Someone's got to try," the housekeeper persisted.

"Excuse me," Mrs. Goodge said, "but like Wiggins, I don't understand what's going on."

"Well," Mrs. Jeffries said hesitantly, "the only way to get this information to the inspector is to let him know what Helen saw, or in this case, what she heard. If instead of leaving that square blank because the girl was sleeping, we can fill in the square with something like 'heard footsteps/front stairs.' That will get the inspector to thinking. Especially when I point it out to him. Because we've only written that she 'heard footsteps,' hopefully the inspector will start asking more questions. At that point, Helen might own up to what she actually saw that night.''

"Won't he remember that he didn't fill it in himself?'' Betsy asked.

"That's the risk we're takin','' Smythe said, "but I think it's worth takin'. Remember, the inspector got tossed off the case before 'e 'ad much of chance to really examine his timetable.''

"That's what I'm counting on.'' Mrs. Jeffries smiled brightly. "Who wants to have a go at it?''

"Not me,'' Wiggins declined. "Me 'andwritin's not anythin' like 'is.''

"Don't look at me,'' Smythe echoed. "You can barely read my writin'.''

Betsy stared at the small, elegant handwriting of her employer and shook her head, as did Mrs. Goodge.

"I know I can't do it,'' Luty declared.

"If I must,'' Mrs. Jeffries said hesitantly, "I suppose I can try . . .''

"That won't be necessary.'' Hatchet picked up the pen and reached for the bottle of ink. Mrs. Jeffries quickly shoved the paper over to him. Opening the ink carefully, he dipped the pen in, gave it a slight shake as he lifted it out and then looked at the housekeeper. "Shall I write 'heard footsteps/ front stairs'?''

"That will do nicely.''

They watched in fascinated silence as he slowly, carefully began to write. When he was finished, he leaned back, stared at his handiwork for a moment and then smiled. "I think this ought to do it," he said, shoving the paper out to the middle of the table where everyone could see it.

"Oh, it's ever so like the inspector's," Betsy crooned.

"Cor blimey, Hatchet, you're ruddy good at this," Smythe agreed.

"Excellent work," Mrs. Jeffries murmured. "Really excellent."

"Nells Bells, Hatchet," Luty cried. "Did ya use to work for a forger?"

Mrs. Jeffries closed the door of her room softly. Pulling her shawl tighter, she turned down the light and went to sit in her chair by the window. Sitting quietly in the darkened room, staring out at the sleeping city, helped her to think. Tonight, she thought, she had much to think about.

They had so much information. Unfortunately, their meeting had been cut short by Aunt Elberta coming into the kitchen in search of a cup of cocoa. But they had had time to hear most of the important news. Betsy had told them that she'd found out that Fiona Hadleigh had rented a house on the same block as the Cameron house. Apparently, the woman had told her personal maid that this time she wasn't going to sit back and wait for Cameron to get over his grief. Fiona Hadleigh was bound and determined to marry the man. Mrs. Jeffries wondered how badly Mrs. Hadleigh wanted him. Badly enough to kill? Betsy had been a bit reticent about where she'd come by her information and it was only the arrival of Aunt Elberta that had kept

Smythe's questions in check. But was Betsy's news anything more than Fiona Hadleigh's "jumping the gun," as it were? Or was it a motive for murder?

The only facts Betsy really had were that the woman was moving into a rented house close to the Cameron house and that if Hannah Cameron had not come along right after Cameron's first wife died, he would have married Mrs. Hadleigh.

Mrs. Jeffries shifted in her chair and stared out at the quiet street. A pale yellow fog had drifted in and now wafted eerily among the gas lamps. She thought about Smythe's report on Connor Reese. Like the coachman, she found herself hoping that Reese wasn't the killer. She rather liked the good doctor herself. Anyone who worked among the poor and destitute of the East End had her admiration. She shook her head, cautioning herself against prejudgment. Reese had a strong motive to kill Hannah Cameron. He hated her and blamed her for his own mother's death. Furthermore, he'd been in the house that night. Reese could easily have slipped the knife into the victim's back and then slipped out the front door. But Cameron claimed the front door was locked and bolted until his butler had raised the alarm. So how did Reese get out? She sighed. There was only one logical answer to that question. Reese must have had help. Namely, Kathryn Ellingsley. She lived in the house. That night, she assumed that everyone was asleep. She could easily have unbolted a door and slipped her lover out. Add to that the fact that Reese was a doctor and would therefore have no trouble knowing the precise spot to stab someone in order to perforate her heart. Death had been instantaneous.

The killer had either been very lucky or very knowledgeable. Dr. Reese might have been both.

But Mrs. Jeffries didn't like that idea either. It didn't really make sense. Why would the governess help commit murder? Kathryn Ellingsley knew that Hannah Cameron was going to try and trap her that night. That's why she didn't go out in the first place. Instead, Reese came in. Surely, then, if she was frightened of losing her position . . . Mrs. Jeffries went still as another thought occurred to her. Why would Kathryn Ellingsley be frightened? If the Camerons sacked her, she could always go back to her uncle in Yorkshire. Or could she?

Mrs. Jeffries stood up. Gracious, she'd been such a fool. Two different pieces of the puzzle tumbled into her mind. Neville Parrington and a stolen box of papers.

She walked over and lit the small lamp she kept on her desk. Sitting down, she pulled open a drawer, drew out her writing paper and picked up her pen. When she'd finished, she looked at the short message and nodded in satisfaction. Tomorrow morning, she'd send this by telegram to her old friend Constable Trent in York. If anyone could find the answer to her questions and find them quickly, it would be him.

Inspector Witherspoon stared at his fried eggs and bacon with something less than his usual enthusiasm. Being taken off the case had quite lost him his appetite.

"Would you like tea, sir?" Mrs. Jeffries asked cheerfully.

"Yes, thank you," he mumbled.

"Here you are, sir," she said, placing his tea next to his plate. "I'm delighted you're taking the time to eat a proper breakfast this morning. It's quite cold outside and I know you've a lot to do today."

Witherspoon looked at her over the rim of his spectacles. "A lot to do today?" he echoed.

"Why, yes, sir." She smiled brightly and drew his timetable out of her pocket. Unfolding the paper, she put it down next to his teacup. "I hope you don't mind, sir, but I was quite curious about this . . ."

"I've been taken off the case, Mrs. Jeffries," he said wearily.

"I know that, sir," she said crisply, "but just because you've been taken off the case doesn't mean you've stopped being a brilliant detective and a true agent of justice in this great land of ours." She watched him carefully as she spoke, hoping her words would perk him up a bit.

He straightened his spine and lifted his chin. She noted that his expression was no longer glum. Instead, he looked puzzled. "I'm afraid I don't follow you." He gave her a brief smile and then slumped back down in the chair. "But thank you for your kind words."

"I'm sorry, sir." She sighed dramatically. "Perhaps I've overstepped my bounds. I shouldn't bother you with this." She started to reach for the paper but he shot back up and snatched it up himself.

"Bother me with what?" he asked, his attention now on the timetable.

She knew she had to be careful here. Their dear

Inspector, despite seeming to be a bit muddled at times, wasn't a fool. "Well, sir, I was so very curious, you see. So when I was dusting your desk, sir, I happened to glance at it . . . and well, I must say I was quite astounded. Absolutely flabbergasted, to tell you the truth."

"Flabbergasted? About what?"

"About your plan, sir. Your timetable." She walked over to stand by his chair. "It worked. You did find something. That's what made me so curious. I don't quite understand why Chief Inspector Barrows took you off the case. It seems to me, sir, he ought to be thanking his lucky stars that he had you on the hunt, so to speak. If not for your magnificient efforts, a grave miscarriage of justice could happen."

Witherspoon squinted at the paper. "Er, thank you, Mrs. Jeffries, but I don't quite see what you're getting at."

"You don't?" She contrived to sound confused. "But right here, sir." She pointed to the square that Hatchet had altered. "Look. Eleven forty-five . . ."

"Oh yes, I see now," Witherspoon interrupted. "Gracious, I don't remember this. How odd. 'Heard footsteps/front stairs'—that was reported by the maid, Helen." He shook his head. "Honestly, I don't remember writing that down, and you're right, of course—it's quite pertinent. Quite pertinent, indeed. That's the precise time, according to my calculations on the timetable, that the killer would have been moving about the house."

"I know sir," Mrs. Jeffries said enthusiastically. "And I shouldn't worry about not remembering writing it, sir. I'm sure your inner voice prompted you to do it almost by rote. You know how you are, sir. When you're on a case, your instincts take over, so to speak. Besides, sir, you've been under a great deal of strain since your discussion with Chief Inspector Barrows. It's no wonder that a few things have slipped your mind.''

Witherspoon nodded vigorously. "You're absolutely right, Mrs. Jeffries. I must pursue this. I'll go and see the Chief Inspector straight away . . .''

"But sir," she interrupted quickly. "Wouldn't it be easier for you to just go and see this maid"—she made a great show of peeking at the timetable again—"Helen. Wouldn't it be far easier politically to do your investigation on the . . . oh dear, what's the right word to describe this situation?"

"Sly?"

"No, no, sir," she replied. "You're far too honorable a man for that. What I was trying to say was perhaps it would be best to be a bit discreet. Until you have some real evidence, that is.''

He looked doubtful. "But this is real evidence," he said. "But perhaps you're right. The situation is delicate." He sighed deeply. "Politics, Mrs. Jeffries. I must be careful here. I don't wish to go against my superiors. But in this case, I've a feeling they are terribly, terribly wrong. Perhaps a bit of discretion wouldn't be amiss. Perhaps I'll just nip out and get Constable Barnes and we'll see what we can find out without stepping on anyone's toes or upsetting any applecarts.''

"Do finish your breakfast before you go," she said happily. "I believe you'll need your strength.''

*   *   *

"Want me to go with ya?" Wiggins asked Helen as he held open the back garden gate for the maid.

"How'd you know I'd be comin' out?" Helen asked. But she was smiling.

He grinned. "I figured 'e'd be sendin' you out with another telegram today."

"Right you are, you cheeky lad." She laughed and linked her arm with his as they started up the street. "Where's Fred?"

"I left 'im 'ome today," he admitted. Fred had stared at him mournfully when Wiggins had left that morning. But it had been ever so early and he'd not wanted to take the dog with him when he went to the post office to send that telegram for Mrs. Jeffries. He didn't reckon the post office much liked dogs. "You seem ever so much 'appier today. 'Ow come?"

Helen laughed again and then sobered. "I shouldn't be laughin', not really. But the truth is, that household is a lot happier now that her nibs is dead. I know it sounds wicked. I mean, she were stabbed and no one ought to die like that. But she were a right old mean hag and that's the truth. Ever since she's been dead, everyone's breathin' a right sight easier. Especially the governess." She giggled. "She can see her young man now without sneakin' about like a thief in the night. Not that she was foolin' anyone . . . We all knew she was sneakin' out to see that Dr. Reese."

Wiggins looked at her. "You mean all the servants knew?"

She shook her head. "Not just us. Mr. Cameron knew too. He's known for months, since right after Miss Ellingsley come to work there."

" 'Ow do you know that?'' Wiggins wasn't sure this was important, but it might be.

" 'Cause I saw 'em,'' she declared.

"You saw 'em? 'Ow?''

"What do you mean, 'ow? With me eyes.'' Helen gave him a sharp look. "You don't believe me?''

" 'Course I do,'' he soothed. "I'm just curious, that's all.''

She stared at him as though debating whether or not to take offense. Then she shrugged. "Well, if you must know . . .''

"I must, I must. I love the way ya tell things. So much more interestin' than when I try and tell somethin'. Go on, what 'appened, then?''

"Well.'' She smiled happily. "It were one night just a few weeks after Miss Ellingsley come there. She's ever such a nice one, she is. Not at all stuck-up or mean like Mrs. Cameron, despite bein' one of the gentry herself.''

"And what 'appened?'' he prodded.

"It were one night late like, and . . . uh . . . well, I got a bit hungry . . .''

"That's all right, Helen,'' Wiggins said kindly. "Don't be embarrassed. I've been 'ungry myself a few times.''

"Yeah, I expect you have.'' She sighed and closed her eyes briefly, then continued. "But like I was sayin', I got hungry and the girl I share with always sleeps like the dead, so I slipped down to the kitchen. Mrs. Cameron was always so stingy with how much we could eat, ya see, and I'd not had much so as soon as Hazel were asleep, I slipped down to the kitchen and got a bit of bread and cold sausage. I'd just nipped back upstairs when I heard footsteps comin' up the stairs behind me. I run lickety split right up to the top landin' and then I nipped in behind the post and stuck me head round to see who it was. I couldn't think who it were and I were scared to death it were Mrs. Cameron. But it weren't. It were Kathryn Ellingsley. I watched her slip up the back stairs and then go on down the hall to her room on the second floor. Below me, then just as she disappeared, I heard more footsteps and it were Mr. Cameron. He were followin' Miss Ellingsley. I stood there, my knees shakin', hopin' he didn't look up and catch me peekin' out from behind that top post, but he didn't. He just stood there staring in the direction where she'd gone, a funny little smile on his face. A few days later, I found out from one of the other servants that Kathryn was sneakin' out at night to meet that nice Dr. Reese.''

"You like Dr. Reese, then?'' Wiggins asked. He found her story quite startling.

"Oh, yes, he's ever so nice. He treated Hazel for bronchitis, you know. Didn't charge her, neither.'' Helen made a face. "She was ever so sick, she was, and that bloody Mrs. Cameron was goin' to sack her. But Miss Ellingsley slipped Dr. Reese in one night when the Camerons were out with that stupid Hadleigh woman, and he give her some medicine. Hazel were right as rain in a few days.''

They'd come to the entrance of the post office. Wiggins opened the door for Helen. "Allow me,'' he said, bowing gallantly. He really did like this girl. He hoped he could still see her once this case was over.

"Thank you." She smiled happily and stepped inside. "I'll only be a minute. It's only Mr. Cameron's telegram up to Yorkshire to see how his old uncle's gettin' on. Won't take more than a few moments. Are you goin' to wait fer me?"

"Right 'ere," he replied. "I've time to walk ya back."

Walking her back would give him a chance to see what, if anything, he could find out about Brian Cameron. He thought it awfully strange that the man knew a woman in his household was slipping out regularly and did nothing to stop it. It didn't seem right, somehow.

Constable Barnes lived in a neat little house on Brook Street near the Hammersmith Bridge. Witherspoon knocked softly on the pristine white door, hoping the constable hadn't already left for the station.

He wasn't sure he was doing the right thing, but he didn't honestly see that he had any choice. His inner voice had told him all along that this wasn't a burglary. But on the other hand, he knew he was taking a great risk by disobeying a direct order to stay off the case. It was a risk he was prepared to take, but did he have the right to involve Constable Barnes? Barnes didn't have a fortune and a big house. Barnes lived on his policeman's salary. Furthermore, he had a wife to support. Witherspoon had just about talked himself into leaving when the door flew open.

"Goodness, Inspector," Barnes said in surprise. "I didn't expect to see you." He was in his shirt-sleeves and braces.

"Oh, well," Witherspoon muttered. "I didn't really expect to be here."

"Come in, sir." He ushered the inspector inside and closed the door. "Would you like a cup of tea? The wife and I are just havin' breakfast."

Witherspoon opened his mouth to answer, to say that he was sorry to have bothered the good constable, that it was all a mistake, when before he could get a word out, a woman's voice came from the room at the end of the hall. "Who is it, dear?"

"It's Inspector Witherspoon, lovey," Barnes replied, gesturing at the inspector to proceed him. "Come to have a cuppa with us."

"Oh, dear," Witherspoon murmured. "I didn't mean to interrupt your breakfast."

"Not to worry, sir." Barnes chuckled. "You didn't and we've plenty of tea."

They entered a small, cheerful room with white walls adorned with shelves of knickknacks and china, a tiny fireplace and bright yellow-and-white lace curtains at the windows. An oak sideboard sat against the wall, and a round table, covered in a white lace tablecloth and set for breakfast, was square in the middle of the room. A woman with gray hair neatly tucked up in a bun and enormous blue eyes smiled up at him. "Do sit down, Inspector," she said, patting the empty chair next to her. "I'm Adelaide Barnes."

He bowed formally. "It's very nice to meet you, Mrs. Barnes. Do forgive me for interrupting your meal."

"We were just finishing, sir. Have a sit down and I'll pour you some tea. Then you two can have a nice natter about this murder you've been working on.''

She got up, went to the sideboard and took out a pink-and-white flowered china cup and matching saucer, then poured the tea.

Not knowing what else to do, the inspector sat down. "Er, your house is very nice, Mrs. Barnes.''

"Thank you, sir.'' She put his tea down in front of him. "Would you like some toast?''

"No, thank you, I've eaten.''

"Good.'' She smiled at her husband. "A man needs a decent breakfast. That's what I always tell my husband. Sometimes he rushes off with nothing more in his stomach than a bite of bread.''

"Now Addie.'' Barnes chuckled. "I've only done that a time or two. I like my food as well as the next man.''

"That's a time or two too many,'' she countered. "I know your work is important, but so is your health. Isn't it, Inspector?''

"Uh, well, yes, of course.'' Witherspoon smiled warily. "I expect it's been my fault that Constable Barnes occasionally misses a meal. I do sometimes drag him off at the oddest times.''

Adelaide Barnes laughed. "And are you here to drag him off again this morning?''

"Er, yes,'' the inspector admitted.

She turned to her husband, a triumphant gleam in her eyes. "It looks like I've won this wager, now, doesn't it? I told you he'd be round.''

Barnes laughed. "That you have, Addie, and come Saturday night, I'll pay up fair and square.''

"You told your husband I'd be round?'' the inspector repeated. "But how could you possibly know that?"

"How could I not know it?" she said as she reached for her husband's empty plate. "Alfred's told me all about you."

"All about me?" The inspector wasn't certain whether he should be complimented or insulted.

"He's only said nice things, sir," she said. She stacked her own plate on top of her husband's. "That's how I knew you'd be round. I knew you'd not give up on this murder. I told him you'd be here by noon today. I was right, wasn't I, Alfred?"

"Yes, dear." Barnes sighed. "You're always right."

CHAPTER 10

Inspector Witherspoon struggled mightily with his conscience as they approached the Cameron house. Despite Constable Barnes's assurances that he was quite willing to come along and do his bit in the interest of justice, the inspector couldn't stop thinking about whether this action could damage Barnes.

They reached the front of the house. Witherspoon took a deep breath and turned to Barnes. "Constable, I think you ought to reconsider going in with me. I don't wish to put you in an awkward position. Inspector Nivens may come along at any moment and I don't want him getting you into trouble because we've disobeyed an order."

"No, we haven't, sir," Barnes said calmly. "We was told that Nivens was now in charge of the case. But if I recall, sir, the Chief Inspector himself said we was welcome to help. Seems to me, sir, that's what we're doin'. Helpin' a bit. That's all. Come along now, sir, you've a few questions to ask.'' Not giving the inspector time to argue the point, he turned on his heel and marched to the front door.

Witherspoon had no choice but to follow.

Hatfield, the butler, let them in, sniffed in disapproval and escorted them into the drawing room. ''If you'll wait here,'' he said, ''I'll see if Mr. Cameron is available to see you.'' He left them standing awkwardly by the settee.

''Do you think we ought to sit down, sir?'' Barnes asked. ''It might look a sight better, make him think we've a perfect right to be back here if Inspector Nivens . . .'' His voice trailed off as they heard footsteps approaching.

Kathryn Ellingsley, a book in her hand, stepped inside. She started nervously when she saw the two policemen. ''Oh, I didn't know anyone was here.'' Her tone was flustered and she didn't look well. There were dark circles under her eyes and her fair skin was pale.

''We've come to ask a few more questions, Miss Ellingsley,'' Witherspoon smiled briefly. ''We're waiting for Mr. Cameron.''

''He's in the study,'' she said, edging back toward the door, ''I'll just get him for you.''

''That won't be necessary.'' Witherspoon wondered what on earth was wrong with the girl. She looked like she wanted to bolt. ''The butler's gone for him. We're sorry to interrupt him while he's working . . .''

''He's not working,'' she said quickly, nervously. ''Oh, do forgive me, Inspector. I'm not myself today. We've had more bad news. My uncle in Yorkshire has taken a turn for the worse.''

"I'm so sorry to hear that," the inspector said sympathetically. "Especially at what must already be a most upsetting time for both you and Mr. Cameron."

She seemed to relax. "Thank you, sir. You're most kind. It's difficult for Brian, of course, considering what's happened recently, but he was never as close to Uncle Neville as I was. I lived with him before I came to London. To be perfectly frank, I'm very concerned, though Brian tells me I'm making too much of it. But Uncle Neville's not a young man."

"You wanted to see me, Inspector?" Brian Cameron strode into the room.

"Yes, I'm so sorry to intrude. Miss Ellingsley has just told me about your concern over your uncle."

Brian smiled at Kathryn. "I've just sent a telegram, dear. They'll let us know straight away if you need to go up to him."

"But Brian, I really think I ought to go . . ."

"Nonsense," Cameron said briskly. "Neville's going to be all right. He's a tough old bird. Besides, my dear, you really must have a bit of a rest before you go up to do sick-room duty. You've had quite a trying time lately. We all have." He turned his attention to the inspector. "Thank you for your concern, Inspector, but I'm sure it's a bit of a tempest in a teapot. As I've told Kathryn, our uncle is quite a sturdy fellow for his years. He's only got a touch of bronchitis. Now, what can I do for you?"

"We'd like to have a word with one of your staff," he replied. "The maid, Helen."

Cameron nodded. "Kathryn, could you run

along and get the girl, please? Ask her to step in here.''

As soon as she'd gone, Cameron asked, "Would you mind telling us why you want to speak to her? I was under the impression that your Inspector Nivens was out there trying to find a burglar.''

Witherspoon was prepared for this question. He'd thought about it all morning. He only hoped his answer made sense to anyone other than himself. "You're correct, sir. Inspector Nivens is doing just that. The constable and I are only helping to tidy a few things up. We have reason to believe that the maid may have heard someone that night but was too frightened to say anything.''

Cameron raised his eyebrows. "Why on earth would one of the servants be frightened?''

"She's scared they'll be back,'' Barnes said calmly, before the inspector could say anything. "It's a common enough reaction,'' he continued. "A murder's been done and young women get frightened. Sometimes they think it's safest not to say too much. So don't be hard on the girl, Mr. Cameron.''

"Brian, what on earth are these policemen doing here?'' Fiona Hadleigh, her face set in an unflattering scowl, stormed into the room. "I thought we were done with all this. Honestly, are we to have no peace here at all? First Kathryn insists on talking to that wretched Mr. Drummond, though why she feels it's necessary for a young woman her age to trouble him about her will, I'll never know. Then you shut yourself up in your study all morning . . .''

"Don't upset yourself, Fiona,'' he interrupted,

reaching over and patting her on the arm. "Everything will be fine. There's nothing wrong."

"Then why are they here?" she pointed in the direction of Witherspoon and Barnes. "I'll not have you tied up all day answering their stupid questions. You promised to accompany me to Regent Street this morning . . ."

"It's all right, dear," he soothed, giving Witherspoon an imploring look for understanding. "They're only doing their job. They've just a couple of things to clear up with one of the servants and then they'll be on their way."

"I should hope so." She sniffed. "We've enough bother here as it is without having policemen under foot all day. I do want your opinion on those curtains I'm thinking of getting for my drawing room."

"Mrs. Hadleigh," Barnes asked suddenly, "now that you're here, there's a question I'd like to ask you."

"Again?"

"Yes, ma'am," Barnes answered as he dug out his notebook. He flipped it open and leafed through the pages. The inspector wondered what he was up to.

"Ah, here it is," the constable said. He glanced up at Mrs. Hadleigh. "In your statement, you said you went up to bed at eleven thirty. Is that correct?"

"As well as I can remember, it was about then." She didn't sound quite so haughty now. "Why?"

"And when you retired, did you read or write a letter perhaps?" he prodded.

Fiona's brows drew together. "That's most impertinent, but if you must know, I got ready for bed.''

"I see," Barnes said. He flipped a page over. "According to both Mr. Cameron's and Mr. Ripton's statements, they retired at little past eleven thirty.''

"What are you getting at, Constable?" Cameron interrupted.

Witherspoon wondered the same thing, but he trusted that Barnes knew what he was doing.

Unruffled, Barnes merely said, "Just tryin' to get a few facts straightened out, sir. You and Mr. Ripton did go up a little past eleven thirty, right?''

Cameron nodded.

"And both of you said that Mrs. Cameron and Mrs. Hadleigh had retired a few minutes earlier. Would it be fair to say they went upstairs at eleven twenty-five?''

"All right, Constable, so we went up to bed at eleven twenty-five," Fiona said curtly. "What of it?''

"Actually, dear." Brian smiled at her fondly. "It was closer to eleven-fifteen when you and Hannah retired.''

"Eleven-fifteen," Barnes mused. "Mrs. Hadleigh, my question is this: if you'd gone up to bed at eleven-fifteen and gotten ready to go to sleep, then why were you fully dressed, still in your evening clothes, when the body was discovered a good forty minutes later.''

"Are ya sure I said that?" Helen peered closely at the timetable, her pretty face confused. "I don't remember tellin' ya that.''

"But I'm sure you did," Witherspoon insisted. Actually, he wasn't, but he thought his inner voice must have had some reason for prompting him to fill in the square. "Are you saying you didn't hear anyone on the front stairs?"

Helen licked her lips and shot a quick glance at the open drawing room door. "No, not exactly. I mean, I did hear someone."

Witherspoon beamed at her approvingly. "Excellent, excellent. I was sure you had."

"I did, but ya see, I didn't exactly hear footsteps . . . but . . . uh . . . well—" She broke off, her face an agony of indecision.

Wisely, the inspector decided not to interrupt this time. He simply looked at her.

Finally, she took a deep breath. "It were a bit more than just hearin' someone, sir," she blurted. "I saw 'im as well."

Witherspoon's spirits soared. His inner voice was right. "Who did you see?" he prompted gently.

"It were Mr. Ripton, sir," she whispered. "I saw him comin' up the front stairs. It were dead on eleven-forty-five too. I know 'cause I looked at the clock in the kitchen when I left to come upstairs."

"Why didn't you tell us this when we spoke to you before?" Barnes asked.

Helen looked down at the carpet. "I guess I was scared, sir. I didn't want anyone to know what I was doin'. You know, roamin' about the house that time of night."

"Exactly what were you doing, Helen?" Witherspoon asked.

Helen twisted her hands together. "Do I have to tell?"

"We can't force you to tell us anything," the inspector said gently, "but I think it would be best if you did."

Helen swallowed heavily. "I were ever so hungry, sir, and so when I thought everyone was asleep, I went down to the kitchen to get something to eat. I only took a bit of bread and sausage. Please don't tell on me, sir. I'll not do it again."

Witherspoon and Barnes exchanged glances. After what they'd seen of this household, neither of them could really blame the girl for holding her tongue.

"We won't say a word," the inspector assured her. "It's no crime to be hungry. Were you afraid you'd be sacked if Mrs. Cameron knew you were taking food?"

She nodded. "Then after I heard she was dead, I was scared someone might think I 'ad somethin' to do with killin' her. I mean, I wasn't in me room when she were gettin' murdered."

"We don't think anything of the sort," Witherspoon said honestly. Of all the people who disliked the late Mrs. Cameron, this frightened girl was one of the least likely people to have killed the woman. "Is there anything else you'd like to tell us?"

"No, sir, that's the only unusual thing that happened. May I go now?"

"Yes, Helen, and thank you for your help."

Hatfield materialized in the doorway as the girl was leaving. "Mr. Cameron would like to see you," he told her.

Helen's eyes got as big as saucers. "He wants to see me?"

"Right now," Hatfield replied. "He's in the study."

The girl, her face paling, nodded and hurried out.

Barnes and Witherspoon exchanged glances and then, without speaking, took off right behind her. Both men feared the same thing, that the butler had run tattling to Cameron about the girl taking food. She was probably going to get the sack.

"He only wants her to take a telegram for him," Hatfield said, stopping both of them in their tracks. "She's not in any trouble."

Witherspoon turned and stared at the butler. His thin face was creased in worry and his shoulders slumped dejectedly. "We're not monsters, you know," he said. "I'd not let the girl lose her position for taking a little food."

"Then you were listening?" Witherspoon charged gently. "You overheard what she told us."

He nodded. "I did. I was curious because you wanted to speak to her." He cleared his throat. "I know I shouldn't have eavesdropped, but some of us here don't like the way this whole situation's been handled. Mrs. Cameron wasn't killed by any burglar, despite what that other policeman says."

"I see," the inspector replied. He was a bit puzzled. He didn't know whether he ought to press the man for more information or not. "Did you hear everything she told us?"

"Yes, sir. But if you're thinking that Mr. Ripton stayed downstairs that night to murder his sister, you're mistaken."

"Mistaken?"

Hatfield shook his head vehemently. "He did come back downstairs. I've no doubt of that, sir. But that was only so he could pinch the rest of the port, sir. I ought to know; the bottle was missing the next day. I found the empty in Mr. Ripton's room."

"You're saying that Ripton stole a bottle of port?" Witherspoon couldn't believe it.

"Oh, yes, sir. He does it every time he stays the night."

"Telegram, Mrs. Jeffries." Mrs. Goodge eagerly handed the housekeeper the small envelope. "You was out when it come so I took it."

"I hope it's a reply from Yorkshire," Mrs. Jeffries said. She ripped the small brown envelope open and pulled out the thin paper. "It is my reply," she said cheerfully. "I do hope it helps clarify things a bit."

But the message really didn't clarify anything.

Parrington in poor health but no sign of foul play. Large estate. Heir is his niece, Kathryn Ellingsley. Hope this helpful.

"What's it mean, then?" asked Mrs. Goodge, who was reading over her shoulder.

"I'm not sure, Mrs. Goodge," she admitted. "I quite expected a different answer."

"What were you expecting?" the cook asked curiously.

"To be frank, I was actually thinking that Brian Cameron would be the heir, not Kathryn Ellingsley.

I mean, Hannah Cameron's murder would make sense if he were expecting to inherit a fortune from a dying uncle. But as it is . . .'' She shook her head, unwilling to say more until she'd had time to think the situation through. She'd obviously made a grave mistake in her reasoning. But she'd been so sure, so very sure. Part of her still was. It was the only thing that made sense. She tucked the telegram in her pocket and started for the coatrack. Taking down her bonnet, she slipped it on and then grabbed her coat.

''Where are you off to, then?'' the cook asked. Her curiosity overcame her desire to have her kitchen empty in case one of her sources came by.

''To the post office,'' Mrs. Jeffries declared. ''To send another telegram.''

''What do you make of Mrs. Hadleigh's statement?'' Barnes asked the inspector as they went down the hall to the front door.

''I suppose she could be telling the truth,'' Witherspoon replied. ''Some people are very devout. But I personally don't think the Almighty cares whether one says one's nightly prayers fully dressed or in one's nightclothes.''

Barnes snorted. ''I can't see that one down on bended knees in an evening dress for a good half-hour, sir,'' he said. ''She just doesn't strike me as bein' that religious a woman.''

But that's precisely what she'd claimed to be doing from the time she went to her room until she heard the commotion downstairs. Praying. With all her clothes on. She'd told them quite haughtily that she didn't think it proper to pray in one's night-clothes.

Like the constable, Witherspoon found it difficult to believe, but even with his timetable, he'd no evidence to dispute her.

They'd reached the front door when the subject of their conversation suddenly stopped them in their tracks.

"I'd like a word with you, if you please," Fiona Hadleigh demanded. Witherspoon dropped his hand from the doorknob and turned. "Yes, Mrs. Hadleigh," he said politely. "What can I do for you."

"There's something you ought to know," she said as she stalked toward them. "It's about Kathryn."

"Miss Ellingsley?" Witherspoon said. "What about her?"

"She isn't quite what she appears to be," she replied. She stopped directly in front of them and took a deep breath. "Brian didn't want me to mention it, but I feel it's my duty . . ."

"Oh, for God's sake, Fiona." Brian Cameron's voice thundered down the hall. "Leave it alone. Kathryn's my cousin. She's family. I'll not have you telling tales to all and sundry about her."

"I'm sorry it displeases you, Brian." Fiona's cheeks turned red. "But it really is our duty to tell the police everything."

"Kathryn has nothing to do with any of this."

"But we don't know that," Fiona insisted. "Hannah was murdered."

"She was killed by a burglar," Cameron shot back. He glared at his guest, his eyes glittering with rage. "And I'll thank you to mind your own business . . ."

"Excuse me." Witherspoon thought he ought to take control of the situation. "But why don't we all sit down and sort this out."

"There's nothing to sort out," Cameron snapped. "Fiona doesn't know what she's talking about."

"I most certainly do," Fiona charged. She lifted her chin and looked at Witherspoon. "Kathryn Ellingsley has been slipping out of the house at night to meet her paramour. Furthermore, she always went out through the small sitting room. The one Hannah was murdered in."

Inspector Witherspoon's head was spinning by the time he got home that evening. He hung up his coat and hat and started down the hall to the drawing room just as Mrs. Jeffries came up the back stairs.

"Good evening, sir," she said cheerfully.

"Good evening, Mrs. Jeffries. I do believe I'll have a sherry before dinner. It's been a most extraordinary day."

She followed him into the drawing room and went right to the cupboard. Pulling out a bottle of Harvey's she poured him a glass and took it over. Sitting it down next to him, she said, "Extraordinary, you say. Well, sir, I'll venture to guess that your continued investigation has been successful."

Witherspoon reached for his drink, took a sip and sighed happily. "I think you may be right, but it's all a bit muddled so far." He'd learned far more than he expected today, but he wasn't quite sure what it all meant.

"Not to worry, sir." She plopped down in the chair opposite him and settled herself comfortably. "You'll sort everything out in no time. You always do. Now, sir, tell me all about it."

At the meeting that night, Mrs. Jeffries didn't waste any time. Before anyone else could start, she told them everything she'd learned from the inspector. She was glad she'd found out such a wealth of information from him. None of the others had found out a thing.

"I still don't think Ripton ought to be let off the hook just because of what the butler says," Luty complained. "Seems to me he's doin' quite nicely now that his sister's dead."

"We're not letting him off the hook," Mrs. Jeffries replied. "But the inspector felt that Hatfield had no reason to lie for John Ripton."

"Well, at least the inspector knows about Kathryn Ellingsley slippin' out of the 'ouse now," Wiggins put in.

"But Kathryn hadn't slipped out that night," Betsy said. "She'd let Dr. Reese in. Seems to me we ought to be thinking of a way to let the inspector know about that."

"I don't think 'e's a killer," Wiggins said defensively. "The only motive 'e's got is that 'e 'ated 'is cousin. But it weren't nothin' new. 'E'd 'ated the woman for years. Why would 'e take it into 'is 'ead to kill that night?"

"He could have done it to protect Kathryn," Hatchet suggested.

Wiggins stubbornly shook his head. "If she sacked Kathryn, Dr. Reese woulda gotten what 'e wanted. 'E'd have just married the girl. Seems to me, that 'e 'ad less of a reason for wantin' the Cameron woman dead than any of 'em.''

"Well, I agree with Betsy. It was downright mean of that Hadleigh woman to tattle on her the way she did," Luty declared. "Hate tattlers. Always did. It's obvious she's tryin' to make the girl look bad. How the dickens did she find out about Kathryn slippin' out anyway?"

"Probably from one of the other servants," Hatchet ventured.

"I don't think so," Mrs. Jeffries replied. "I think the ones that knew Kathryn's secret kept it to themselves. Remember, Kathryn had slipped Dr. Reese into the house one other time when one of the maids was ill. His care kept that girl from being sacked. No, I think Mrs. Hadleigh found out accidentally. Perhaps from Brian Cameron."

"Funny, isn't it?" Betsy said. "But everyone in that house except Hannah Cameron knew about Kathryn. She didn't find out until right before she was killed."

"I think Mrs. Hadleigh did it," Mrs. Goodge declared. "She's the one that's really benefitting. She'll finally get her hooks into Brian Cameron, though why the woman wants the man, I'll never know. And that silly excuse she gave the inspector for being fully dressed.." She *harrumphed* indignantly. "Praying, indeed. Twaddle, that is. The Archbishop of Canterbury doesn't stay on his knees for that long in prayer. Especially not on a cold, hard floor."

"I still think we ought to keep an eye on Ripton," Smythe mused. "It don't take more than a minute or two to pinch a bottle. What was 'e doin' downstairs that whole time?''

''Maybe he wasn't,'' Luty said. ''Maybe he went upstairs with Brian Cameron, waited till he thought the coast was clear and then went back down to get his liquor.''

As the others argued and debated, Mrs. Jeffries let her mind drift. Suddenly, something Betsy said a few moments ago popped into her head. She looked at the maid. ''What did you just say about Hannah and Kathryn?''

''Me?'' Betsy looked at her in surprise. ''I just said that everyone but Hannah Cameron knew about Kathryn slipping out at night. Why? Is it important?''

''Yes, yes, I think it could be,'' Mrs. Jeffries replied. She didn't quite see how that piece of the puzzle fit, but she was suddenly certain that it was very important. She hoped the telegram she'd sent might give her an answer, but it would only if her basic assumption was correct. Was she right? That was the question. But there was another avenue of inquiry she could take. It was dangerous, but it might provide the one piece of evidence she needed.

She realized that all of them were looking at her expectantly. ''Hatchet,'' she said. ''Are you dreadfully tired?''

Hatchet, to his credit, didn't so much as raise an eyebrow at the odd question. ''Not at all, Mrs. Jeffries. Why? Is there something I need to do tonight?''

She hesitated. What she was going to request was totally wrong. Practically immoral. Patently illegal. But it might be the only way to catch the killer. She had to know this information. It was imperative and impossible at the same time. If she could have found a way to have the inspector get it, she would have. But there simply wasn't enough evidence for him to seek a search warrant.

Yet she couldn't bring herself to put someone else in harm's way. If this was going to be done, she'd do it herself. "No," she replied as she got to her feet, "there's nothing you need to do. I'm going to do it."

Alarmed, Smythe got up. "What are you up to, Mrs. J.?"

"Nothing, Smythe," she replied airily. "Besides, the less you know about it, the better you'll be. But if I could trouble you to call me a hansom . . ."

"If you need to go out tonight," he interrupted, "you'll be takin' me with ya. You're up to somethin'."

"And me." Hatchet rose as well. "Whatever you're planning, you'll have to let us in on it."

Luty leapt to her feet. "Is it dangerous? I'll go home and git my gun. Oh, lordy, I can tell, this is goin' to be fun."

"You'll not be leaving me here, either," Betsy declared. "Whatever it is you're planning, I'm going to be right there."

Exasperated, Mrs. Jeffries didn't know whether to laugh or to box their collective ears. "I'm trying to protect you all," she cried. "For goodness' sakes, I could be absolutely, positively wrong about this whole matter."

"I don't care if you is wrong," Wiggins said

staunchly. "You ain't gettin' outta this 'ouse tonight without me and Fred."

Fred, upon hearing his name, jumped up from
his warm spot by the stove and dashed over to the
table. He bounced excitedly at Wiggins's feet, hoping everyone getting up meant he was going to go
out.

"Where are you planning on going, Mrs. Jeffries?" Hatchet asked calmly. "And more importantly, what do you want us to do?"

She had two choices. Either let them in on her
scheme or give it up altogether. But if she did that,
a murderer might go free. More important, if she
was right, someone else—someone innocent—
might die. She stood there for a moment in indecision.

"I'm not sure precisely where the place is," she
replied. "But I think it should be quite simple to
find that information."

"What information?" Smythe pressed.

"The address of a solicitor," she replied. "You
see, it's quite imperative that I have a look at someone's will."

In the end, it was Hatchet and Smythe who went.
Armed with various small kitchen utensils, a pocket
knife, and Inspector Witherspoon's old policeman's
lantern, they went out into the night with assurances to the ladies that they'd be fine.

Luty, Mrs. Goodge, Betsy, Wiggins and Mrs.
Jeffries prepared to wait.

Mrs. Goodge put on the kettle and got out her
knitting.

Wiggins got his pen and paper and set to work writing a poem for Helen.

Luty pulled out a pack of playing cards and started playing Patience.

Mrs. Jeffries went up to her room to have a nice long think and Betsy began to pace.

"This is it," Hatchet murmured. He glanced over his shoulder at Smythe. They were in the back of a block of offices on Connaught Street. The alley was quiet; the area was deserted at this time of night. Hatchet reached for the door handle, gave it a turn and wasn't in the least surprised to find the thing locked solid. "It's locked."

But Smythe wasn't listening. He was standing on an overturned wooden crate he'd found and had a wicked-looking knife out. He was busy prying open a smallish window on the far side of the door. "This is'n," he muttered, "but it'll be a tight job for us to get through it. It's right small, but I think we can manage."

Hatchet looked doubtful.

"Ah, there she goes," Smythe murmured as he wedged the bottom of the window open far enough to get his fingers under. With a grunt, he shoved it all the way up, tossed Hatchet a quick grin and then shoved his head inside.

Hatchet watched in amazement as the rest of the big man followed. He heard a loud thump.

"Are you all right?" Hatchet whispered.

"Yeah. I landed on me 'ead. It's a bit of a drop. Do you think you can make it through?"

"I'll give it try," he replied. He stepped up on the box, grasped the side of the window and emulated Smythe by just diving straight in, putting his arms straight out in front of him as soon as his torso had cleared the frame.

He was saved from a nasty bump on the head by Smythe, who grabbed him before his forehead connected solidly with the floor.

Getting up, Hatchet brushed his coat off.

Smythe was already moving down the hall. He'd switched the lantern on and was shining the dim light on the doors as he walked. Hatchet hurried to catch up with him.

"This is it." Smythe stopped and handed the lantern to Hatchet. " 'old this." He pulled his pocket knife out, eased it between the lock and the door and then applied pressure. There was a faint click as the lock disengaged.

Impressed, Hatchet asked, "Where did you learn to do that?"

"Picked it up 'ere and there." Smythe shrugged. "Not much to it, really. Wouldn't work on a decent lock. Lucky for us this 'ere's a cheap one. You ready?"

"As ready as I'll ever be." Hatchet took a deep breath, thanked his lucky stars there wasn't a night watchman in this building and opened the door.

"What's takin' them so long?" Betsy wailed. "They've been gone for hours."

"They've only been gone for two and a half hours," Mrs. Jeffries assured her. "And I'm sure they're just fine."

"But what if they got caught?" she moaned.

Mrs. Jeffries was thinking the same thing.

They'd be ruined. All of them. And it would all be her fault.

"They ain't gonna get caught," Luty said. "Hatchet's too smart and fer that matter, so is that feller of yours."

"Mine?" Betsy stopped pacing and stared at Luty. "What are you talking about?"

Luty chuckled. "We ain't blind, ya know. Everyone can see you two are sweet on each other. 'Course he's not much to look at . . ."

"I think he's fine to look at," Betsy said indignantly. "His appearance isn't ordinary, but I think he's quite handsome."

"You think Smythe is 'andsome?" Wiggins exclaimed. "Our Smythe?"

"Yes, our Smythe," Betsy shot back. "And furthermore, if you repeat one word of this to him, I'll have your guts for garters."

From the flaming red in her cheeks and the glint in her eyes, Wiggins was sure she meant what she said. "I can keep a secret," he retorted. "I've kept 'em for Smythe often enough. You should ask me what 'e says about you."

"What does he say?" she demanded.

Wiggins grinned. "Can't tell ya. It's a secret."

Mrs. Jeffries smiled at Luty, grateful the woman had distracted everyone with her remarks. Luty winked at her.

They continued the vigil.

Mrs. Goodge yawned. Wiggins scribbled. Luty played another hand of Patience and Betsy continued to pace. Mrs. Jeffries's thoughts swirled around the case. What if she was wrong? What if Smythe and Hatchet got caught?

The clock had just struck the half hour when they heard the back door open. Betsy almost cried in relief when the two men, grinning like they'd just conquered a mountain came into the kitchen.

"Did you have any difficulties?" Mrs. Jeffries asked anxiously.

"Not a one, madam," Hatchet said. "No one will even know we were ever there." That wasn't quite the truth. Someone might notice the scratches on the window, but he didn't think it likely.

"You were right, Mrs. Jeffries," Smythe said as they all took their seats at the table. "She did have a will. Lucky for us she'd seen her solicitor recently too. It were right on 'is desk."

"Unfortunately, we did waste some time looking for the wretched thing in the file cabinets," Hatchet added. "Until I suggested we have a look at Drummond's desk."

"I'd a sussed that out eventually," Smythe told him testily.

"Were you able to determine who her heir is?" Mrs. Jeffries said quickly. She crossed her fingers. The suspense was killing her. "Is it Brian Cameron?"

Smythe looked Hatchet, waited for him to nod and then said. "Sorry to disappoint ya, Mrs. J., but you were off the mark with that one."

She stared at him in disbelief. She simply couldn't believe it. "Are you certain?" she whispered.

"Quite sure," Hatchet said. "The will is very simple. I'm sorry to say the heir is Connor Reese. On her death, everything goes to him."

CHAPTER 11

Mrs. Jeffries didn't sleep well. How could she? She'd been wrong. Dreadfully so. She got up the next morning grumpy and still angry at herself for being so foolish as to think that only her solution was the right one. She'd put Hatchet and Smythe in terrible danger and she wasn't going to forgive herself easily.

But as she puttered about the drawing room, halfheartedly running a feather duster over the mantel, she couldn't help thinking that she couldn't have been that wrong. She was sure she knew who murdered Hannah Cameron. She sighed as she glanced at the clock, wondering if the inspector was having a better day than she was.

He'd been so excited by his discoveries yesterday that he'd not even had a proper breakfast this morning. He'd just grabbed a slice of toast and dashed off.

Her shoulders slumped and she put the duster down on the table. In a short while, she'd have to tell the others. Admitting she was wrong wasn't going to be pleasant, but she owed them the truth. Luckily, it had been so late last night when Hatchet and Smythe had returned, she'd been able to get everyone to hold their questions until today. They were due to meet back here at four for tea. Everyone, except herself, was out snooping about, doing their very best to bring this case to a just conclusion. She sighed again and shook her head. Too bad she hadn't a clue about how to go about it.

"Dr. Reese," Witherspoon said, "we're sorry to bother you, but we've a few questions to ask."

"Can you be quick about it?" Reese looked pointedly at his waiting room, which, as the inspector and Barnes knew because they'd come in that way, was filled with patients wanting to see the doctor. "Some of those people out there are very ill. I don't like to keep them waiting."

They were in the doctor's surgery—in his examination room to be precise. It was quite small. There was a privacy screen in one corner. A table covered with a clean linen cloth stood in the center of the room and beyond that was a desk beside a glass cupboard filled with medical texts. Next to the door was a cupboard and a sink. The room smelled heavily of disinfectant. But despite its size, the inspector was quite impressed. The surgery was obviously clean and well equipped. Not really what one would expect for an East End practise.

"We won't keep you long, sir," Witherspoon assured him. "Uh, this is a bit awkward, Doctor, but can you tell me where you were on the night your cousin was murdered?''

Reese hung his coat in the cupboard and pulled out a clean, white apron. He slipped it over his head. He looked surprised, but not unduly alarmed by the question. ''May I ask why you want to know?''

''We've had it on good authority that you're . . . uh . . . er . . .''

''You're courting Miss Ellingsley.'' Constable Barnes took pity on Witherspoon and interrupted. ''We've heard that she's been sneakin' out at night to see you. Is this true?''

''It is,'' Reese replied. He walked over to the table, pulled a drawer open and began taking instruments out. ''I imagine you know all about Kathryn and I. Otherwise you wouldn't be here.''

Witherspoon nodded.

''I imagine you also know that I loathed my cousin,'' he continued. ''But I've loathed her for years. I'd hardly bother to murder her now.''

''Nevertheless, she was murdered,'' Barnes said.

''Kathryn and I had nothing to do with Hannah's death,'' Dr. Reese stated flatly.

''But it was because of Mrs. Cameron that you had to sneak about to see each other,'' Barnes charged. ''Seems to me that gives you a bit of a motive, sir.''

''Hannah tried to make it impossible for us to see one another,'' he said curtly. ''But that didn't stop us. We started meeting secretly. That was Kathryn's idea. I wanted her to marry me. But Kathryn felt she should stay on at the Cameron house for awhile longer for the children's sake. She was hoping that Brian would send them away to boarding school next term.''

"Even the little girl?" Witherspoon asked. He thought eight years old was quite young to send a child away from her home.

"Ellen would be better off at school than she was living with that woman," he said disgustedly. "But that's not the issue, is it? I'm just explaining why we met secretly. Why Kathryn didn't just chuck the position and marry me. She's devoted to those children.''

Witherspoon wondered how a devoted governess could sneak out and leave her charges unattended. "Wasn't she worried about the children when she slipped off to be with you? I mean, what if one of them woke up and needed her?"

"Ellen and Edward sleep very well," he replied, going to the sink and turning on the water. He picked up a bar of carbolic soap and started scrubbing his hands. "They never wake up. But please don't think Kathryn is in any way negligent. Hazel, one of the housemaids, would slip up and stay in Kathryn's room by the nursery. The children were always well looked after.''

"How often did you and Miss Ellingsley see one another?" Witherspoon asked. He had no idea what prompted the question, but he felt he ought to ask something. He was rather surprised by the doctor's candor. He'd expected the man to hem and haw and deny everything.

"Not often enough to suit me." Reese dried his hands. "Look, Inspector. Kathryn and I are going to be married. I'll not have you thinking she's loose or doesn't have the highest of morals. When we did manage to see one another, all we ever did was walk and talk.''

"You're engaged?" Witherspoon asked. That probably wasn't pertinent either, but it never hurt to ask.

"Yes." Reese sighed. "We were going to announce it last week, but then Kathryn's uncle took ill and she didn't want to announce our engagement publicly till she told him privately. Now, if there's nothing else, I've a room full of patients.''

"You haven't answered the question, sir," Barnes reminded him. "Where were you on the night that your cousin was murdered?''

Reese smiled. "I think you already know the answer to that question. I was visiting Kathryn. Only this time, instead of her slipping out to meet me, she'd let me into the house.''

"This come for ya, Mrs. Jeffries," Wiggins said as he came into the kitchen. He handed her a small brown envelope, the twin to one the housekeeper had received yesterday.

"Thank you, Wiggins," Mrs. Jeffries replied. She dreaded this meeting. She wasn't sure what to say. One part of her was still convinced she had to be correct.

"Been a lot of telegrams today," Wiggins continued cheerfully. "Helen was tellin' me that Kathryn Ellingsley's 'ad one as well. 'Ers was bad news, though. Her uncle's not expected to last through the night.''

"Who's not going to last?" Aunt Elberta, wrapped in her coat and hat, thumped into the kitchen and headed purposely toward the table.

"Thought I'd find the lot of you here," she continued, not waiting for an answer to her question. "Can't see how you get any work done. Every time I come in here you're sittin' around drinking tea."

"Aunt Elberta," Mrs. Goodge cried in alarm. "What are you doing here? You're supposed to be at the British Museum with Effie!"

She waved her hand dismissively. "Got boring, that did. Told Effie to bring me home." She stopped beside the cook. "I'm tired. That girl's dragged me all over London."

"Would you care for a cup of tea?" Mrs. Jeffries asked.

Aunt Elberta shook her head. "No, I'm going to go lay down for a bit. I just come in to let you know I'll be goin' home tomorrow."

"But I thought you were staying the week," the cook said.

"Changed my mind," Aunt Elberta replied with a yawn. "No offense meant, but I've decided I'm too old for sightseein'." She smiled wearily. "Now, if you don't mind, I'll go have a nap before I start my packing."

"Really." Mrs. Goodge sniffed as soon as the woman left the room. "This is a bit of a surprise. She seems quite anxious to leave."

"Not to worry, Mrs. Goodge," Mrs. Jeffries said. "I think she's had a nice visit. But when a person gets to be your aunt's age, they like their own home."

"At least Effie'll stop complainin' about havin' to ride herd on the woman," Luty commented. Then she looked at the envelope in the housekeeper's hand. "Well? Ain't ya gonna open it?"

"Oh, yes, of course." Mrs. Jeffries smiled bravely and tore the ruddy thing open, though she didn't expect that this answer would be much better than the one she'd had last night. She pulled the paper out and stared at the brief message.

"Who's it from?" Betsy asked curiously.

"Constable Trent," Mrs. Jeffries murmured. Her mind was racing with questions. "He's a family friend. He used to work with my late husband."

"What's it say, then?" Luty demanded.

But Mrs. Jeffries paid no attention to her friend. Instead, she looked at Wiggins. "You say Kathryn Ellingsley got a message that her uncle isn't expected to last through the night?"

"Right," Wiggins said. "She and Mr. Cameron are fixin' to go to Yorkshire tonight. They're leavin' for the station in a bit. Helen told me the 'ouse was in an uproar, that Mrs. Hadleigh were 'avin' fits about 'im goin' off with Miss Ellingsley . . ."

"Do you know what time?" Mrs. Jeffries interrupted. "Think, Wiggins. It's very important. A life might depend on it."

Wiggin's gaped at her for a moment. "I think Helen said they was leavin' on the six o'clock train. But truth to tell, Mrs. Jeffries, I really wasn't payin' all that much attention. Helen does rattle on a bit and I was more concerned with gettin' back 'ere on time than listenin' to 'er."

"What's goin' on, Mrs. J.?" Smythe asked.

"Get the horse and carriage," she told him. "Get back here as quickly as you can."

She knew the answer now. But unless they moved quickly, someone else was going to die.

Smythe didn't question her. He leapt to his feet and bolted for the back door. "I'll be back in 'alf an 'our," he promised.

"Thank goodness the inspector is upstairs," Mrs. Jeffries muttered. "At least now I won't have to track him down. Wiggins, run upstairs and get my notepaper. Hurry, and don't let the inspector see you."

Sensing her urgency, he nodded and moved quickly to do her bidding.

"Hatchet," Mrs. Jeffries said, "I'm going to need your services again. I want you to write a note, and here's precisely what I want it to say. We'll have to move quickly and we'll have to take some risks. If we don't, an innocent person is going to die tonight."

"Do you know, Mrs. Jeffries, he admitted it straight out," Witherspoon told his housekeeper. "Dr. Reese made no pretenses whatsoever. He said he was in love with the girl and he was going to marry her. They were going to announce their engagement last week, but then her uncle became ill so they postponed it."

Mrs. Jeffries was only half listening. Her eye was on the clock and her head was cocked toward the front door. Two minutes to go. Then Wiggins would pound on the knocker and run for all he was worth. She crossed her fingers, hoping that none of their neighbors would see the lad and mention it to the inspector later.

"At least Dr. Reese didn't lie to you, sir."

There was a loud pounding on the front door. Mrs. Jeffries leapt to her feet. "I'll get it sir." Wiggins was a bit premature, but it really didn't matter.

She flew down the hall, threw open the door and blinked in surprise. "Hello? Can I help you?"

The tall, white-haired man inclined his head slightly. "My name is Bartholomew Pike and I'd like to see Mr. Smythe if he's available."

"He's not," she said quickly, wanting to get rid of him. "But I'll be happy to tell him you called around."

He frowned in disappointment. "Please ask him to contact me immediately. The matter is most urgent."

Mrs. Jeffries saw Wiggins hotfooting it down the street towards the front door. "I'll do that, Mr. Pike."

He nodded brusquely, turned and left, passing Wiggins as the lad dashed up the stairs. Mrs. Jeffries snatched the note out of his hand and hurried back into the house.

"Who was it?" the inspector asked.

"I don't know, sir." Mrs. Jeffries took a long, calming breath. "But it was a gentleman, sir. He didn't give his name but he did ask me to give you this." She handed the inspector the note and watched while he unfolded it.

Witherspoon's mouth opened as he read. "Gracious! Mrs. Jeffries, what sort of man was it who gave you this?"

"He looked like a gentleman, sir. Quite respectable, really. Why, sir? What's wrong?"

Witherspoon waved the note in the air. "This note says that if I don't get to the Cameron house immediately, Kathryn Ellingsley will die."

"Then you'd better go, hadn't you?" She was

itching to grab his coat and hat for him, but held herself in check. It wouldn't do to look too anxious.

"But what if it's someone's idea of a joke?"

"I shouldn't think the man who brought it was playing a joke, sir. He looked as somber as a banker. Perhaps, sir, you'd best go. Isn't it lucky that Smythe just happened to pick today to give the horses a good run? He's got the carriage right outside."

"I do hope this isn't someone's idea of a prank," the inspector muttered as he climbed out of the elaborate carriage in front of the Cameron house. Wiggins held the door open for him. Fred, who'd jumped into the carriage before anyone could stop him jumped down and began to prance excitedly at the footman's feet.

A hundred feet up the road, a hansom had stopped in the middle of the street and was picking up a man and a woman. Witherspoon started for the front door.

"Excuse me, sir," Wiggins hissed, "but isn't that Mr. Cameron and Miss Ellingsley getting into that cab?"

The inspector squinted through his spectacles. Night had fallen and he couldn't see very well. The man was helping the woman inside. "I do believe you're right, Wiggins. I say." Witherspoon raised his voice. "Mr. Cameron, we need to have a word with you."

Cameron looked back at them and then quickly jumped into the cab and slammed the door. "Drive on," he cried. The hansom took off.

"Well, really," Witherspoon snapped. "I know

the fellow heard me. This is terrible. I've got the most dreadful feeling about this . . ."

But Wiggins wasn't listening. He was bolting after the cab. The inspector watched in stunned amazement as his footman nimbly grabbed the back of the thing and leapt on.

Fred, barking his head off, took off after his beloved friend.

"Get in, sir," Smythe shouted. "We'll catch them up."

They raced after the hansom, thundering through the streets at a breakneck pace. Witherspoon, his head stuck out the window, kept his eye on the running dog as they careened around a corner and into the heavy traffic of Park Lane. But a heavy carriage was no match in speed for a lightweight hansom and they soon lost sight of their quarry completely. Inspector Witherspoon feared the worst.

Wiggins breathed a sigh of relief as the hansom slowed to a reasonable pace. It felt like he'd ridden for hours, though in fact, they'd only come down to the docks. The vehicle turned onto a small, dark street. Wiggins shivered. In the distance, he could hear a dog barking. The hansom slowed further and finally pulled up aross the street from a building next to a wharf.

"Here's an extra five for your trouble," he heard Brian Cameron say to the driver. "Thank you."

Wiggins dropped off the back and, taking care to stay out of sight, dashed behind an empty coopers van parked by the side of the road. He watched as Cameron got out and then turned and helped

Kathryn Ellingsley down. "But why are we stopping here?" he heard her ask her cousin. "We'll
be late for the train."

"We've plenty of time, my dear," Cameron replied. "And I must pick up some important papers.
Uncle Neville wanted me to bring them to him."

They crossed the road as soon as the hansom
pulled away. Wiggins started to follow them. But
instead of going toward the front door of the building, Cameron suddenly grabbed the girl's arm and
started pulling her toward the wharf.

"Brian," she cried, "what are you doing?"

Wiggins froze.

"Let's go have a look at the water," Cameron
said. "It's quite lovely. I think you'll enjoy the
view."

"Are you mad?" Kathryn tried to free her arm,
but he held fast. "Let me go, I tell you."

"I'm sorry it has to be this way." Cameron
grabbed her around the waist and dragged her further out onto the wharf. "But you're in the way.
You've got to die before Uncle Neville does. It's
most inconvenient. You should have been in that
room that night. Not Hannah."

"Let me go," Kathryn cried, struggling in ear-
nest now. "Brian, what are you doing?"

Wiggins started across the street at a dead run.
But they were almost across to the end of the wharf
now.

Kathryn Ellingsley was fighting him, fighting
hard, but it wasn't doing her any good. Cameron
grabbed her around the neck and drug her toward
the water. She flailed at him with her fists and tried
to kick, but he slapped her hard and picked her up.

"Hey," Wiggins yelled as they got to the edge of the dock. "Leave her alone, I tell ya." He charged across the wood pilings.

Cameron, with one frantic look at his pursuer, dropped her into the river. Kathryn screamed as she hit the water.

Wiggins leapt for the edge.

But Cameron was ready for him. He grabbed him around the knees and pulled him back, throwing him onto the wharf hard enough to knock the wind out of his lungs. Wiggins kicked out with one leg, catching the man on the thigh and toppling him over. He landed smack on Wiggins. The two men rolled across the wharf. Cameron smashed a fist into Wiggins's face. Wiggins tried punching him in the stomach, but his arm was held down by the bigger man's weight. Cameron's hand shot up and grabbed Wiggins's throat. He squeezed hard. Wiggins finally got his own hand free and clawed at Cameron's arm. But his own strength was failing and the pressure increased, choking the life out of him. His vision clouded and the night turned blacker and blacker.

Suddenly, the pressure was gone as sixty pounds of furious dog leapt onto Brian Cameron's back. Fred, snarling and barking, clamped his jaws onto the arm squeezing the life out of his master.

Cameron screamed and rolled to one side, trying desperately to get away from the enraged beast. Witherspoon and Smythe raced across the wharf. "Are you all right, Wiggins?" the inspector shouted.

Wiggins tried to sit up and point to the river. "Drownin', she's drownin'!"

Smythe didn't hesitate. He continued running. Wiggins slumped back as he heard the sound of a body hitting water. He prayed the coachman would be in time to save the drowning woman.

"I've got 'er," Smythe called.

Witherspoon blew hard on his police whistle and then dropped to his knees beside his fallen footman. "Dear God, Wiggins. Are you all right?"

"I'm fine. Don't let him get away," Wiggins moaned. He lifted his head and looked over at his dog. Then he smiled.

Fred, still snarling dangerously, had driven Cameron back against the side of the building. The man cringed there, held at bay by the animal who lunged at him every time he moved.

Witherspoon jumped up and rushed to the edge of the wharf. "Is she all right?"

Smythe nodded. "She's alive, but this water is freezin'. We've got to get her out of here."

Heavy footsteps pounded across the wharf as two police constables responded to Witherspoon's whistle. One of them recognized the inspector.

"Over here," the inspector shouted.

Within moments, they had Kathryn and Smythe out of the water and wrapped in blankets while the inspector tended to Wiggins.

As soon as the inspector realized that Wiggins was really going to be all right, he got up and walked over to Brian Cameron.

He wasn't in the least worried that Cameron would try to make a run for it. Not with Fred standing guard. The man had flattened himself against the building, his face a mask of terror as the dog snarled viciously at him.

"It's all right, Fred," he told the dog. "You've done a good job, but we'll take over now." Fred didn't budge.

"Here, boy," Wiggins called softly, and the animal, with one last snarl at the cowering man, trotted over and began licking the footman's cheek.

"Brian Cameron," the inspector said firmly, "you're under arrest for the murder of Hannah Cameron and the attempted murder of Kathryn Ellingsley and Cuthbert Wiggins."

It was very late by the time they were all gathered around the kitchen table. The inspector was still at the station, but Wiggins, wrapped in one of Mrs. Goodge's knitted afghans and with a cup of cocoa in front of him, was quite happily enjoying being the center of attention.

Smythe, who'd very much liked the way Betsy had fussed when he'd arrived home in wet clothes and wrapped in a blanket, was quite content to sit back and enjoy a glass of fine Irish whiskey while the footman retold the tale several times over.

"All right." Luty put down her glass and stared at Mrs. Jeffries. "Tell us how ya figured it out."

"Actually"—she smiled briefly—"there was one fact that kept bothering me. It was something Betsy said yesterday. Namely, that everyone in that household except Hannah Cameron knew that Kathryn Ellingsley went out at night."

"I don't follow ya," Smythe said. "What does that 'ave to do with anythin'?"

"But that was the key to the puzzle," she replied. "Don't you see, Brian Cameron didn't know his wife knew about Kathryn. He'd no idea she was

in the room. He wanted to murder Kathryn Ellingsley all along. I figured it out yesterday, but then
when I found out who Kathryn's heir was, I wasn't
sure I was right. You see, I'd gotten the inheritance
sequence wrong.''

''What does that mean?'' Wiggins asked.

''It means that we were confused from the
start,'' she replied. ''We kept focusing on Hannah
Cameron . . .''

''She was the one that was murdered,'' Hatchet
interrupted, somewhat testily. He and Luty were
both annoyed that they'd missed the action down
on the wharf.

''Yes, I know,'' Mrs. Jeffries said. ''But that was
a mistake. You see, Cameron knew about Kathryn.
He went into that room that night, expecting to find
Kathryn slipping in. Instead, his wife was standing
by the door waiting to catch the girl in the act, so
to speak. In the darkness, he stabbed her. But she
was the wrong one.''

''I still don't understand why 'e'd want to kill a
nice girl like Miss Ellingsley,'' Wiggins said.

''He wanted her dead so that he could inherit
their uncle's fortune,'' Mrs. Jeffries said. ''That's
why he kept sending all those telegrams to Yorkshire. He was running out of time. But I got confused. I thought his plan was to murder Kathryn
and then wait until their uncle died and then inherit
her share of the estate. Last night, when you found
out who her heir was, that it was Connor Reese, I
still didn't understand until it was almost too late.''

''I'm confused,'' Mrs. Goodge complained. ''I
can't make heads nor tails of it.''

''It's very simple, really,'' Mrs. Jeffries said.

"Neville Parrington had a burglary six months ago." She pulled the telegram out of her pocket and read it to the them.

> Ellen and Edward Cameron inherit after K.E.
> Parrington's will stolen in London burglary six months ago.
> Hope this helpful and keep up the good work.
> Cheers, Edwin Trent

She shook her head disgustedly. "But even with this, it still didn't make sense because I was still focusing on the wrong thing. You see, I didn't realize until Wiggins came along and told us today that Neville Parrington was on his deathbed. It was then that the shoe dropped."

"I'm glad you know what you're talkin' about." Mrs. Goodge sniffed. "I don't. What does Parrington's burglary have to do with our murder?"

"I'm not explaining it very well." She sighed. "And I've no proof, but I'm sure that Brian Cameron was the one that stole his uncle's will. The circumstances were very much the same."

"That's true," Hatchet said. "According to my source, that burglary wasn't done by a professional. Neither was the one at the Cameron house."

"No, both of them were done by Cameron. He stole his uncle's will to find out one thing—who was Parrington's heir? I expect he was a bit annoyed to find out it was Kathryn Ellingsley and not himself."

"But why'd Cameron wait six months to kill her?" Betsy asked.

"He didn't want to arouse suspicion," Mrs. Jeffries stated. "We know he fired his governess to give her a position in his house and I expect he was absolutely delighted when she fell in love with Dr. Reese. If you'll recall, Kathryn and Dr. Reese met at the Cameron house."

"But Dr. Reese had gone there to 'ave a go at Mrs. Cameron," Wiggins interjected. "It's not like 'e were a guest."

"True." Mrs. Jeffries grinned. "But I'll wager that Cameron noticed they were attracted to each other and I'll bet if you asked Dr. Reese, you'd find out that it was Brian Cameron who gave him Kathryn's Yorkshire address so that Reese could correspond with her."

"You mean he connived to get the girl to come?"

"That's it precisely. He wanted Kathryn in London. I expect that he was planning on her having an unfortunate 'accident.' Let's remember what we know about Brian Cameron. He needs money. But it wouldn't do him any good to kill his wife. He'll not get anything from her estate, but he would get quite a bit of money if Kathryn Ellingsley were dead. And she had to die before Neville Parrington did. Don't you see, she'd left her estate to her fiancé, Dr. Reese. If Parrington died before Kathryn did, she'd inherit. There was no point in killing her then. All the money would go to Reese. If she died before Parrington, the estate would go to Cameron's children. Essentially, he'd have control of a huge amount of money to do with it what he pleased.'' She sat back and smiled.

They looked at her blankly.

"Oh, I know it's a bit muddled. But I'm certain of it.''

"But why were you so confused when you found out Reese and not Cameron was her heir?'' Betsy asked. "You looked ready to spit nails last night when Hatchet and Smythe come in.''

"Because, like most people, I'd assumed that Kathryn left her money to her family. If not to Cameron then to his children. That's all the family she had. It was only when I thought about it and found out from Wiggins today that Cameron was taking Kathryn to Yorkshire that I realized what he was up to. He had to kill her before Neville Parrington died. Otherwise, Cameron would get nothing. I'd suspected he was the killer, but I was a bit confused as to the details. But not to worry. We sorted it out in the end.''

Luty shook her head. "I'm still confused.''

"Me too,'' Smythe muttered, but he didn't mind all that much. Good Irish whiskey could take the edge off anything. That and the fact that Betsy had kissed him when the others weren't looking.

"I still think it shoulda been that Hadleigh woman,'' Mrs. Goodge muttered.

"She was a strong suspect,'' Mrs. Jeffries said, "but she really had a very flimsy motive. She hated Hannah Cameron, but from what we learned, she'd hated her for a long time. Besides, I didn't think it was her because she was still fully dressed when the inspector arrived.''

Wiggins cocked his head to one side. "Huh?''

"Remember, the victim was stabbed. That means the murderer probably got blood on his clothes. Even the cleanest of stabbings involves some blood spurts. There wasn't any blood on her clothes when the inspector got there. Brian Cameron was wearing a heavy dressing gown over his clothing. I expect there was a drop or two of blood on that shirt of his. But he didn't dare take it off in case the police searched the house, so he did the cleverest thing possible. He kept the shirt on and put on a dressing gown."

" 'E was takin' a bit of a risk," Smythe commented.

"Not really," Mrs. Jeffries said. "He'd done his best to make it look like a burglary. If Chief Inspector Barrows hadn't come onto the scene so quickly and spotted that it was murder, Cameron would have gotten away with it. Can you really see Inspector Nivens asking a gentleman to remove his dressing gown?"

"Gracious, are you all still up?" Inspector Witherspoon, smiling broadly, stepped into the kitchen. "Oh, I'm so glad to see that Wiggins and Smythe are all right. I can't tell you how worried I've been."

"We didn't hear you come in, sir." Mrs. Jeffries wasn't sure what to do.

"Oh, that's all right. I expected to be at the station all night." Witherspoon ambled over to the table and pulled out a chair. "But Chief Inspector Barrows insisted I come home. I think he could tell I was a bit concerned about Wiggins and Smythe. By the way, he sends his heartiest regards to you two." He nodded at them. "If not for your bravery, that young woman would be dead now. You should be very proud of yourselves. Very proud indeed.''

Wiggins grinned foolishly.

Smythe blushed. ''It weren't nothin','' he muttered.

''It was so.'' Betsy chided the coachman. ''Just ask Miss Ellingsley.''

''Is that whiskey?'' Witherspoon peered over his spectacles at the open bottle sitting smack in the middle of the table.

''Uh, yes, sir, it is,'' Mrs. Jeffries admitted.

''Hatchet and I are right lucky we come by to visit,'' Luty said quickly. ''Otherwise we'd a missed hearin' all about yer excitin' evenin'. When I heard this one''—she jerked her thumb at Smythe—''had been swimmin' in the Thames and that this one''—she nodded at the footman—''had almost had the life squeezed outta him, I talked Hepzibah into breakin' out a bottle of yer best whiskey. I didn't think you'd mind. Celebratin', ya know. They ain't dead.''

''Excellent idea, Mrs. Crookshank.'' The inspector shuddered at the memory. He'd come close to losing two people who were very dear to him. ''May I have some too?''

''I'll get another glass,'' Betsy said, getting up.

''What happened at the station, sir?'' Mrs. Jeffries asked.

''Brian Cameron's refused to make any statement at all,'' he replied. ''Thank you, Betsy,'' he said as she put the glass of whiskey in front of him.

''Oh, dear, sir,'' Mrs. Jeffries commented. ''That will make it difficult for you.''

''Not really. We've a lot of evidence against

him. Miss Ellingsley managed to make a statement.
Cameron's references to her possible inheritance
from her uncle give him quite a strong motive.
We're sure he meant to murder Kathryn that night,
instead of Mrs. Cameron. But even if we can't con-
vict him of his wife's murder, and I think we can,
we've got the evidence of his attempted murder of
Miss Ellingsley and Wiggins, of course.'' He
tossed the whiskey down his throat and then
coughed. "Oh dear, this isn't at all like sherry.
Quite strong, isn't it?''

"Is Miss Ellingsley all right?'' Wiggins asked
anxiously. He still felt bad that he hadn't been able
to prevent Cameron from tossing her into the
Thames.

"She's fine, Wiggins,'' Witherspoon assured
him. "She managed to keep from drowning by
grabbing a piling. But if Smythe hadn't jumped in
and pulled her out when he did, she probably
would have died. We've a number of heroes in this
house.'' He paused and looked curiously around
the room. "Where's Fred? Surely he should be
here too.''

"He's in the larder eatin' a beefsteak,'' Mrs.
Goodge said. "A great big thick one I got from the
butcher this mornin'. I figured he deserved it.''

"He most certainly does,'' Witherspoon agreed
with a laugh. Then he sobered and looked at Smythe and Wiggins. "Now that I know you two aren't
suffering any ill effects from our adventure, I can
rest easy.'' He yawned widely.

"Inspector.'' Mrs. Jeffries had to ask. "Was Inspector Nivens at the station?''

"He did come by,'' the inspector replied. "He

didn't seem at all pleased that we'd solved the case, either. As a matter of fact, he quite rudely told me he wasn't coming to my dinner party.''

"What a pity, sir." She fought hard to keep from smiling.

"Yes, isn't it?" Witherspoon murmured. "Too bad, really. I was going to seat him next to cousin Edwina. But she's not coming either."

Knowing that she couldn't keep a straight face, Mrs. Jeffries looked down at her half-empty glass.

" 'Ow come she's not comin'?" Wiggins asked.

"Oh, she's decided to buy her clothes in Edinburgh so she won't be coming to London to shop for her trousseau. But not to worry; we'll have plenty of guests," Witherspoon said cheerfully. "I've invited Chief Inspector Barrows and his wife. They're quite looking forward to it." He started to get up, frowned and popped back down in his seat. "But there is one thing I'm still very puzzled about."

"What's that, sir?" Mrs. Jeffries asked.

"I can't help wondering who that man was who came with the note."

"I've no idea, sir." Mrs. Jeffries shrugged. "As I told you"—she glanced at Smythe—"he looked very much like a banker."

Smythe, who'd just taken a sip of whiskey, had the good grace to choke.